PENGUIN BOOKS

WHY HAVEN'T YOU WRITTEN?

Nadine Gordimer was born and lives in South Africa. She has written ten novels, including *A Sport of Nature*, *Burger's Daughter*, *July's People*, and *The Conservationist* (co-winner of the Booker Prize in England). Her short stories have been collected in nine volumes, and her nonfiction pieces were published together as *The Essential Gesture*. Gordimer has received numerous international prizes, including the 1991 Nobel Prize in Literature. In the United States, she has received the Modern Literature Association Award and the Bennett Award. Her fiction has appeared in many American magazines, including *The New Yorker*, and her essays have appeared in *The New York Times* and *The New York Review of Books*. She has been given honorary degrees by Yale, Harvard, and other universities and has been honored by the French government with the decoration Officier de l'Ordre des Arts et des Lettres. She is a vice president of PEN International and an executive member of the Congress of South African Writers.

NADINE GORDIMER

WHY HAVEN'T YOU WRITTEN?

Selected Stories 1950–1972

PENGUIN BOOKS

PENGUIN BOOKS
Published by the Penguin Group
Viking Penguin, a division of Penguin Books USA Inc.,
375 Hudson Street, New York, New York 10014, U.S.A.
Penguin Books Ltd, 27 Wrights Lane, London W8 5TZ, England
Penguin Books Australia Ltd, Ringwood, Victoria, Australia
Penguin Books Canada Ltd, 10 Alcorn Avenue, Suite 300,
Toronto, Ontario, Canada M4V 3B2
Penguin Books (N.Z.) Ltd, 182–190 Wairau Road,
Auckland 10, New Zealand

Penguin Books Ltd, Registered Offices:
Harmondsworth, Middlesex, England

This collection first published in Penguin Books (U.K.) 1992
Published in Penguin Books (U.S.A.) 1993

1 3 5 7 9 10 8 6 4 2

The Soft Voice of the Serpent first published in the United States of America by
Simon & Schuster 1952
Published by The Viking Press in a Compass Book edition 1962
Copyright Nadine Gordimer, 1951, 1952
"A Watcher of the Dead" first appeared in *The New Yorker*.

Livingstone's Companions first published in the United States of America by
The Viking Press 1971
Copyright © Nadine Gordimer, 1965, 1966, 1967, 1969, 1971
"A Third Presence" first appeared in *Cosmopolitan;* "The Bride of Christ" and
"A Satisfactory Settlement" in *The Atlantic Monthly;* "A Meeting in Space"
(as "Say Something African") and "Why Haven't You Written?" in
The New Yorker; and "Otherwise Birds Fly In" in *Cornhill.*

ISBN 0 14 01.7657 8
(CIP data available)

Printed in the United States of America
Set in 10/12 pt Monophoto Sabon

Contents

From

The Soft Voice of the Serpent
(1953)

The Kindest Thing to Do

In the warm stupor of early Sunday afternoon, when the smell of Sunday roast still hangs about the house, and the servants have banged the kitchen door closed behind them and gone off, gleaming and sweaty in tight Sunday clothes, to visit at the Location, the family comes out dreamily, slackly, to lie upon the lawn. The hour has drained them of will; they come out at the pull of some instinct, like that which sends animals creeping away to die. They lie, suspended in the hour, with the cushions and books about them. The big wheels have turned slower and slower; now they cease to turn, and hang motionless. Only the tiny wheels still turn; silent and busy and scarcely noticeable, the beetles climbing in the grass blades, the flowers fingered gently by small currents, as they lift, breathing up to the sun. The little world is still running, where the birds peck, stepping daintily on their twigs of claws in the flower beds.

'Have you got Micky there?' The voice came clearly from the bedroom window and it almost made her wince, it almost penetrated, but there was no resistance to it: in the fluid, heavy, resurgent air the steel blade of sound slid through and was lost. Her head, drooping near the drooping, bee-heavy, crumpled paper chalices of the poppies, lifted half-protestingly, her lazy hand brushed the grey specks of insects which flecked the pages of Petrarch's 'Laura in Death'. In her mind's eye, she saw Micky, head to tail, asleep, somewhere near ... On the grass, at her back, at her side; somewhere ... She grunted and waved in assent, already back in the book, in the mazy spell of steady warmth and flowers fixed in the hypnosis of the sun, and grass blades, seen from their own level, consumed in dark, blazing light along the edges. The pulses slackened and the blood ran sweet and heavy in the veins; the print danced and the mind almost swooned. It swerved away, off into thoughts half-formed, that trailed and merged.

In one of the neighbouring houses that enclosed the garden on three sides, some poor child began to practise the piano. The unsure notes came hesitantly across the air, a tiny voice that disturbed the afternoon no more than would a fly, buzzing about the ear of a sleeping giant. The Sunday paper lay about. The father lay rolled on to his back, suddenly asleep in the defenceless fashion of the middle aged, with his mouth half open and the stretched folds of his neck relaxed like the neck of an old turkey. The little boy had grass in his hair, that was itself like winter grass, pale and rough. The others read, dozed, dreamed, and lay on their backs, the sky and the trees and the house and the bright dots of poppies reflected in their eyes as in an old-fashioned convex mirror – the kind of mirror that in Victorian days reflected the room it looked down upon as another world into which one might climb, like *Alice Through the Looking-glass*. There it was, the shining white house, the shining green fir, the shining blue sky, in the little round mirror of each eye.

She read on, lost, drowsing, flicking minute creatures from the pages, scratching mechanically at her leg, where the grass pricked her.

And the next moment it was gone; the beautiful lassitude turned sick and sour within her, the exquisite torpor hung heavy around her neck, she struggled free of the coils of the dead afternoon. 'But I was sure . . .' she said, stunned; feeling beaten down before the figure of her mother. Her mother stood, almost too much to bear, purposeful and hard as reality, demanding and urgent. Her glance was too insistent, it came like a pain, piercing the spell. 'Well, there you are . . .' the mother spoke with scornful resignation, angrily, 'I might have known you wouldn't bother to look.'

'But I thought . . .'

'Yes, of course "you thought" – surely it wasn't asking too much of you to see whether the dog was with you? Well, it's done now, and the poor little bird's bleeding and half torn to bits and still alive, too.'

The girl sat up. She was dizzy. The afternoon suddenly sang and was orange-coloured. The great wheels started turning, the world creaked and groaned and rushed into confusion and activity, the clamour started up again.

Yesterday they had found a bird – an injured dove, its wing damaged by some small boy's catapult. Once before they had found a hurt bird, and had kept it in a cage and fed it until it was able to fly again, and so this time they brought out the old cage and put the sullen soft grey dove inside with food and water, confident that with care it would soon be healed. Now this afternoon, the mother – always mindful of the small responsibilities that everyone else so easily forgot after the first ardour of sympathy – had gone out to the shed to see how the bird was progressing, and seeing it sulking, puffed up resentfully in a corner of its cage, had decided to let it out to peck about the back garden for a while, intending to return it to the cage if it were still unable to fly. But of course Micky, who eyed the doves upon the wall longingly, and chased them ineffectually when they alighted upon the path or the grass, must be kept out of the way. The mother had made sure that Micky was safely on the front lawn with the family. She had called out of the bedroom window . . .

'I was sure he was here,' the girl repeated. 'I felt sure he was here. I thought . . .'

'I had a feeling he'd gone round there after the bird, and when I went out, sure enough, there he was worrying it as if it were a bone.'

'Little beast . . .' the girl shuddered.

'It's alive, poor creature, too – I'm sure I don't know what's to be done for it now.' The mother kept her accusing gaze on the girl, washing her hands of the whole affair.

'You didn't kill it . . .?' the girl asked, almost pleadingly.

'*I* can't kill the thing,' she said. She had always done everything unpleasant for her children; she had always stood between them and the ugliness of life: death, sickness, despair.

The girl looked for something in her mother's face and this time did not find it.

Suddenly she wished, wished she could have the last half-hour back, she wanted it over again, desperately, childishly, uselessly, so that she might look up from her book and say: No, Micky isn't here.

In a kind of sulky horror she got up and started to walk round the side of the house. 'Where?' she said drearily, pausing and turning. Her hair was rumpled and grass clung to her clothes, her right cheek was flushed with sun. 'Just near the hedge,' said the mother.

She tried to prepare herself to imagine what the bird would look like, but her mind turned away from the thought. It was upset, too lately, roughly woken to serve her. The narcotic sun stared hatefully upon her and she sickened from it, as a man turns from the smell of liquor he has drunk too freely the night before. She did not *care* about the bird; she did not want to be bothered with it. She wanted to go away into the house, or out, somewhere, and pretend it hadn't happened. If you ignored something, put it utterly from you, and went on to the next thing, it was as if it had never happened. If she walked away now, life would grow over the incident, covering it, hiding it smoothly.

I am weak, she said, self-pitying.

I'll have to kill it.

Something lifted and turned over inside her as she realized the thought. Fear prickled right over her body, from her head to her toes.

Then she came out round the screen of the hedge and into the shade of the hedge and she looked upon the ground, that was damp and mossy in patches, and she could not see the bird. She looked here and there, and poked at a drift of dead leaves with her foot, but she did not find it.

And then she turned and there it was, lying in a stony hollow just behind her. There it was, and it was not a bird, it was a flattened mess of dusty feathers, torn and wet with the dog's saliva, oozing dark blood from wounds that lay hidden, making sodden the close soft down of – ah, what was it, was it the breast, the tail; what part was recognizable in the crushed wad of that small body . . .

Only the head. And as she saw the head a thrill of such vivid, terrifying, utter anguish contracted in her that she felt that some emotion she had never used before had been called up from her soul. It was unbearable. It was the emotion that bursts the human heart. The emotion from which men hide their heads in despair. For the head of the bird lay sunken in the last humility, down upon its broken breast; the beak rested piteously in the feathers, and the eyes were closed strangely, resignedly, in the final martyrdom of suffering. A passionate desperation of agony had passed over that small grey head, had blazed up in the little being of the bird, making it great, bigger than itself, and breaking it, bringing its head down upon its broken breast.

She felt that nothing could expiate this, ever; nothing, nothing; no tears, no sorrowing, no compensation of other joys could wipe out this thing that existed in life.

She saw that the bird still lived; that it was; that it experienced the awfulness of its own annihilation. And cowardly and trembling, knowing that each moment she delayed out of cowardice it suffered to the full, she slowly drew off her sandal. Very slowly, almost whimpering, she lifted the sandal and brought it down upon the bird's head. She had not known it would be so terrible – that beneath the blow of the sandal she would feel the shape of the small grey head, the particular horror of the resistance of the delicate-boned skull and the softness of the outer covering of feathers, all at once, at the moment of contact. And in an agonized instant life asserted itself vainly and for the last time in the tiny creature, and it half-raised itself, opening the thin mute beak in a wild flutter. Wildly she brought the sandal down again; once, twice, three times. The bird was dead.

And now it was nothing; it was a dead bird.

She put her sandal on again, feeling the dust on her bare foot uncomfortable against the inner sole. (soul)

She looked at the bird. How strange a thing that was – she had killed, had battered the life out of something. She thought: killing is a strange thing; it is terrible, until you do it, right up to the moment of doing it.

She had read so many times of murder, and it had meant nothing to her; it was as emotionally incomprehensible to her as a passionate love affair would be to a child of seven. But now with a slow cold trickle of fear that ran – and could not be checked, could not be fought – through her soul, leaving its cold awful imprint, a dark knowledge came to her. She felt it open, a Lethean flower of knowledge, that she feared and did not want, chilling her soul with a strange cold sap. It came coldly because it was a dreadful cold thing, the understanding of the fulfilment of the will to kill. I could kill anything now, she thought, and the words seemed light and easy. They were the words of no-feeling, and she was afraid of them. She was deadened under the weight of this cold knowledge, that would never leave her now, once it was discovered. Ah, the hopelessness, the awfulness of knowing . . . The passion of pity she had felt for the bird was nothing compared with this; gladly, gladly would she feel that again. But she could not; only the calm reasonableness of the clear thought: I could kill anything now.

She came round to the front garden, breathing warmly, with her face drawn in a wry frown. They watched her from the lawn. 'Well, what happened?' they asked, watching her face. 'I killed it. It's dead,' she said.

'Ugh . . . How awful . . . How could you?'

'It was the kindest thing to do,' said someone else sensibly. 'She had to put the poor thing out of its misery – what else could she do?' The mother got up and went round to the back to dispose of the body.

She went inside because she could not bear the lazy, sprawling sun, that blazed as horribly now as an electric light left burning right on into daylight. She washed, and combed her hair, and let the water run over her hands. And later, in the evening, she went out, and laughing and talking in a group of those social acquaintances who are vaguely referred to as 'friends', she said with a grimace – 'I had to do something ghastly this afternoon – I had to kill a bird.' 'How brave of you!' said the young man, laughing, with mock heroic emphasis. 'For a girl – yes,' said another, spearing an olive on a coloured toothpick. 'Women are terrified of squashing a beetle. God knows, they can be cruel and ruthless in their own devious subtle fashions – but when it comes to killing any sort of little creature, they're the most craven cowards.' 'Well, I did,' she said stoutly, carelessly; and laughing like a woman of spirit, she took the olive from him and popped it into her mouth.

The Defeated

My mother did not want me to go near the Concession stores because they smelled, and were dirty, and the natives spat tuberculosis germs into the dust. She said it was no place for little girls.

But I used to go down there sometimes, in the afternoon, when static four o'clock held the houses of our Mine, and the sun washed over them like the waves of the sea over sand castles. I felt that life was going on down there at the Concession stores: noise, and movement, and – yes, bad smells, even – and so I would wander down the naked road, with the hot sun uncomfortably drying the membrane inside my nose, seeing the irregular line of narrow white shops lying away ahead like a jumble of shoe boxes.

The signs of life that I craved were very soon evident: rich and careless of its vitality, it overflowed from the crowded pavement of the stores, and the surrounding veld was littered with sucked-out oranges and tatters of dirty paper, and worn into the shabby barrenness peculiar to earth much trampled upon by the feet of men. A fat, one-legged native, with the patient detachment of the business man who knows himself indispensable, sat on the bald veld beside the path that led from the Compound, his stock of walking-sticks standing up, handles tied together, points splayed out fanwise, his pyramids of bright, thin-skinned oranges waiting. Sometimes he had mealies as well – those big, hard, full-grown ears with rows of yellowish tombstones instead of little pearly teeth – and a brazier made from a paraffin tin to roast them by. Propped against the chipped pillars of the pavement, there were always other vendors, making their small way in lucky beans, herbs, bracelets beaten from copper wire, knitted caps in wonderful colours – blooming like great hairy petunias, or bursting suns, from the needles of old, old native women – and, of course, oranges. Everywhere there were oranges; the pushing, ambling crowds filling the pavement ate them as they stared at the windows, the gossips, sitting with their blankets drawn close and their feet in the gutter, sucked at them, the Concession

9

store cats sniffed at the skins where they lay, hollow-cheeked, discarded in every doorway.

Quite often I had to flick the white pith from where it had landed, on my shoe or even my dress, spat negligently by some absorbed orange-eater contemplating a shirt through breath-smudged plate glass. The wild, wondering, dirty men came up from the darkness of the mine and they lay themselves out to the sun on the veld, and to their mouths they put the round fruit of the sun; and it was the expression of their need.

I would saunter along the shopwindows amongst them, and for me there was a quickening of glamour about the place: the air was thicker with their incense-like body smell, and the sudden rank shock of their stronger sweat, as a bare armpit lifted over my head. The clamour of their voices – always shouting, but so merry, so angry! – and the size of their laughter, and the open-mouthed startle with which they greeted every fresh sight: I felt vaguely the spell of the books I had read, returning; markets in Persia, bazaars in Cairo ... Nevertheless, I was careful not to let them brush too closely past me, lest some unnameable *something* crawl from their dusty blankets or torn cotton trousers on to my clean self, and I did not like the way they spat, with that terrible gurgle in the throat, into the gutter, or, worse still, blew their noses loudly between finger and thumb, and flung the excrement horribly to the air.

And neither did I like the heavy, sickening, greasy carrion-breath that poured from the mouth of the Hotela la Bantu, where the natives hunched intent at zinc-topped forms, eating steaming no-colour chunks of horror that bore no relation to meat as I knew it. The down on my arms prickled in revulsion from the pulpy entrails hanging in dreadful enticement at the window, and the blood-embroidered sawdust spilling out of the doorway.

I know that I wondered how the storekeepers' wives, who sat on soap boxes outside the doorways of the shops on either side of the eating-house, could stand the breath of that maw. How they could sit, like lizards in the sun; and all the time they breathed in the breath of the eating-house: took it deep into the recesses of their beings, whilst my throat closed against it in disgust.

It was down there one burning afternoon that I met Mrs

Saiyetovitz. She was one of the storekeepers' wives, and I had seen her many times before, sitting before the deep, blanket-hung cave of her husband's store, where a pile of tinsel-covered wooden trunks shimmered and flashed a pink or green eye out of the gloom into the outside – wearing her creased alpaca apron, her fat insteps leaning over her down-at-heel shoes. Sometimes she knitted, and sometimes she just sat. On this day there was a small girl hanging about her, drawing on the shopwindow with a sticky forefinger. When the child turned to look at me, I recognized her as one of the girls from 'our school'; a girl from my class, as a matter of fact, called Miriam Saiyetovitz. Yes, that was her name: I remembered it because it was ugly – I was always sorry for girls with ugly names.

Miriam was a tousled, black-haired little girl, who wore a red bow in her hair. Now she recognized me, and we stood looking at one another; all at once the spare line of the name 'Miriam Saiyetovitz', that was like the scrolled pattern of an iron gate with only the sky behind it, shifted its perspective in my mind, so that now between the cold curly M's and the implacable A's of that gate's framework, I saw a house, a complication of buildings and flowers and figures walking, where before there was nothing but the sky. Miriam Saiyeto-vitz – and this: behind her name and her school self, the hot and buzzing world of the stores. And I smiled at her, very friendly.

So she knew we had decided to recognize one another and she sauntered over to talk to me. I stood with her in the doorway of her father's store, and I, too, wrote my name and drew cats composed of two capital O's and a sausage tail, with the point of my hot and sticky finger on the window. Of course, she did not exactly introduce me to her mother – children never do introduce their mothers; they merely let it be known, by referring to the woman in question off-hand, in the course of play, or going up to speak to her in such a way that the relationship becomes obvious. Miriam went up to her mother and said diffidently: 'Ma, I know this girl from school – she's in class with me, can we have some red lemonade?'

And the woman lifted her head from where she sat, wide-legged, so that you couldn't help seeing the knee-elastic of her striped pink silk bloomers, holding over the cotton tops of her stockings, and said, peering, 'Take it! Take it! Go, have it!'

Because I did not then know her, I thought that she was angry, she spoke with such impatience; but soon I knew that it was only her eager generosity that made her fling permission almost fiercely at Miriam whenever the child made some request. Mrs Saiyetovitz's glance wavered over to me, but she did not seem to be seeing me very clearly: indeed, she could not, for her small, pale, pale eyes narrowed into her big, simple, heavy face were half-blind, and she had always to peer at everything, and never quite see.

I saw that she was very ugly.

Ugly, with the blunt ugliness of a toad; the ugliness of seeming not entirely at home in any element – as if the earth were the wrong place, too heavy and magnetic for a creature already so blunt; and the water would be no better: too subtle and contour-swayed for a creature so graceless. And yet her ugliness was without repellence. When I grew older I often wondered why; she should have been repellent, one should have turned from her, but one did not. She was only ugly. She had the short, stunted yet heavy bones of generations of oppression in the ghettos of Europe; breasts, stomach, hips crowded sadly, no height, wide strong shoulders, and a round back. Her head settled right down between her shoulders without even the grace of a neck, and her dun flat hair was cut at the level of her ears. Her features were not essentially Semitic; there was nothing so *definite* as that about her: she had no distinction whatever.

Miriam reappeared from the shades of the store, carrying two bottles of red lemonade. A Shangaan emerged at the same time, clutching a newspaper parcel and puzzling over his handful of change, not looking where he was going. Miriam swept past him, the dusty African with his odd, troglodyte unsureness, and his hair plastered into savage whorls with red clay. With one swift movement she knocked the tin caps off the bottles against the scratched frame of the shopwindow, and handed my lemonade to me. 'Where did you get it so quickly?' I asked, surprised. She jerked her head back toward the store: 'In the kitchen,' she said – and applied herself to the bottle.

And so I knew that the Saiyetovitzes lived there, behind the Concession store.

Saturday afternoons were the busiest. Mrs Saiyetovitz's box stood vacant outside and she helped her husband in the shop. Saturday afternoon was usually my afternoon for going down there, too; my mother and father went out to golf, and I was left with the tick of the clock, the purring monologue of our cat, and the doves gurgling in the empty garden.

On Saturdays every doorway was crowded; a continual shifting stream snaked up and down the pavements; flies tangled overhead, the air smelled hotter, and from the doorway of every store the high, wailing blare and repetition of native songs, played on the gramophone, swung out upon the air and met in discord with the tune of the record being played next door.

Miriam's mother's brother was the proprietor of the Hotela la Bantu, and another uncle had the bicycle shop two doors down. Sometimes she had a message to deliver at the bicycle shop, and I would go in with her. Spare wheels hung across the ceiling, there was a battered wooden counter with a pile of puncture repair outfits, a sewing-machine or two for sale, and, in the window, bells and pumps and mascots cut out of tin, painted yellow and red for the adornment of handlebars. We were invariably offered a lemonade by the uncle, and we invariably accepted. At home I was not allowed to drink lemonades unlimited; they might 'spoil my dinner'; but Miriam drank them whenever she pleased.

Wriggling in and out amongst the grey-dusty bodies of the natives – their silky brown skin dies in the damp fug underground: after a few months down the mine, it reflects only weariness – Miriam looked with her own calm, quick self-possession upon the setting in which she found herself. Like someone sitting in a swarm of ants; and letting them swarm, letting them crawl all over and about her. Not lifting a hand to flick them off. Not crying out against them in disgust; nor explaining, saying, well, I *like* ants. Just sitting there and letting them swarm, and looking out of herself as if to say: What ants? What ants are you talking about? I giggled and shuddered in excitement at the sight of the dried bats and cobwebby snake-skins rotting in the bleary little window of the medicine shop, but Miriam tugged at my dress and said, 'Oh, come on –' I exclaimed at the purple and red shirts lying amongst the dead flies in the wonderful confusion of Saiyetovitz's store window, but Miriam was telling me about her music exam in September, and only frowned at the interruption. I was approaching the confusion of adolescence, and sometimes an uncomfortable, terrible, fascinating curiosity – like a headless worm which lay shamefully hidden in the earth of my soul – crawled out into my consciousness at the sight of the animal obviousness of the natives' male bodies in their scanty covering; but the flash of my guilt at these moments met no answer in Miriam, although she was the same age as I.

If the sight of a boy interrupting his conversation to step out a yard or two on to the veld to relieve himself filled me with embarrassment and real disgust, so that I wanted to go and look at flowers – it seemed that Miriam did not see.

It was quite a long time before she took me into her father's store.

For months it remained a vague, dark, dust-moted world beyond the blanket-hung doorway, into which she was swallowed up and appeared again, whilst I waited outside, with the boys who looked and looked and looked at the windows. Then one day, as she was entering, she paused, and said suddenly and calmly: 'Aren't you coming . . .?' Without a word, I followed her in.

It was cool in the store; and the coolness was a surprise. Out of the sun-naked pavement – and into the store that was cool, like a cellar! Light danced only furtively along the folds of the blankets that hung from the ceiling: crackling silent and secret little fires in the curly woollen furze. The blankets were dark sombre hangings, in proud colours, bold and primal. They hung like dark stalactites in the cave, still and heavy, communing only their own colours back to themselves. They brooded over the shop; and over Mr Saiyetovitz there beneath, treading the worn cement with his disgruntled, dispossessed air of doing his best, but . . . I had glimpsed him before. He lurked within the depths of his store like a beast in its lair, and now and then I had seen the glimmer of his pale, pasty face with the wide upper lip under which the lower closed glumly and puffily.

John Saiyetovitz (his name wasn't John at all, really – it was Yanka, but when he arrived at Cape Town, long ago, the Immigration authorities were tired of attempting to understand and spell the unfamiliar names of the immigrants pouring off the boat, and by the time they'd got the 'Saiyetovitz' spelt right, they couldn't be bothered puzzling over the 'Yanka', so they scrawled 'John' on his papers, and John he was) – John Saiyetovitz was a gentle man, with an almost hangdog gentleness, but when he was trading with the natives, strange blasts of power seemed to blow up in his soul. Africans are the slowest buyers in the world; to them, buying is a ritual, a slow and solemn undertaking. They must go carefully; they nervously scent pitfalls on every side. And confronted with a selection of different kinds of the one thing they want, they are as confused as a child before a plate of pastries; fingering, hesitating, this or that . . .? On a busy Saturday they must be allowed to stand about the shop endlessly, looking up and about, pausing to shake their heads and give a profound 'ow!'; sauntering off; going to press their noses against the window again; coming back. And Mr Saiyetovitz – always the same, unshaven and collarless – lugging a blanket down from the shelves, flinging it upon the counter – and another, and then another, and standing, arms hanging, sullen and smouldering before the blank-faced purchaser. The boy with his helpless stance, and his eyes rolling up in the agony of decision, filling the shop with the sickly odour of his anxious sweat, and clutching his precious guitar.

Waiting, waiting.

And then Mr Saiyetovitz swooping away in a gesture of rage and denial; don't care, sick-to-death. And the boy anxious, edging forward to feel the cloth again, and the whole business starting up all over again; more blankets, different colours, down from the shelf and hooked from the ceiling – stalactites crumpled to woollen heaps to wonder over. Mr Saiyetovitz throwing them down, moving in jerks of rage now, and then roughly bullying the boy into a decision. Shouting at him, bundling his purchase into his arms, snatching the money, gesturing him cowed out of the store.

Mr Saiyetovitz treated the natives honestly, but with bad grace. He forced them to feel their ignorance, their inadequacy, and their submission to the white man's world of money. He spiritually maltreated them, and bitterly drove his nail into the coffin of their confidence.

With me, he was shy, he smiled widely and his hand went to the stud swinging loose at the neck of his half-buttoned shirt, and drew as if in apology over the stubbled landscape of his jaw. He always called me 'little girl' and he liked to talk to me in the way that he thought children like to be talked to, but I found it very difficult to make a show of reply, because his English was so broken and fragmentary. So I used to stand there, and say yes, Mr Saiyetovitz, and smile back and say thank you! to anything that sounded like a question, because the question usually was did I want a lemonade? and of course, I usually did.

The first time Miriam ever came to my home was the day of my birthday party.

Our relationship at school had continued unchanged, just as before; she had her friends and I had mine, but outside of school there was the curious plane of intimacy on which we had, as it were, surprised one another wandering, and so which was shared peculiarly by us.

I had put Miriam's name down on my guest list; she was invited; and she came. She wore a blue taffeta dress which Mrs Saiyetovitz had made for her (on the old Singer on the counter in the shop, I guessed) and it was quite nice if a bit too frilly. My home was pretty and well-furnished and full of flowers and personal touches of my mother's hands; there was space, and everything shone. Miriam did not open her eyes at it; I saw her finger a bowl of baby-skinned pink roses in the passing, but all afternoon she looked out indifferently as she did at home.

The following Saturday at the store we were discussing the party. Miriam was telling Mrs Saiyetovitz about my presents, and I was standing by in pleasurable embarrassment at my own importance.

'Well, please God, Miri,' said Mrs Saiyetovitz at the finish, 'you'll also have a party for your birday in April ... Ve'll be in d'house, and everyting'll be nice, just like you want.' – They were leaving the rooms behind the shop – the mournful green plush curtains glooming the archway between the bedroom and the living-room; the tarnished samovar; the black beetles in the little kitchen; Miriam's old black piano with the candlesticks, wheezing in the draughty passage; the damp puddly yard piled with empty packing-cases and eggshells and banana skins; the hovering smell of fish frying. They were going to live in a little house in the township nearby.

But when April came, Miriam took ten of her friends to the Saturday afternoon bioscope in celebration of her birthday. 'And to Costas Café afterwards for ice-cream,' she stated to her mother, looking out over her head. I think Mrs Saiyetovitz was disappointed about the party, but she reasoned then, as always, that as her daughter went to school and was educated and could speak English, whilst she herself knew nothing, wasn't clever at all, the little daughter must know best what was right and what was *nice*.

I know now what of course I did not know then: that Miriam Saiyetovitz and I were intelligent little girls into whose brains there never had, and never would, come the freak and wonderful flash that is brilliance. Ours were alabaster intellects: clear, perfect light; no streaks of dark, unknown granite splitting to reveal secret veins of brightness, like thin gold, between stratum and stratum. We were fitted to be good schoolteachers, secretaries, organizers; we did everything well, nothing badly, and nothing remarkably. But to the Saiyetovitzes, Miriam's brain blazed like the sun, warming their humbleness.

In the year-by-year passage through school, our classmates thinned out one by one; the way seedlings come up in a bunch to a certain stage in their development, and then by some inexplicable process of natural selection, one or two continue to grow and branch up into the air, whilst the others wither or remain small and weedy. The other girls left to go and learn shorthand-and-typewriting: weeded out by the necessity of earning a living. Or moved, and went to other schools: transplanted to some ground of their own. Miriam and I remained, growing straight and steadily . . .

During our matriculation year a sense of wonder and impending change came upon us both; the excitement of coming to an end that is also a beginning. We felt this in one another, and so were drawn together in new earnestness. Miriam came to study with me in the garden at my house, and oftener than ever, I slipped down to the Concession stores to exchange a book or discuss work with her. For although they now had a house, the Saiyetovitzes still lived, in the wider sense of the word, at the store. When Miriam and I discussed our schoolwork, the Saiyetovitzes crept about, very quiet, talking to one another only in hoarse, respectful whispers.

It was during this year, when the wonder of our own capacity to learn was reaching out and catching into light like a veld fire within us, that we began to talk of the University. And, all at once, we talked of nothing else. I spoke to my father of it, and he was agreeable, although my mother thought a girl could do better with her time. But so long as my father was willing to send me, I knew I should go. Ah yes, said Miriam. She liked my father very much; I knew that. In fact she said to me once – it was a strange thing to say, and almost emotionally, she said it, and at a strange time, because we were on the bus going into the town to buy a new winter coat which she had wanted very badly and talked about longingly for days, and her father had just given her the money to get it – she said to me: You know, I think your father's just right – I mean, if you had to choose somebody, a certain kind of person for a father, well, your father'd be just the kind you'd want.

When she broached the subject of University to her parents, they were agreeable for her to go, too. Indeed, they wanted her to go almost more than she herself did. But they worried a great deal about the money side of it; every time I went down to the store there'd be a discussion of ways and means, Saiyetovitz slowly munching his bread and garlic polony lunch, and worrying. Miriam didn't worry about it; they'll find the money, she said. She was a tall girl, now, with beautiful breasts, and a large, dark-featured face that had a certain capable elegance, although her father's glum mouth was unmistakable and on her upper lip faint dark down foreshadowed a heavy middle age. Her parents were peasants; but she was the powerful young Jewess. Beside her, I felt pale in my Scotch gingery-fairness: lightly drawn upon the mind's eye, whilst she was painted in oils.

We both matriculated; not so well as we thought we should, but well enough; and we went to the University. And there, too, we did well enough. We had both decided upon the same course: teaching. In the end, it had seemed the only thing to do. Neither of us had any particular bent.

It must have been a hard struggle for the Saiyetovitzes to keep Miriam at the University, buy her clothes, and pay for her board and lodging in Johannesburg. There is a great deal of money to be made out of native trade concessions purchased from the government; and it doesn't require education or trained commercial astuteness to make it – in fact, trading of this sort seems to flourish in response to something very different: what is needed is instinctive peasant craftiness such as can only be found in the uneducated, in those who have scratched up their own resources. Storekeepers with this quality of peasant craft made money all about Mr Saiyetovitz, bought houses and motor-cars and banded their wives' retired hands with diamonds in mark of their new idleness. But Mr Saiyetovitz was a peasant without the peasant's craft; without that flaw in his simplicity that might have given him cheques and deeds of transfer to sign, even if he were unable to read the print on the documents . . . Without this craft, the peasant has only one thing left to him: hard work, dirty work, with the sweet, sickly body-smell of the black men about him all day. Saiyetovitz made no money: only worked hard and long, standing in his damp shirt amidst the clamour of the stores and the death-smell from the eating-house always in his nose.

Meanwhile, Miriam fined down into a lady. She developed a half-bored, half-intolerant shrug of the shoulders in place of the childish sharpness that had been filed jagged by the rub-rub of rough life and harsh contrasts. She became soft-voiced, where she had been loud and gay. She watched and conformed; and soon took on the attitude of liberal-mindedness that sets the doors of the mind slackly open, so that any idea may walk in and out again, leaving very little impression: she could appreciate Bach and Stravinsky, and spend a long evening listening to swing music in the dark of somebody's flat.

Race and creed had never meant very much to Miriam and me, but at the University she sifted naturally toward the young Jews who were passing easily and enthusiastically, with their people's extra-ordinary aptitude for creative and scientific work, through Medical School. They liked her; she was invited to their homes for tennis parties, swimming on Sundays, and dances, and she seemed as unimpressed by the luxury of their ten-thousand-pound houses as she had been by the contrast of our clean, pleasant little home, long ago, when she herself was living behind the Concession store.

She usually spent part of the vacations with friends in Johannesburg; I missed her – wandering about the Mine on my own, out of touch, now, with the girls I had left behind in the backwater of the small town. During the second half of one July vacation – she had spent the first two weeks in Johannesburg – she asked me if she could come and spend Sunday at my home, and in the afternoon, one of the medical students arrived at our house in his small car. He had come from Johannesburg; Miriam had evidently told him she would be with us. I gathered her parents did not know of the young man's visit, and I did not speak of it before them.

So the four years of our training passed. Miriam Saiyetovitz and I had dropped like two leaves, side by side into the same current, and been carried downstream together: now the current met a swirl of dead logs, reeds, and the force of other waters, and broke up, divided its drive and its one direction. The leaves floated clear; divergent from one another. Miriam got a teaching post in Johannesburg, but I was sent to a small school in the Northern Transvaal. We met seldom during the first six months of our adult life: Miriam went to Cape Town during the vacation, and I flew to Rhodesia with the first profits of my independence. Then came the war, and I, glad to escape so soon the profession I had once anticipated with such enthusiasm, joined the nursing service and went away for the long, strange interlude of four years. Whilst I was with a field hospital in Italy, I heard that Miriam had married – a Dr Somebody-or-other; my informant wasn't sure of the name. I guessed it must be one of the boys whom she had known as students. I sent a cable of congratulation, to the Saiyetovitzes' address.

And then, one day I came back to the small mining town and found it there, the same; like a face that has been waiting a long time. My Mother, and my Dad, the big wheels of the shaft turning, the trees folding their wings about the Mine houses; and our house, with the green, square lawn and the cat watching the doves. For the first few weeks I faltered about the old life, feeling my way in a dream so like the old reality that it hurt.

There was a feel about an afternoon that made my limbs tingle with familiarity . . . What . . .? And then, lying on our lawn under the hot sky, I knew: just the sort of glaring summer afternoon that used to send me down to the Concession stores, feeling isolated in the heat. Instantly, I thought of the Saiyetovitzes, and I wanted to go and see them, see if they were still there; what Miriam was doing; where she was, now.

Down at the stores it was the same as ever, only dirtier, smaller, more chipped and smeared – the way reality often is in contrast with the image carried long in the mind. As I stepped so strangely on that old pocked pavement, with the skeleton cats and the orange peel and the gobs of spit, my heart tightened with the thought of the Saiyetovitzes. I was in a kind of excitement to see the store again. And there it was; and excitement sank out at the evidence of the monotony of 'things'. Blankets swung a little in the doorway. Flies crawled amongst the shirts and shoes posed in the window, the hot, wet, sickening fatty smell came over from the eating-house. I met it with the old revulsion: it was like breathing inside someone's stomach. And in the store, amongst the wicked glitter of the tin trunks, beneath the secret whispering of the blankets, the old Saiyetovitzes sat glumly, with patience, waiting ... As animals wait in a cage; for nothing.

In their delight at seeing me again, I saw that they were older, sadder; that they had somehow given themselves into the weight of their own humbleness, they were without a pinnacle on which to fix their eyes. Whatever place it was that they looked upon now, it was flat.

Mr Saiyetovitz's mouth had creased in further to the dead folds of his chin; his hair straggled to the rims of his ears. As he spoke to me, I noticed that his hands lay, with a curious helpless indifference, curled on the counter. Mrs Saiyetovitz shuffled off at once to the back of the shop to make a cup of tea for me, and carried it in, slopping over into the saucer. She was uglier than ever, now, her back hunched up to meet her head, her old thick legs spiralled in crêpe bandages because of varicose veins. And blinder too, I could see: that inquiring look of the blind or deaf smiling unsure at you from her face.

The talk turned almost at once to Miriam, and as they answered my questions about her, I saw them go inert. Yes, she was married; had married a doctor – a flicker of pride in the old man at this. She lived in Johannesburg. Her husband was doing very well. There was a photograph of her home, in one of the more expensive suburbs; a large, white modern house, with flower borders and a fishpond. And there was Miri's little boy, sitting on his swing; and a studio portrait of him, taken with his mother.

There was the face of Miriam Saiyetovitz, confident, carefully made-up and framed in a good hairdresser's version of her dark hair, smiling queenly over the face of her child. One hand lay on the child's shoulder, a smooth hand, wearing large, plain, expensive diamond rings. Her bosom was proud and rounded now – a little too heavy, a little over-ripe in the climate of ease.

I could see in her face that she had forgotten a lot of things.

When his wife had gone into the back of the shop to refill my teacup, old Saiyetovitz went silent, looking at the hand that lay before him on the counter, the fingers twitching a little under the gaze.

It doesn't come out like you think, he said, it doesn't come out like you think.

He looked up at me with a comforting smile.

And then he told me that they had seen Miriam's little boy only three times since he was born. Miriam they saw hardly at all; her husband never. Once or twice a year she came out from Johannesburg to visit them, staying an hour on a Sunday afternoon, and then driving herself back to town again. She had not invited her parents to her home at any time; they had been there only once, on the occasion of the birth of their grandson.

Mrs Saiyetovitz came back into the store: she seemed to know of what we had been speaking. She sat down on a shot-purple tin trunk and folded her arms over her breast. Ah yes, she breathed, ah yes . . .

I stood there in Miriam's guilt before the Saiyetovitzes, and they were silent, in the accusation of the humble.

But in a little while a Swazi in a tobacco-coloured blanket sauntered dreamily into the shop, and Mr Saiyetovitz rose heavy with defeat.

Through the eddy of dust in the lonely interior and the wavering fear round the head of the native and the bright hot dance of the jazz blankets and the dreadful submission of Mrs Saiyetovitz's conquered voice in my ear, I heard his voice strike like a snake at my faith: angry and browbeating, sullen and final, lashing weakness at the weak.

Mr Saiyetovitz and the native.

Defeated, and without understanding in their defeat.

A Watcher of the Dead

When my grandmother died, in 1939, Uncle Jules took over. There was no man about our house; my father, a poor provider, uncomplainingly suffered by my mother, apologetically aware of his own unimportance, had run away and left us eight years before. Uncle Jules was my father's brother, and he seemed to materialize in response to family crises, such as weddings and funerals. In Johannesburg, where we lived, there were numerous other relatives on my father's side, but we did not see them often. Quite suddenly, out of the vague comings and goings of some sort of business (diamond buying? travelling in jewellery?) that kept Uncle Jules out of Johannesburg and sometimes even out of South Africa, he appeared and made all the necessary arrangements.

Although my grandmother was an old lady with the soft-pink colour that comes from growing up in rainy England and the friendly, Cockney quickness of speech that comes from being a Londoner, and although she had friends on our street, in the unfashionable part of Johannesburg, who were Scotch and Afrikaner and Italian, when she died, she was Jewish; all the other things were gone and she was only Jewish. Her race and the religion she had lightheartedly ignored claimed her for initiation at last, an initiation that we did not understand and that took her away from us as her death, by itself, had not yet done.

I was a girl of sixteen and the eldest of the three children, but to me, as to my brother William and my sister Helen, being Jewish had simply meant that we had a free half-hour while the other children at our convent school went to catechism. If Mother had ever known any Jewish customs – and I doubt it – she had forgotten them long before we were born. Jewish funerals are simple and austere – no flowers; just a short service at the graveside, and the plain wooden coffin goes down into the grave. In South Africa, at least, it is not usual for Jewish women to go to funerals, even of their closest friends. Uncle Jules arranged for a rabbi to conduct the service at the cemetery, had the death notice put in the paper, and telephoned all the relatives to tell them when the funeral would be. We could do nothing. We didn't even believe that my grandmother was dead. She had been mashing a banana for Helen, and tasting more than she mashed, when the fork simply failed to reach her mouth. A blood clot, the doctor said, but it seemed to us that she had merely been interrupted and would presently return, saying, 'Now, what was I doing when . . .'

The afternoon of the day she died, the family and two embarrassed neighbours sat around the living-room, where my grandmother's sword ferns, in the windows, made the light green. Uncle Jules, preoccupied, came and went. At last he paused and sat down in the brown armchair, alert, drumming with his fingers and biting nervously at the inside of his cheek. His eyebrows gathered in a frown as things to be done passed in review before his mind. Suddenly his eyebrows arched, his mouth pursed, and he said. 'We'll have to get a *wacher*.'

'A what?' asked William.

'A *wacher*,' Uncle Jules said. 'I'll have to go and phone the synagogue to . . .' Mumbling to himself, he went to the telephone.

I got up and went out into the passage after him. 'What's a *wacher*?' I whispered, catching his coat sleeve.

'Good God! Don't you know?'

'Sh-h-h!' I said, and tugged at him, not wanting my mother to hear.

With a glance toward the room where the others sat, he said softly, 'A watcher of the dead.'

These words, coming from that matter-of-fact man's mouth, seemed to me like an incantation carelessly repeated by someone who has merely overheard it somewhere and says it again, not knowing what it is that he says. A watcher of the dead. *Who* watches, I wondered, and for what does he watch? For that which has happened to them already? For some sign of where they have gone? What kind of man can watch where there is nothing to watch at all, only what is past, blank, behind, and what is unknown, blank, ahead? A watcher of the dead.

'How long will he stay?' I asked.

'Sunset to sunrise, I think it is,' my uncle said. Then he dragged the telephone directory from beneath the magazines that always piled up on top of it on the rickety hall table.

The synagogue sent an elderly gentleman who dwindled from a big stomach, outlined with a watch chain, to thin legs that ended in neat, shabby brown shoes, supple with years of polishing. He wore glasses that made his brown eyes look very big, he had a small beard, and his face was pleasantly pink and planned in folds – a fold beneath each eye, another fold where the cheek skirted the mouth, a fold where the jaw met the neck, a fold where the neck met the collar. There was even a small fold beneath the lobe of each ear, as if the large, useful-looking ears had sagged under their own weight and usefulness over the years.

He took off his hat and put down his cane, and at once busied himself about the room in which my grandmother lay, in the peculiar silence of one who does not breathe, on her own side of the old double bed that she had brought with her when she came to live with us. He moved her body on to the floor, lit a candle, altered the position of a chair. I almost expected him to begin humming softly to himself. My mother stood in the doorway, biting the joint of the first finger of her clenched hand, exactly the way my ten-year-old sister sometimes did. We children did not know that this placing of the body on the floor was a gesture of the Jewish faith, signifying the renunciation of worldly comforts. We said nothing. Even my mother said nothing, but only looked at the figure on the floor, as people look after the retreating bundle of a sick person wheeled away down a hospital corridor to some unimagined treatment in some un-imagined room.

A little later, Uncle Jules, who had been out of the house arranging about the funeral, which was to take place next afternoon, came into the living-room again. 'The what-d'you-call-'em's come,' William said.

'The *wacher*? Good!' Uncle Jules said, and dropped his raincoat into a dark corner of the hall.

The darkness of the first night – the first night that she was not there – was welling up in all the rooms of the house. As the lights came on, now in this room, then in that; as the family went into bedrooms, into the kitchen, into the bathroom, and, without thinking, touched each room into light, my grandmother began really to be dead. The electric light opened up every shadowy room and found her not there.

Always before at this time in the evening, there had been a smell of frying in the house; the door of my room would fly open and there she would be, saying, 'Darling, shall we have chips?' Her cheeks were always pinker when she cooked; the tiny diamond earrings that had grown into her lobes over forty years before came winking alive against her pink ears. She would look anxiously and respectfully at my schoolbooks, waiting for me to make up my mind. Then she would leave me to my studies, and a moment or two later I would hear her talking to Helen in the hall.

My grandmother had lived with us and kept house for us ever since my father disappeared. Mother ran a little stationery shop and came home every night, like the man of the family, to hear from my grandmother what had happened during the day and to make the decisions and check the bills. It was just as it had been with my father. My grandmother did not like to have to make up her mind. She had never had to while my grandfather was alive; she had never lived, as my mother had lived, with a man who abdicated all authority, a man to lean on whom would have been to fall against empty air. She had trembled joyfully in the shadow of her husband all her life, and she respected my mother enormously.

Though it didn't show, I realized later, out of my knowledge of my own life as a woman, that there was a wistfulness in my mother's acceptance of her mother's respect. My little grandmother was feminine as a dove, with her full bosom, in her grey dress; vain of her two new hats, winter and summer; moved easily to tears by the Shirley Temple films she and Helen followed around the small suburban cinemas; remembering from fifty years back the happy, vulgar, innocent music-hall songs we children loved to hear. Mother cherished her, in the true sense of the word, as a man cherishes a woman, a woman a child, but also saw in her something that she herself did not have – the easy tears, the gentle weakness, the submission to sex.

Uncle Jules went into my grandmother's room to speak to the watcher, and we children, unable to settle down anywhere, even in our own rooms, went in search of my mother, who was in the kitchen getting dinner. All day long she had been doing something; I could not have said what it was that she was doing, but she moved about, there were objects in her hands, and her eyes were lowered in concentration. She was busy at the kitchen table when we went into the kitchen, and the cat was arching itself plaintively against her legs, begging for food. Our house was small, and all on one floor, and Uncle Jules had hardly gone into my grandmother's room when I heard him coming back along the passage.

'Haven't you given him anything?' he asked urgently.

My mother looked at Uncle Jules and said, 'What does he want?'

'He doesn't *want* anything. But, good Lord, it's always done.' My uncle felt that he must not get exasperated and was unsure what feeling he *could* display toward my mother. All attitudes are equally embarrassing and affronting before the fact of death.

'Should I cook him something?' asked my mother.

'No, no, you must have something for him to drink. It's usual. A bottle of brandy. They're always given a bottle of brandy.'

'What?' said my mother.

'Haven't you got a bottle of brandy, or something, in the house?' Uncle Jules asked patiently. 'Surely you've got *something*.'

'Oh, yes,' said my mother. 'He's going to drink brandy? You mean to tell me he's going to drink brandy tonight?'

My uncle smiled and shrugged his head on one side. 'Well,' he said, 'it's the custom. It's always done.'

'There's a bottle not opened yet,' my mother said. 'It's put away. I'll get it.' She went out of the kitchen. The cat stalked around and around the table leg. In a moment, my mother was back. 'Is this all right?' she asked anxiously, handing a new bottle of brandy to my uncle.

'Of course, of course,' he said. 'What should he expect – Napoleon?' From his expression, it was clear that he felt he had said the wrong thing again. He sighed and left the kitchen, carrying the bottle of brandy by its neck.

'Here you are, then, my cat,' said my mother, taking a pat of ground meat out of the refrigerator and sitting down on the kitchen-chair, so that the cat might feed easily from her hand. In a brief series of gobbles, the meat disappeared; the cat went on licking at the empty fingers. My mother began to cry, her face pulled awry, looking more like Helen than ever, and tears ran down into her mouth. Helen, William, and I stood still, on the other side of the kitchen table, afraid to touch her.

'I don't want her to be with him! I don't want her to be with him!' my mother said. Nobody answered, nobody spoke or moved.

Presently, she got up and blew her nose and went over to the sink to wash her hands.

The family and Uncle Jules sat beneath the round yellow ceiling-light, gathered at table for supper. Everything tasted very good; everyone was very gentle and attentive. Love rose into consciousness between us children and within us; William's hand, passing the butter, was my hand; my little sister's hair, resting along her back, was my hair. This was an exciting discovery, and the more exciting for being a shared one. We could not share it with my mother, though. She sat, serving, spiritually and physically alone at the head of the table.

Afterward, we trooped into the living-room and sat in silence, William and Helen pretending to read, Mother and I merely sitting. Uncle Jules stared down between his knees at the floor. An hour or two ago, there had come the knowledge of my grandmother *not there* – lack, absence, the *goneness* of someone well loved, familiar. Now there was something, someone, again. I felt the presence of our dead grandmother, like a stranger in the room near by.

Before my mother went to bed, she walked into the room where my grandmother lay, and we children followed. The watcher, who had taken off his glasses and was resting his eyes, got up from his chair. There was something of the air of a museum attendant about him; I felt that he might say, 'Now, is there anything in particular you would like to see? Any information you wish?'

My mother went over to my dead grandmother and bent down and touched her hair.

'Excuse me,' said the old gentleman. With a thrill of fear, I remembered the notices they put on exhibits: 'Please do not touch!'

'What?' asked my mother.

'It is not allowed,' the old gentleman said regretfully.

'I'm not doing anything,' my mother said. 'I've come to kiss my mother good night.'

'It is not allowed – to touch the dead,' said the watcher.

My mother stood bent over the dead woman, with her head turned to him. Her look seemed to draw a line around herself and her mother that the old gentleman, blinking without his glasses, quietly within his rights, didn't dare to cross. I knew he could not take one step nearer to my mother, to the place where my grandmother lay. He moved his hands with the apologetic, imploring denial of the small official. And, like all small officials, he clutched at the authority behind him. 'It's against the Jewish religion,' he said with a shrug and a smile of distress.

My mother drew a deep breath and then said sharply, 'But she didn't die of anything contagious! I couldn't get anything from her!'

The watcher looked shocked. His attitude toward death was abstract, the abstraction of the professional; my mother's approach was individual, the approach of the amateur. He shrugged once more.

'Why? Why?' insisted my mother. And before he could answer, she asked again, 'Why? Why shouldn't I?' She was excited and angry, with the impossible, aggressive anger that feeds on itself and does not even want to be placated. I thought she might stamp her feet, grind her teeth.

'There's no reason, is there? *Is* there?' she repeated, shrilly.

I felt sick and my heart beat terribly fast. 'But, Mother,' I said, 'he can't help it. It's not *his* fault.' I looked at my grandmother, so deep asleep.

My mother's eyes flashed pure venom at the watcher, who stood there tugging at one ear, like a simple, obstinate mule who doesn't even know, or pretends he doesn't know, that all the shoving, pushing, and shouting of the mule driver is directed at him. 'No,' she said, her voice trembling. 'I know it isn't his fault.' And I saw that because it wasn't his fault, because he couldn't help it, she hated him. She wanted to flay him for his innocence.

In the power of her inconsolable rage, she swept to the door. Then she remembered, and turned for one look at my grandmother, alone on the floor, and, with a terrible shock of sorrow, found that she had forgotten her, that she had lost her last moment with her, lost it in anger.

Lying in my bed in the dark, I felt that perhaps in the morning the watcher, the poor old gentleman with the well-polished shoes, would be dead, too – killed silently and innocently in his chair by the rage of my mother's grief.

But in the morning all things are different. In the morning, unbelievably and reassuringly, my mother was cooking a big breakfast of kippers and fried eggs. 'Bring me the brass tray from the breakfast-room,' she said. 'He'll want something to eat early, before he goes, poor old thing. He's not so young, to be sitting in a chair all night.'

I looked at her. Her face, over the stove, was quiet.

Her hands moved slowly and were very cold to the touch. She arranged the tray and carried it into the breakfast-room and put it before the old gentleman. He sat patiently at the table, with his napkin tucked into the V of his waistcoat, while she poured tea for him. The flaps beneath his eyes were more pronounced; he ate steadily, like an obedient child. When he had finished, he wiped his mouth very thoroughly, put the crumpled napkin by his place, and thanked her.

He went out to get his hat and stick, and she stood, her hand on the teapot, looking after him. Uncle Jules paid the watcher his two-guinea fee, and the old gentleman left, carrying a neat paper parcel that must have been the bottle of brandy – opened or intact, one could not tell.

My mother took the breakfast tray out to the kitchen and I followed her. She looked very tired; a nerve jumped beneath her left eye. 'Poor old thing,' she murmured gently. 'He must be old, you know.'

'Mmm. And being up all night –' I said.

A pallid smile lifted the corner of her mouth, which looked dry and thin. 'He had eaten an apple,' she said. 'There was the skin of an apple curled on a bit of newspaper beside him. Shame! He'd been eating an apple. I only just remembered, now, seeing it there.'

'But didn't he –' I said, hardly knowing what I was saying but beginning to understand.

'Asleep,' she said. 'Asleep all the time. Fast asleep.'

There was a moment of silence – kitchen silence, composed of the small hissings of the cooking pots, the scraping of a knife, the drizzling tap. 'Mother,' I said, 'did you –' Her back was to me – perhaps she did not even hear me – and I never asked her what I had started to ask her.

I have never asked her to this day. At the time, I thought, shocked, she means this morning; it was this morning that she went into the room and found him. I could see, as if I had been there, the dark, withdrawn house, the room of the dead, with the candle burning, the old man asleep, with his chin sunk sidewise into its own folds, the green coil of apple peeling, with the faint scent of vanished apple in the room, and my mother, alone with my grandmother for the last time.

Treasures of the Sea

There was a beach on the South Coast of Natal where there was time for the sand to record every footstep. At the end of the day, there they were, interlaced perhaps, but clear with the stamp of the foot that impressed them; the quick, kicked-up track of a running child, the fancy dapple of the big dog's paws, the even clefts left by the hard bony feet of an Indian fisherman. They asserted authority over the beach as little as a flag, stuck by an explorer into a mound of snow, over the white, baffling supremity of the Pole. The beach, the sea, the madly singing bushes were the live, the real, the supreme here; the light dabs of human feet had not stepped out a beautiful background for a frieze of figures, running, cavorting, and clowning, but had merely succeeded in feeling lightly over one curve, one convolution of a composition so enormous that they would never be able to feel out the whole of it. There was white sand all around the few, far, faint footsteps, sand drying thin-crusted and bright in the wind, looped from rocks to rocks along each inlet, mile after mile.

It was here that they had brought her when she was two years old, to sit in a hat of plaited mealie leaves with her feet plastered over with a mound of heavy wet sand. It was here that she fought and struggled and screamed against the touch of the sea, until the feel of it, rising cool and enclosing against the small of her little back, and the scent of it prickling her nose with froth woke a new pleasure in her, and as she was brought back year after year, seemed to egg her on to show off, to dive and tumble and scream. It was at this beach, or another like it, that she first discovered a hint of the activity of the sea, the strange thick wet rubbery foliage, the red flowers buttoned along the undersides of rocks, the silent fish and lethargic dabs of mucus living in perfect shells, the hundreds of shells individually fashioned and coloured to a whim. All this delicate craftsmanship, done by the sea. She had discovered it led by her native nanny along the tiny low-tide beaches where between the rocks, the wash turned over hundreds of thousands of shells with the sound of money gently clinking, and sucked back away gustily whilst they sprang into wet colour under the sun. The nanny collected brown-backed cowrie shells like tiny tortoises to trim milk-jug covers, but the child stuffed her pockets with whatever they would hold. When she got back to her room and turned them all out upon the bed, her pockets were wet with a curious heavy salt wetness. It was the glitter off the shells. Now they lay with the sand upon the bedcover, dull as any china. A few winkles that she had found room for were crusted disgustingly in their little towers, dead.

She threw the lot out of the window.

But next day and next year she was back hunched down with her knees up to her chin again, gathering up the unbelievable satin pink shimmer of the mother-of-pearl oyster shells, wet from the sea.

When she grew up she travelled, but more stirring than all the dead palaces, the mountains and cities, pictures and monuments, the ballet, the theatre, the opera, and the stirring talk of café philosophers; eliciting from her the tug of a warm crude response rooted in the kernel around which her adult layers of taste, discernment, and appreciation had folded, was the sight of small boys in southern ports who swam out to the ship and dived for passengers' coins. She hung with the rail pressing into her stomach, flinging her coins as far and hard as her excitement. And she seemed to feel the thin rim of the coin cutting down hard through the enormous green weight of water, and the bubbles flying from the boy's ears as he went after it and beat it to the bottom. The sea was so immense, so weighted in favour, able to hide whole ships and never return them, yet the boy got the mere fleck of a penny back from it. He beat the sea to the bottom. One day when they were far out, she went to the rail and dropped a penny, away from her hand into ten thousand miles of endless grey water. Gone, lost, taken by the sea and too infinitesimal to be taken account of.

'Wishing, my dear young lady?' said a delicate old gentleman, passing by. And she smiled the brilliant smile of accession to other people's impressions that we all gratefully employ to distract the world from ourselves. He took the sunburst of a smile and put it away with his collection of the characteristics of young women.

In America the nature of the sea's fascination for her was mistaken for a physical zest something like that she had felt when, almost a baby and still learning to distinguish different sensory discoveries, she had been dipped into a new and buoyant element, less staid than air. They rushed her to Florida beaches and sent her scudding over the backs of long rollers balanced on a piece of fragile board, watching her face for the furious pleasure which they awaited as their triumph. They laid her on a sprung-rubber chaise longue under a fringed canopy, to absorb the sting of sun and the abrasive of salt in close company with thousands who flocked to the benefits of another kind of Ganges. Offering them the sunburst, she supposed it must be what she enjoyed. But when, in a determination to give her everything they had contracted the sea to offer in the way of a kick, they took her deep-sea fishing off Florida Sound, enjoyment of a very personal kind came up and seized her as she landed a great fish, heaving with life, out of the depths of the sea. They wanted to take photographs of her, holding it tail to shoulder. But she wanted it stuffed, she called, throwing it in tight triumph where it could not jump back into the sea.

After that, wherever she went she fished, and the record of the beautiful, shiny, gaping creatures she had hooked out of the sea grew almost at the pace of her collection of hundreds of thousands of shells, picked up alone on beaches all over the world, and thrown into boxes and old pillowcases. At home now she had a special aquarium built, and in it she tried to persuade salt-water fish and sea plants to grow as they did for the sea. But transported by airplane in special containers, and deluded by lights and artificial currents in the big box of water, they refused to adapt themselves to the slightest degree. Every time she returned to the white beaches where hundreds of anemones closed themselves away at her touch in every pool, and fish so small and finely made that you could see their threads of skeletons through the opalescent flesh flickered in easy survival through raging tides and the menace of bigger creatures, she smiled at the triumph of the sea. The sea kept its treasures to itself. Threw them carelessly upon the beach in the knowledge that the abundance was never-ending, that there would always be more, more, more; in the confidence that whoever took them away would find that he had taken nothing: the very discarded shells and stones that children gathered left the colour for which they had been prized behind them on the beach; the seaweed broken away from the slowly waving mesh became an unrecognizable putrid stickiness; the splendid fish, once out and on land, gross and stupid enough only to be eaten.

It was about this time that she met a man whose idea of her was so much what she wanted herself to be that she fell deeply in love with him. He was young and he was beautiful, and through him, she felt herself vulnerable for the first time. She did not want him to fly; she was suddenly afraid for him to swim out beyond the breakers. He had soaked up her life like a sponge, and she looked forward to living in the interstices of his being for the rest of her time. Her friends were neglected, her books unread, her aquarium a greenish and dried-up piece of clutter.

They wanted to marry as soon as possible, but before they could hollow a warm place for themselves in their world, there was a business obligation in Rhodesia he had to fulfil. She could not decide which would be more pleasure: to go with him, or to wait for him for two short weeks in certainty in some place that she loved. He decided for the latter, and she took the added pleasure of accepting his deciding for her. It was suddenly all quite perfect; she would go down to the deserted South Coast village where she had been so often before. She would play in the sun on the sand (he found her delight in rock-pools and shells and quaint sea-things an astonishing and precious streak of child in a person so definitely moulded by the world) and he would come to her there.

What else was there to decide? His forehead was wrinkled, arranging it all. Oh, a ring! She must have his ring to signal that she was waiting for him. What kind of a ring did she want? What about a sapphire?

Oh no! she said swiftly with the happiness of inspiration. A pearl! A big pink pearl.

Of course, a pearl would be just the thing for her!

Lying flat on a smooth black rock watched by unseen black crabs petrified by the very displacement of air her motionless body caused, her happiness grew round the rosy pearl as the pearl had itself grown round a tiny piece of grit. Lustre on lustre, warmth on warmth, the pearl on her finger was the core of her life, the fact of love round which the future gathered itself. And as the human self, watchful of stingier times perhaps ahead, nets in all possible satisfactions attending a happiness which is already great enough in itself, she added a delicate but strong nuance to her happiness by the knowledge that here, lying with the softness of the sea air touching at her armpits, with her happiness beating steadily inside her, the symbol of that happiness which she wore in the pink pearl on her finger was also the most beautiful possession of the sea. The sea made nothing more lovely than a pearl. And though no longer belonging to the sea, the pearl was as lovely as it had ever been. All that was best, fullest, at the peak and most perfect welled up to the brim of her life. And the most precious treasure of the sea hung on her finger. She smiled slowly the long slow relaxed smile that seemed to pass from her face to the warm rock beneath her, and set for ever in the seams of that rock, in the sand of that shore, on the shore of that sea.

The days themselves passed with a slowness that she treasured, for she could wait. Waiting had become a positive state, the balance of a drop ready to fall. All day long she wandered on the beach watching her footsteps fill with ooze, and lay for afternoons high on the rock with her hand dipping the lapping water as a bird. She was too full to want anything: to want to fish, or explore the life of the pools, or endear herself to the big old dog by throwing a piece of driftwood for him. She lay with her eyes half-shuttered against the sky, and sometimes, although she was silent, she thought she felt herself singing. Sometimes she fell asleep. And when she woke up she saw circles and splotches of dark, and as she lifted her stiff head, the sea and the sky lurched as if from the porthole of a boat on a rough passage.

One afternoon she woke from a quick light sleep and saw, as she rested, from the corner of her eye, something pinkish move on a rock just across the pool from the one on which she lay. It might have been a crab, but it didn't seem to be. She sat up to get a better view. It moved again. She smiled to herself, in that warm weakness for all life which her own present joy in life engendered. Getting on her haunches and clambering to the edge of her rock, she put her hand out to steady herself and leaned out over the pool to see. The water glittered up at her. The brightness was replaced with blackness. Dizzy, she caught out at what seemed to be a point of rock, a piece of triangular dark. With a surprised intake of breath like a child tumbling, she fell into the pool.

The pool was very shallow, shallow enough for a child to paddle in, and she lay for a moment with one arm over the rock on which she had struck her head, the sand clouding up into the water, the tiny crabs scuttling away from the risen water-line. Then her body slid down, the water hid her face, and the drop of blood, from the scratch made on her chin by a fragment of shell, stained the water faintly like a tiny drop of cochineal. The water hardly covered her back. But later in the afternoon the tide rose, and the waves climbed over the rocks into the pool and turned her over and over, handling her curiously.

All night long the sea lifted and laid, lifted and laid her body, until there was no part of her that was not touched by the sea. And in the morning, when the tide ran out with the rising of the sun, she lay quietly, sheltered, in the pool, and a soft current rippled beneath her floating hand, playing her fingers delicately as a reed instrument, threading in and out with the softest touch possible about the cold finger on which the pearl still shone, very beautiful in the water.

The Prisoner

When I went to school at Mrs Keyter's I used to sit next to the old push-up-and-down window that looked out on the yard. But it was too high for me to see out. I was in the front row at the end, right under the corner of Mrs Keyter's eye, but I could watch her too; the rough wood of our benches, clawed along the grain with scrubbing and deeply indented with furrows tooled by pencils and pocket knives, rubbed smooth with dirt and the glistening waterways of sweat that play mapped out on our palms, nipped at my thighs; the children breathed over their scribblers; the three-legged alarm ticked on the cupboard; without lifting my head, my pencil lead cold to my tongue, my hand as if shielding what I had written, I sat doing nothing, watching her.

Her left hand went slowly up to the side of her chin, and began to pull at the hair. The hair was a single bristle, albino, that caught the light. Her thumb and first finger tried to nip it, to get a grip between the two nails. But it slipped through, seemed to be not there. Yet when the pad of her first finger felt for it again, there it was – the prick of it. She tried again.

A little aureole of red rose round the invisible hair; made clumsy with impatience, the thumb and first finger sometimes pinched the skin in a quick white pleat that went redder again.

Then her head turned swiftly and she picked up a ruler or a pencil with a click against her table: stir. Like bubbles breaking up to the surface, the attention of the children rose; glazed eyes lifted, heads bobbed, the calm concentration rippled with refractions, bright, choppy. – My head bent furiously to finish the work I had not even begun. When the ruler came down against the table and the voice opened: 'Now –' A spurt of panic sent my pencil black and hasty over the empty lines. 'Everybody finished?' – It was a high, slow, questioning voice that only made statements. The jostle of the other children's released attention buffeted my harassed mind. 'Close your books.' QUESTION 1, she was chalking on the blackboard, in sweeping strokes as if she used a brush. Then the a, in parentheses, enclosing like claws . . .

Although I have forgotten what it was like to be a child, I can always remember this. And remembering it is like opening up an old seam, worked out and closed off long ago; feeling your way along the dark, low passages there are smells, objects you stumble over, the sudden feel under your hand of a surface you know. Round the side of the house there were dank stones under the hedge, pincushions of moss between them; putting up your hand to leave the room, you could go round there in summer and sit on the cool stones. A light greyish dust bloomed everything in the schoolroom; chalk blew like pollen from the old towel with which the children took it in turns to clean the blackboard. Mrs Keyter's hand, resting on your book as she bent to explain something, made a smooth dry sound on the paper; if it touched you it was dry as fine sea-sand. But outside, the yard where we screamed at playtime was red-earthed and damp because over it all was a great apricot tree, and in the apricot tree, an owl.

The owl belonged to Mark, Mrs Keyter's little boy. He went to her school along with the rest of us. And along with the rest of us he left when he was nine or ten and old enough to go to a real school with bells and uniforms and proper classrooms. We went back to see her sometimes, during our first year or two at the Government school; and then we began to have nothing to say to her, and in our gyms and badges, with fountain pens sticking out of our blazer pockets, we smiled at the little house with the black-and-white linoleum down the passage, the bare-board schoolroom with the unsteady scrubbed benches and forms.

We forgot about her altogether at thirteen or fourteen. Except to meet her in the street, with the trapped, embarrassed grin of children for their former teachers; a kind of momentary paralysis of self-confidence, as if in the eyes of the teacher the child reads always its own guilt, a secret the other will never forget. Mrs Keyter trotted quietly on, her paper shopping bag swinging from the small dry hand, her greenish coat flapping. She had mild tired eyes deep beneath a hat that was always the same shape.

Perhaps it was always the same hat; the Keyters were peculiar

people, our mothers said. Mrs Keyter still kept her little school, year
after year, taking other people's third and fourth children. She
herself had never had another child. And it seemed that they led a
very odd life, without friends, without change since the days when
we, the eldest children, the same age as her Mark, had been small.
Keyter was a black-haired handsome man with black eyes under
brows that guarded them heavily, and he was some sort of minor
official at the post office. He had been there ever since anyone could
remember. '— My, but he was a handsome young man all the same —'
my mother used to say. We giggled disbelief. He had once had a
sweeping moustache and worn dress trousers with braid down the
sides at a Masonic dance. 'Mind you, he was surly. There was
something morose about him, he danced with you as if he didn't
know you were there.' — We had been afraid of Mr Keyter when we
went to Mrs Keyter's school; 'Mark's father' was a phrase of threat
to Mark, we knew, and if we met him in a doorway, we stood dead
still, our ribs blowing in and out our only movement, unable to
speak. He seldom spoke either. He went by as he might have stepped
over a mouse.

Now our parents didn't go to Masonic gatherings any more, but
were members of a country club and played golf; they had cocktail
parties and Rotary dinners. We no longer lived in the township
where we had been just down the road from Mrs Keyter's little
school. With the money that had come suddenly — like the reward
pouring out of a slot machine when luck presses the innocent-looking
but right button — from gold shares or the sale of squares of weedy
ground in the town made suddenly valuable by new gold mines
thrown up like mole-workings all around us, our parents had built
new houses. Most families owned an American car.

But the Keyters found no new pleasures and those they had had
sank into disuse. He went to work and walked home again. She
taught school in the mornings, walked into town to do her household
shopping in the afternoons. She kept her head down, not submis-
sively, but as if she minded her own business and wanted other
people to mind theirs. They kept the same old house in the same old
street — how close the houses were together! How had we ever
breathed there? — and the grass grew tall round the garage in which

41

were housed an old kitchen-table and some spare forms not in use in the schoolroom. People said they had lost on the share market. How else could it be that they lived so quietly, so dully? They had never got on well together (so people said). How on earth had he come to marry her, in the first place? She was not the sort to marry. And he was a disagreeable creature; what had made her marry him? They never went out together, yet out of school hours, when her high, reasonable voice and the following chant of the children sang out, no one had ever heard anything but silence issuing from that small house on the street. There was a rumour that they did not speak. They had not spoken to one another for several years – a native girl who had worked for them had told it to someone else's servant.

The one link that kept the Keyters alive to the community, made them belong still, was their son Mark. Or rather Mrs Keyter's Mark; his father had never paid any attention to him when he was a baby or a small boy, now that he was growing up they had for one another the strangeness of daily intimates who do not know one another. It was Mrs Keyter and Mark.

Mark was a big, black-haired, handsome boy, as big as a grown man at fourteen. He had his father's face, his father's body, his father's walk. But it was as if the father's body had been snatched up and put on – any old outward form will do – by a wild, careless, loving streak of life. Keyter's heavy handsomeness was fired up and tossed around by Mark; a wonderful deep colour spread like visible energy from the neck of his old jersey, up from his curiously healthy bright ears, up his cheeks. In winter it was quick and rosy, in summer warm and mellow as the sun-coloured skin of a fruit. His dark eyes were always lit up, as if he had been running. – In fact that was the total impression of him; you had caught him in the splendid moment of activity.

Mark went to boarding-school in the Free State, and he matriculated, of course, about the same time as we did. Mrs Keyter, who, as our old teacher, was interested in what we were going to do, told us that he was to take a degree in engineering.

But he never came to the University. Three of us met him on the train the day we had been in to Johannesburg to register as students. We were sitting close together over time-tables and suggested reading lists for the courses on which we had decided, when the train door opened at a siding and Mark jumped in. He was carrying one of those tin lunch cases with a wire handle. He was working at a steel foundry.

When we came home with our piece of news, our mothers countered it with another: old Keyter had gone to live at the Cape. Since when? Transferred down there since the beginning of the month, someone said. – Well, they were a queer bunch ... We shrugged. Our own affairs were fascinatingly absorbing just at that time; there is perhaps nothing in family life, except a marriage of one of the daughters, so happily fingered-over as the aura which surrounds the first child to be sent up to a university. Everyone from the servant to the grandmother must reach out to touch it; a faint nimbus of distinction, like a smear of phosphorescence rubbed on through contact, glimmers from them as well.

So it was not until much later that we heard that Mark's father had denied any interest in furthering Mark's education at the University, and, completely withdrawing his support, had gone off to live as he wished at the coast. It was at examination time at the end of the first year, when my mother had been greatly impressed by my distracted air and the strip of light showing under my door until two o'clock in the morning, and meeting Mrs Keyter, had kept her talking in lower and lower tones outside the grocer's. My mother is such a determined giver of confidences that the burden of her unburdening must in the end completely disarm the most reticent; it becomes impossible to withhold at least some return of confidence without appearing hurtfully mistrusting and positively insulting. So Mrs Keyter, with her eyes gently smiling faraway in her head and her coat hanging flatter to her slighter body, told in a low voice of statement how Mr Keyter had refused to help her let Mark become an engineer. She could not afford to do it on her own. Now he was her young workman, coming home to her; she smiled. He didn't mind it so much; the work was – well ... He couldn't be expected to take much interest in it. But perhaps, who knows, Mr Keyter might change his mind later? That was what she told Mark. But he's young of course, and he feels bitter about it ...

My mother came home tight-lipped and wide-nostrilled. She'd talk about him politely and call him 'Mr Keyter' if he belonged to her! — That poor woman, sticking to such a creature. No feeling even for his own child. What a shame. Mrs Keyter became 'old Mrs Keyter'; the epithet of compassion, nothing to do with age; she was no older than my mother. On the infrequent occasions when Mr Keyter was spoken of, people prefixed 'old' to his name too; scornfully, the dismissal, the condemnation by society of an unnatural father. 'Old Keyter? Oh, he's mad . . .' my mother would say with impatience, having to find a name for something she could not understand.

But Mark did not have to stay in his black overalls at the steel foundry long.

The war came and at once he left and joined the Air Force. He occurs in every war. He must have been at Waterloo, at Balaklava, at Ladysmith, at Gallipoli; an archetype of great physical beauty, energy, gaiety, magnificent in an officer's uniform, some germ that springs up to life from the morbid atmosphere of war like those extraordinary orchid-fungi that appear overnight out of the sodden soil of dark hidden places. He is the manifestation of the repellent fascination of war; wonderful enough to be worthy of sacrifice as an offering — at the same time too much a tantalization of what life might be like to be given without a pang and a doubt. Utterly innocent himself, everyone who looks at him gains a spurious nobility. Your heart beats with excitement and at the same time tears rim your eyes.

When Mark came home on leave and walked out of the broken gate of his mother's little house he seemed to fill the street. The two dirty little girls who played in the gutter opposite stood looking out from under their brows as he passed. The rheumatic old retriever who had belonged to the people up the road for ten years came out to sniff at his shoes and not remember him. He was an officer. His uniform lay on him like the plumes of a cock. His cap cut a slanting line above the line of his eyes: black, deep, friendly, male — not cajoling, but simply drawing to the surface like a blush, a melting of response from everyone who met them. And the smile; with pleasure at the sight of it was mixed envy: how could anyone feel such a smile inside himself? What capacity for joys did it shine off?

There's Mark Keyter! people would say. He's a lovely boy —! the old ladies said with astonishment. He's grown a fine man, the men remarked reflectively. The young women said nothing: – I saw Mark today. There was no knowing what women felt at the sight of him; the shopgirls – perhaps they had known him as children; I'm Lily Burgess . . . Kathleen Pretorius . . . Meg . . . they might offer suddenly, shyly, as they tied the string round the parcel. And he would lean across the counter, smile with surprise – there was a curious little blush, just round the eyes, when he smiled, very warm – and ask and answer the usual questions of past acquaintance, laughing, pleasant. Beside him was his mother, to whom he belonged. Small, stooped, in the greens, browns, and greys that had faded on her for years, she went about with him, handing her parcels up to his arms, talking to him in her questioning voice, listening quietly with a smile beneath her lowered hat as they walked. She seemed to take on a gently vigorous frailty, like a god resting in the sight of his creation.

If no woman in our town knew more of Mark than the lift of his handsome head beside his mother in the cinema, or the quickness of his legs along the street, we knew that in the town near the airport where he was stationed he took all the tributes to which his attractions entitled him. When you met other men who had been stationed at the same place and you mentioned Mark's name, they laughed and jerked their heads knowingly. 'They fight over him. He's always got some new girl on the string. Some of the chaps' wives, too, wouldn't say no to a crooked finger from Keyter. And he doesn't care a damn. – But he's a good chap – Who could blame him? Anybody else with his advantages would be a fool not to do the same.' Then, of course, Mark got married; in every woman in wartime there rises the instinct to mate with a man like Mark. He married one of the pretty girls and brought her home to visit, to Mrs Keyter's old house behind the dying hedge. 'She's a dear girl,' Mrs Keyter told my mother. 'Young people must marry quickly in these times.'

And then there was a baby. It was a boy, and Mrs Keyter went down for the christening. Several people saw photographs of the tiny thing, brought out of a leather case in her handbag. She twisted her head to smile over them once again whilst you were looking at them. She carried around with her a roll of knitting in a fawn silk scarf. She seemed armed against her aloneness, her solitary comings and goings, the clamour of the pupils and the silence of her empty after-noons.

When the baby was three or four months old Mark was sent away to a fighter command in Egypt; it was surprising that he had been kept in South Africa as long as he had. I was buying some bulbs in the local florist's one morning soon after when Mrs Keyter came in and stood waiting beside the little ledge where the florist kept a pen and ink and the printed cards for greetings and the black-bordered cards for wreaths. She stood with her handbag held in front of her between her two hands rather the way a person does who comes steeled to an interview for a job, or some sort of interrogation ... She had her tongue pressing her lower lip and she did not seem to see me for a moment; then she looked sideways with a start and smiled slowly. 'They're lovely, aren't they?' – with the slight self-consciousness of the past child for the teacher, I indicated a great bucket of chrysanthemums. But she cut past that. Ignoring it, turning straight to me as a woman she said: 'I'm so annoyed; it's wrong of them. Mark has been reported missing, and people keep sending me flowers. – As if someone were dead, flowers and messages of sympa-thy. I'm going to tell the florist please not to send any more.' The lids of her familiar sunken eyes were infinitely finely wrinkled, delicate as the fine shining skin cast by some newly emerged insect. Under them her eyes held me with reasonableness. I brought an edge of hysteria to it with the over-vehemence of my agreement. I felt that *she* must be looking at *me* curiously; I was the one whose face must be watched for the appearance of disaster, like a rash. I know that I left that shop stupidly, backing away as if from some fearful sight.

Mark Keyter was never found. As well expect to have returned to you a garland you have dropped into the sea. Because he was never reported killed he died slowly; for some people – with a shrug, after two or three months; for others, only at the end of the war, when they realized he wasn't back; for his mother, nobody knows when. And because of this, his legend was without the fitting close it should have had. No stir of mourning for his youth and beauty rose because everybody found its loss at a different time. And then again because of that there is no starting point for his memory; we do not know when absence became non-existence, we cannot say: Mark Keyter died here, and build up a pyre of recollection on that spot. We talked about him now and then for a year or two, and then we stopped talking of him.

Mrs Keyter has kept on teaching school. She did stop for a short while – round about the time of Mark's death, it must have been – but now she has been at it again for a long time. Old Keyter came back, too. Not directly after Mark was reported missing, but soon. He has become a recluse; he never goes out, except at night. My brother saw him once turn round suddenly under a street lamp. He said that the old man is as handsome as ever, and that for that instant, he felt again exactly as we did when we were children, and we met him in a doorway. We seldom see Mrs Keyter; only my mother does, of course – she bumps into everybody. When I got back from my trip to Europe last month and came home to stay with the family for a few weeks, she reproached me: 'You know, it would be nice if you went to see old Mrs Keyter for a minute while you're here. She's always asking after you. Whenever I've seen her, she's wanted to know where you were, and what you were doing. Poor old thing, she's got so little in her own life. She's very thrilled just now, mind you – she's got Mark's little boy with her.'

The only way you can escape from the necessity of taking up the everyday life that waits for you again is to go round visiting people, telling over and over the fortnight in Paris, the Rembrandts in Holland, the plays in London. I had seen everybody; the dwindling end of my return began to open out on days that would have to be taken up and lived ... Then I remembered Mrs Keyter; mother, I haven't been round to see Mrs Keyter! – I went that same afternoon, justified in the assumption of a guilt.

When I stood at the old green front door with the red glass fleur-de-lis inset, standing ajar into the hall, I smiled to see the sameness of that house. A patch of new wire net shone water-marked like moire on the old rusted veranda screening; the black-and-white linoleum jumped up and down before your eyes. Through the hall archway came the same Mrs Keyter, the gentle, precise, inquiring walk, the soft inquiring laugh – the pleasure of surprise as she took my hand in hers. We went into the living-room that was still evidently the schoolroom as well; while we talked and she sat on the edge of her chair with her head tilted, nodding sympathetic noises in her throat, my eyes as they moved in animation caught the curling map of Africa, the stack of beaded counting boards, the blackboard turned against the wall. It was like not being able to prevent oneself seeing the words of someone else's letter, left before one on a table. I wanted to look and look around that room. I wanted to get up and go and touch things. The amused, half-patronizing wish to renew contact with what you have succeeded in leaving far, far behind; confinements that seem too small, too frail ever to have bounded you.

Hanging on the wall amongst the old spotted prints (a dead fly was caught under the glass of one) there was a clear studio portrait of Mark in his officer's cap. I said: 'Mother tells me you've got Mark's little boy with you for a while –'

Out of her eyes, that seemed as if sleeping (I remembered her eyes that day at the florist's), life, the grip of living people on everyday things came and currented that quiet, inert body, long ago folded away into resignation like a set of neat, faded clothes. Inner joy and content showed miraculously in a face that no longer thought itself capable of expressing such emotions, should they still exist anywhere.

'For good,' said Mrs Keyter.

It was more than joy; it was the tender acceptance of a miracle by someone without hope. I was filled with a light-hearted relief, the selfish relief of not having to feel sorry for someone else, of not having to be guilty of one's own happiness. Mrs Keyter was not imprisoned in the pale disappointments of her unrewarded age, her loss of lover and son, the one by failure of relationship, the other by death. It did not matter that she was old, poor, and shabby. For she in her turn held something cupped in her life; the quick, fluttering being of a child. She went out to call him from the yard. I smiled after her, at ease.

She was gone five minutes; ten. It was quiet in that room.

It had always had a watching air, that room, the watching air of a clock.

Suddenly, the wind of my life that roared through my ears with voices, places, experiences, attainments, dropped –; I fell through in the space, the silence; through time; I found myself becalmed in the waiting, the emptiness of childhood. It was a most curious feeling; a tingling in my hands. I sat breathing the dryness of chalk; there was chalk filming the table in front of me, chalk beneath my palm on the arm of the old leather chair, chalk, chalk, silting the floorboards and all the surfaces, high and low, rubbed by hands every day, or hidden away out of reach for years on the tops of cupboards. Chalk dried the blood. People powder away. There was a torpor of life as if I crouched, with secret stiff hands acting a lie, watching a small, dry, chalk-ingrained hand go up to a face to finger a hair. A single colourless hair. Nothing has changed. It repeated itself with horror. *Nothing has changed.* In poverty and drabness nothing changes. Wood does not wither. Chalk does not rust. What is dead and dry lives on for ever and is for ever dead.

I looked up with a start. A small boy had come into the room. He stood just in the doorway, eating a piece of cake. He stood obediently, a child who has been sent. 'Hullo,' I said quickly, and remembered that I didn't know his name. 'Have you come to say hullo to me?' 'Yes,' he said, going on eating. 'And what's your name?' 'Charles,' he said. He was looking at the last piece of cake as if he wanted to impress himself with the finality of the bite to come. He was a thin little boy with dirty knees, not like Mark at all. He had a pale neck like a stem, and his eyes, pale blue, lifted round and round the room away from me. The chapped knobs of his wrists stuck out far beyond the sleeves of a stern dark-grey jersey. He had finished the cake. He had finished the lingering crumbs round his mouth. He stood there, quietly. Fortunately, Mrs Keyter came in at that moment for I could not think of anything to say to him. She came in smiling her distant gentle smile, like a far-off sun whose warmth one cannot feel, and she put her hands on the narrow yoke of his shoulders. 'Grandma,' he said in his little hoarse voice, 'can I have anuller piece –'

The hands were drawn with chalk, as a washerwoman's hands are drawn with years of water.

When I came out of the gate into the early twilight a streetlight went on suddenly just outside. It caught Mark's little boy in the shadow of the gatepost, hunched back against it with one small foot turned in slightly before him, the other lifted resting back on the crumbling concrete. He had a pocketful of stones and he was throwing them, slowly, one by one, at the pole.

The Amateurs

They stumbled round the Polyclinic, humpy in the dark with their props and costumes. 'A drain!' someone shouted, 'Look out!' 'Drain ahead!' They were all talking at once.

The others waiting in the car stared out at them; the driver leaned over his window: 'All right?'

They gesticulated, called out together.

'– Can't hear. Is it OK?' shouted the driver.

Peering, chins lifted over bundles, they arrived back at the car again. 'There's nobody there. It's all locked up.'

'Are you sure it was the Polyclinic?'

'Well, it's very nice, I must say!'

They stood around the car, laughing in the pleasant little adventure of being lost together.

A thin native who had been watching them suspiciously from the dusty-red wash set afloat upon the night by the one streetlight, came over and mumbled, 'I take you ... You want to go inside?' He looked over his shoulder to the Location gates.

'Get in,' one young girl nudged the other toward the car. Suddenly they all got in, shut the doors.

'I take you,' said the boy again, his hands deep in his pockets.

At that moment a light wavered down the road from the gates, a bicycle swooped swallow-like upon the car, a fat police-boy in uniform shone a torch. 'You in any trouble there, sir?' he roared. His knobkerrie swung from his belt. 'No, but we've come to the wrong place –'

'You having any trouble?' insisted the police-boy. The other shrank away into the light. He stood hands in pockets, shoulders hunched, looking at the car from the streetlight.

'We're supposed to be giving a play – concert – tonight, and we were told it would be at the Polyclinic. Now there's nobody there,' the girl called impatiently from the back seat.

'Concert, sir? It's in the Hall, sir. Just follow me.'

Taken over by officialdom, they went through the gates, saluted and stared at, and up the rutted street past the Beer Hall, into the Location. Only a beer-brazen face, blinking into the car lights as they passed, laughed and called out something half-heard.

Driving along the narrow, dark streets, they peered white-faced at the windows, wanting to see what it was like. But, curiously, it seemed that although they might want to see the Location, the Location didn't want to see them. The rows of low two-roomed houses with their homemade tin and packing-case lean-tos and beans growing up the chicken wire, throbbed only here and there with the faint pulse of a candle; no one was to be seen. Life seemed always to be in the next street, voices singing far off and shouts, but when the car turned the corner – again, there was nobody.

The bicycle wobbled to a stop in front of them. Here was the hall, here were lights, looking out like sore eyes in the moted air, here were people, more part of the dark than the light, standing about in straggling curiosity. Two girls in flowered head-scarves stood with their arms crossed leaning against the wall of the building; some men cupped their hands over an inch of cigarette and drew with the intensity of the stub-smoker.

The amateur company climbed shrilly out of their car. They nearly hadn't arrived at all! What a story to tell! Their laughter, their common purpose, their solidarity before the multifarious separateness of the audiences they faced, generated once again that excitement that so often seized them. What a story to tell!

Inside the Hall, the audience had been seated long ago. They sat in subdued rows, the women in neat flowered prints, the men collared-and-tied, heads of pens and pencils ranged sticking out over their jacket pockets. They were a specially selected audience of schoolteachers, who, with a sprinkling of social workers, two clerks from the administrative offices, and a young girl who had matriculated, were the educated of the rows and rows of hundreds and hundreds who lived and ate and slept and talked and loved and died in the houses outside. Those others had not been asked, and were not to be admitted because they would not understand.

The ones who had been asked waited as patiently as the children they taught in their turn. When would the concert begin?

In an atmosphere of brick-dust and bright tin shavings behind the stage, the actors and actresses struggled to dress and paint their faces in a newly built small room intended to be used for the cooking of meat at Location dances. The bustle and sideburns of a late-Victorian English drawing-room went on; a young woman whitened her hair with talcum powder and pinned a great hat like a feathery ship upon it. A fat young man sang, with practised nasal innuendo, the latest dance-tune whilst he adjusted his pince-nez and covered his cheerful head with a clerical hat.

'You're not bothering with make-up?' A man in a wasp-striped waistcoat came down from the stage.

A girl looked up from her bit of mirror, face of a wax doll.

'Your ordinary street make-up'll do – they don't know the difference,' he said.

'But of course I'm making-up,' said the girl, quite distressed. She was melting black grease paint in a teaspoon over someone's cigarette lighter.

'No need to bother with moustaches and things,' the man said to the other men. 'They won't understand the period anyway. Don't bother.'

The girl went on putting blobs of liquid grease paint on her eyelashes, holding her breath.

'I think we should do it properly,' said the young woman, complaining.

'All right, all right.' He slapped her on the bustle. 'In that case you'd better stick a bit more cotton-wool in your bosom – you're not nearly pouter-pigeon enough.'

'For God's sake, can't you open the door, somebody,' asked the girl. 'It's stifling.'

The door opened upon a concrete yard; puddles glittered, one small light burned over the entrance to a men's lavatory. The night air was the strong yellow smell of old urine. Men from the street slouched in and out, and a tall slim native, dressed in the universal long-hipped suit that in the true liberalism of petty gangsterdom knows no colour bar or national exclusiveness, leaned back on his long legs, tipped back his hat, and smiled on teeth pretty as a girl's.

'I'm going to close it again,' said the fat young man grimly.

'Oh, no one's going to eat you,' said the girl, picking up her parasol.

They all went backstage, clambered about, tested the rickety steps; heard the murmur of the audience like the sea beyond the curtain. 'You'll have to move that chair a bit,' the young woman was saying, 'I can't possibly get through that small space.' 'Not with that behind you won't,' the young man chuckled fatly. 'Now remember, if you play well, we'll put it across. If you act well enough, it doesn't matter whether the audience understands what you're saying or not.' 'Of course – look at French films.' 'It's not that. It's not the difficulty of the language so much as the situations ... The manners of a Victorian drawing-room – the whole social code – how can they be expected to understand ...' – the girl's eyes looked out behind the doll's face.

They began to chaff one another with old jokes; the clothes they wore, the slips of the tongue that twisted their lines: the gaiety of working together set them teasing and laughing. They stood waiting behind the makeshift wings, made of screens. Cleared their throats; somebody belched.

They were ready.

When would the concert begin?

The curtain screeched back on its rusty rings; the stage opened on Oscar Wilde's *The Importance of Being Earnest*.

At first there was so much to *see*; the mouths of the audience parted with pleasure at the sight of the fine ladies and gentlemen dressed with such colour and variety; the women? – gasp at them; the men? – why laugh at them, of course. But gradually the excitement of looking became acceptance, and they began to listen, and they began not to understand. Their faces remained alight, lifted to the stage, their attention was complete, but it was the attention of mystification. They watched the players as a child watches a drunken man, attracted by his babbling and his staggering, but innocent of the spectacle's cause or indications.

The players felt this complete attention, the appeal of a great blind eye staring up at their faces, and a change began to work in them. A kind of hysteria of effort gradually took hold of them, their gestures grew broader, the women threw great brilliant smiles like flowers out into the half-dark over the footlights, the men strutted and lifted their voices. Each frowning in asides at the 'hamming' of the other, they all felt at the same time this bubble of queerly anxious, exciting devilment of over-emphasis bursting in themselves. The cerebral acid of Oscar Wilde's love scenes was splurged out by the oglings and winks of musical comedy, as surely as a custard pie might blot the thin face of a cynic. Under the four-syllable inanities, under the mannerisms and the posturing of the play, the bewitched amateurs knocked up a recognizable human situation. Or perhaps it was the audience that found it, looking so closely, so determined, picking up a look, a word, and making something for themselves out of it.

In an alien sophistication they found there was nothing *real* for them, so they made do with the situations that are traditionally laughable and are unreal for everyone – the strict dragon of a mother, the timid lover, the disdainful young girl. When a couple of stage lovers exited behind the screens that served for wings, someone remarked to his neighbour, very jocular: 'And what do they do behind there!' Quite a large portion of the hall heard it and laughed at this joke of their own.

'Poor Oscar!' whispered the young girl, behind her hand. 'Knew it wouldn't do,' hissed the striped waistcoat. From her position at the side of the stage the young girl kept seeing the round, shining, rapt face of an elderly schoolteacher. His head strained up toward the stage, and a wonderful, broad, entire smile never left his face. He was asleep. She watched him anxiously out of the corner of her eye, and saw that every now and then the movement of his neighbour, an unintentional jolt, would wake him up: then the smile would fall, he would taste his mouth with his tongue, and a tremble of weariness troubled his guilt. The smile would open out again: he was asleep.

After the first act, the others, the people from outside who hadn't been asked, began to come into the hall. As if what had happened between the players and the audience inside had somehow become known, given itself away into the air, so that suddenly the others felt that *they* might as well be allowed in, too. They pushed past the laconic police-boys at the door, coming in in twos and threes, barefoot, bringing a child by the hand or a small hard bundle of a baby. They sat where they could, stolidly curious, and no one dared question their right of entry, now. The audience pretended not to see them. But they were, by very right of their insolence, more demanding and critical. During the second act, when the speeches were long, they talked and passed remarks amongst themselves; a baby was allowed to wail. The schoolteachers kept their eyes on the stage, laughed obediently, tittered appreciatively, clapped in unison.

There was something else in the hall, now; not only the actors and the audience groping for each other in the blind smile of the dark and the blind dazzle of the lights; there was something that lived, that continued uncaring, on its own. On a seat on the side the players could see someone in a cap who leaned forward, eating an orange. A fat girl hung with her arm round her friend, giggling into her ear. A foot in a pointed shoe waggled in the aisle; the people from outside sat irregular as they pleased; what was all the fuss about anyway? When something amused them, they laughed as long as they liked. The laughter of the schoolteachers died away: they knew that the players were being kept waiting.

But when the curtain jerked down on the last act, the whole hall met in a sweeping excitement of applause that seemed to feed itself and to shoot off fresh bursts as a rocket keeps showering again and again as its sparks die in the sky. Applause came from their hands like a song, each pair of palms taking strength and enthusiasm from the other. The players gasped, could not catch their breath: smiling, just managed to hold their heads above the applause. It filled the hall to the brim, then sank, sank. A young woman in a black velvet head-scarf got up from the front row and came slowly up on to the stage, her hands clasped. She smiled faintly at the players, swallowed. Then her voice, the strange, high, minor-keyed voice of an African girl, went out across the hall.

'Mr Mount and his company, Ladies and Gentlemen' – she turned to the players – 'we have tried to tell you what you have done here, for us tonight' – she paused and looked at them all, with the pride of acceptance – 'we've tried to show you, just now, with our hands and our voices what we think of this wonderful thing you have brought to us here in Athalville Location.' Slowly, she swung back to the audience: a deep, growing chant of applause rose. 'From the bottom of our hearts, we thank you, all of us here who have had the opportunity to see you, and we hope in our hearts you will come to us again *many times*. This play tonight not only made us see what people can do, even in their spare-time after work, if they *try*; it's made us feel that perhaps we could try and occupy our leisure in such a way, and learn, ourselves, and also give other people pleasure – the way everyone in this whole hall tonight' – her knee bent and arm outstretched, she passed her hand over the lifted heads – 'everyone here has been made *happy*.' A warm murmur was drawn from the audience; then complete silence. The girl took three strides to the centre of the stage. 'I ask you,' she cried out, and the players felt her voice like a shock, 'is this perhaps the answer to our Juvenile Delinquency here in Athalville? If our young boys and girls' – her hand pointed at a brown beardless face glazed with attention – 'had something like this to do in the evenings, would so many of them be at the Police Station? Would we be afraid to walk out in the street? Would our mothers be crying over their children? – Or would Athalville be a better place, and the mothers and fathers full of pride? Isn't this what we need?'

The amateurs were forgotten by themselves and each other, abandoned dolls, each was alone. No one exchanged a glance. And out in front stood the girl, her arm a sharp angle, her nostrils lifted. The splash of the footlights on her black cheek caught and made a sparkle out of a single tear.

Like the crash of a crumbling building, the wild shouts of the people fell upon the stage; as the curtain jerked across, the players re-collected themselves, went slowly off.

The fat young man chuckled to himself in the back of the car. 'God, what we didn't do to that play!' he laughed.

'What'd you kiss me again for?' cried the young woman in surprise. '– I didn't know what was happening. We never had a kiss there, before – and all of a sudden' – she turned excitedly to the others – 'he takes hold of me and kisses me! I didn't know what was happening!'

'They liked it,' snorted the young man. '*One* thing they understood anyway!'

'Oh, I don't know –' said someone, and seemed about to speak.

But instead there was a falling away into silence.

The girl was plucking sullenly at the feathered hat, resting on her knee. 'We cheated them; we shouldn't have done it,' she said.

'But what could we *do*?' The young woman turned shrilly, her eyes open and hard, excitedly determined to get an answer: an answer somewhere, from someone.

But there was no answer.

'We didn't know what to do,' said the fat young man uncertainly, forgetting to be funny now, the way he lost himself when he couldn't remember his lines on the stage.

A Present for a Good Girl

On an afternoon in September a woman came into the jeweller's shop. The two assistants, whose bodies had contrived, as human bodies doggedly will, to adapt the straight, hard stretch of the glass showcases to a support, sagged, hips thrust forward, elbows leaning in upon their black crêpe-de-Chine-covered stomachs, and looked at her without a flicker, waiting for her to go. For they could see that she did not belong there. No woman in a frayed and shapeless old Leghorn hat, carrying a bulging crash shopping bag decorated in church bazaar fashion with wool embroidery, and wearing stained old sandshoes and cheap thick pink stockings that concertinaed round her ankles, could belong in the jeweller's shop. They knew the kind; simple, a bit dazed, shortsighted, and had wandered in mistaking it for the chemist's, two doors up. She would peer round stupidly, looking as if she had stumbled into Aladdin's cave, and when she saw the handsome canteens of cutlery, with their beautifully arranged knives spread like a flashing keyboard in their velvet beds, and the pretty little faces of the watches in their satin cases, and the cool, watery preening of the cut glass beneath its special light, she would mumble and shamble herself out again. So they stood, unmoved, waiting for her to go.

But, uncomfortably, she didn't go. She advanced right in, half-defiantly, half-ingratiatingly – she gave a little sniff to herself as if to say: Come on, now! Well, why *shouldn't* I – and put the shopping bag down on the counter. Then she gave the hat a pull, and stood waiting, not looking at the young ladies.

But still they did not move. Their half-closed eyes rested with faint interest upon the crash shopping bag, as upon some fossil discovery.

The third assistant, who was sitting at a table threading wedding rings in order on a velvet rod, pushed the rings aside and got up, thinking with as much crossness as lethargy could muster, Well, someone must see what the old creature wants.

'Yes?' she said.

It was all ready in the woman's mouth; as a child comes threshing up out of water with bulging cheeks, and lets out all its mouthful of breathlessness and enthusiasm in one great gasp, she said: 'Good afternoon, Miss, there's a green bag in the window, Miss – in the corner, right down near the front. I want to get one for my daughter, she's always talking about a green one – and I wondered, you see, it's really only for Christmas, but I thought . . .' – and her pupils that seemed to swim like weak small fish in the colourless wetness of her eyes with their underlids drooping down in a reddish peak, darted wildly. Like a beggar exhibiting valuable sores, she smiled on a mouth of gaps and teeth worn like splinters of driftwood.

'You want the green handbag in the window?' asserted the assistant, looking up, then down.

'Well, how much is it?' said the woman, in the coy tone of a confessed secret, screwing up one eye.

But the young assistant would not be drawn into such intimacy.

'I'll have a look . . .' she said, resigned to wasting her time, and came out from behind the counter. Slow and measured, she unfastened the window catches, leaned in, and drew out the bag. The old woman pressed forward over the counter, her tongue feeling anxiously along the dark canyons of her teeth. She leaned on her elbow and her left hand, with the bones and great knobs that punctuated each joint sliding beneath tough slack skin like that of a tortoise, had taken up a curious pose, hanging indolent from the wrist, like the hand of a Louis XVI dandy pinching up snuff. 'Mmm,' she said, fumbling the air round the bag, wanting to touch it. She breathed hard down her nose, and whilst the assistant parted the bright locked fangs of the zipper and felt for the price-tag inside, the girl held her breath against the fusty sourness of the old woman's breath.

'Four-fifteen,' said the assistant at last.

'Four-fifteen, four-fifteen,' nodded the woman sucking in her lower lip.

'Ninety-five shillings,' said the assistant, hand on hip.

'Ah,' said the woman, lifting her eyebrows under the flop of the zany hat, as if that explained away any difficulty. 'It's got a mirror?' she asked.

'Yes,' said the assistant ironically. You can't afford it, said the hand on her hip.

'Oh, I'm sure she'll like it,' chatted the woman, fidgeting with the pockets and gadgets of the leather interior. 'She loves green, you know. Everythink must be green. All her dresses and everythink. When I tell her it's supposed to be unlucky, she just says, Mum, you're old-fashioned. She's always wanted a green bag –'

'Then you should certainly take it for her, madam,' said the assistant. Another minute or two and the old thing would be gone, muttering she'd see . . . she'd speak to her husband . . .

'You see, I thought I'd get it for her for Christmas,' said the woman. She played with the knobbly string of yellow beads that stood up like boulders on the bony plateau of her chest.

'Yes, better take it when you see it.' Habit prompted the assistant. 'It might be gone, if you wait. You can put it away till Christmas.'

'Oh well, I couldn't take it *now* –' she said. 'You see I haven't got the money on me now.'

'Well, we could put it aside for you until tomorrow,' said the assistant.

The woman stood blinking at her subserviently, with the smirk of cunning innocence worn by the beggar whilst you read his tattered 'testimonial'. 'You see, dear,' she said in a hushed small voice, 'I thought perhaps you'd let me pay for it, like.' Her face was drawn into a question.

'Can't do that, Miss Pierce,' chimed in the other two assistants at once, like the representatives of some great power waking up half-way through a conference in time to boom a veto on some mewling little voice they haven't even heard. 'Mr Cano isn't in.'

'You see, the manager isn't in at the moment,' offered the assistant.

'Oh, I don't expect you to let me *take* it –' protested the woman, smiling at the young ladies as if they had just done her the most charming favour. 'I just wanted to pay somethink down on it, then you could keep it here for me, and I'd come in every week and pay somethink more off it.'

She grinned at them all like a cornered urchin.

'I see,' said the girl Miss Pierce, not prepared for this.

'You can't do it without Mr Cano's permission,' stated the other two. 'You can't do it without him.'

'All right, all right, I know,' said Miss Pierce. '– How much did you want to pay now?' she asked the woman.

Subdued with tension, the old creature grappled down in the shopping bag and dragged up a thin purse. 'I could let you have ten bob,' she said.

'And how long to pay the balance?'

'Well, until Chr – until just about the fifteenth of December.'

'It's out of the question, Miss Pierce,' said one of the others in a high voice.

The girl heard it behind her; in front of her the old woman grinned on her bad teeth, like a dog continuing to wag its tail even at the person who approaches to take away the bone that enchants it.

'All right,' said the girl suddenly.

Silently the woman took a ten-shilling note from the flat stomach of her purse, and waited in silence whilst the receipt was made out. The moment she had the receipt in her possession, and was folding it away in the purse and the purse away in the crash bag, a mood of light-hearted talkativeness seized her. She opened up into confidential mateyness like a Japanese paper flower joyously pretending to be a flower instead of a bit of paper as it swells with water.

She spoke only of her daughter. What her daughter always said, and what she always told her daughter.

'You must know my daughter –' she said, pooh-poohing the remote notion that the girl mightn't. '*You know*, dear, she's the cashier at the Grand Lyceum – fair girl, got a very good figure . . .?' – She had a peculiar way of speaking; each 'd' was a little step before which her voice hesitated, then hastily tripped over.

'Yes,' murmured Miss Pierce, who was actually quite a frequent patron of the cinema in question, but who was never reduced to buying her own seat, and so had never seen the cashier. 'Yes, I think I have seen –'

'Wears a lot of green? Got a quiet way of talking?' went on the woman. 'Of course you know her. It's a good job, you know. She's a clever girl – sharp as a needle. She's been a good daughter to me, I must say. Not like some. That's why I'm glad I got that bag for her.

She's been wanting a green one for a long time; I seen her, when we've been walking along, stopping to look in the shopwindow. And when I've asked her, she's said, no, nothin', just looking generally. But I knew what it was all right; sure enough, somewhere in the window there was always bound to be a green bag . . .'

When she had shambled out with her flattened heels leaning over the sides of the old sandshoes, the two assistants stood looking at Miss Pierce. 'Well, don't say *we* said it was all right. You know Mr Cano –'

'Peculiar-looking woman,' reproached the other one. 'Did you see the way she was dressed! She looks to me as if she drinks, too.'

'Well, why don't you ever do anything, anyway? Why do you always wait for me to come forward?' flashed out Miss Pierce, in a sudden temper.

Two weeks went by and then the woman came in, with an air of wanting to get her ten-shilling note safely paid in before it 'went' on other things. She asked to see the bag again, and repeated to her fellow conspirator, Miss Pierce, the details of her daughter's taste, colour preferences, and mental powers. To get rid of the woman, the girl pretended to have taken particular note of the fair-haired cashier the last evening she had visited the Grand Lyceum. The mother became almost speechless with an excess of quiet pride: she seemed to go off into a sort of dream, leaning on the counter, saying very low, Yes, I'd like to see her face on Christmas morning . . . I'd like to see her face . . . That I would . . . Putting away her second receipt with the greatest of care, she went slowly out of the shop, as if she were walking straight off the edge of a cloud.

'Funny old stick,' said Miss Pierce, writing 'Balance, £3 15s.' on the parcel.

The next time the woman came in she was embarrassingly garrulous, and insisted on offering Miss Pierce a cigarette from an enamelled tin case picturing two yellow cockatoos and fastened with a catch which was evidently rather tricky because she fumbled such a long time over getting it open. Under the same frayed Leghorn hat, she looked queerer than ever; her face was stiff, as if carefully balanced, and there was a streak of mauvish lipstick on her mouth.

She paid only five shillings, with profuse apologies: 'As God's my witness, I'll pay the lot off at the beginning of the month,' she said loudly, raising her right hand. 'As God's my witness ...' Her hand dropped and suddenly she smiled, sweetly, sweetly. 'For my little girl ... my little girl,' she whispered, evidently to herself. Poor Miss Pierce smiled back fiercely in embarrassment. And suddenly the woman was gone.

The fourth time she came it was in the morning, and it seemed to the young Miss Pierce that the woman was really much older than she had noticed: she walked so falteringly, the crash shopping bag was much too heavy for her, and her eyes looked red in her bluish-pale face. Had she been crying, perhaps? Miss Pierce thought perhaps the poor old thing had to work very hard at housework; there was a faint smell of methylated spirits about her – she must have been cleaning windows. Four-pounds-fifteen! Why it must be a fortune to her! Miss Pierce wondered if a peroxide-blonde cashier from the Grand Lyceum was worthy of it. Anyway, the green handbag was another fifteen shillings nearer being paid for.

And that, it seemed, was as far as it would ever get.

Weeks went by, and the woman did not appear; Miss Pierce hid the bag away from the businesslike eyes of Mr Cano: 'What's this?' he would say. '*How* long –? – Put it back into stock. Return the woman's deposit to her ...' So the green bag lay waiting behind a pile of hand-tooled leather writing-cases.

An intoxication of buying grew upon the town as every day Christmas moved up a notch nearer, and soon the three assistants were elbowing one another out of the way as they smiled, persuaded, suggested, to the timorous, the vacillating, the imperious who came to buy. Miss Pierce really did not even have time to wonder if the woman would come for the bag; her shopgirl's attention was already wrangled into half a dozen divisions by half a dozen equally demanding customers as it was; there was no small shred left that was not immediately snatched up by someone who had been waiting fully three quarters of an hour to see a tortoiseshell powder-bowl.

But in the fine high frenzy of half past four on the last Saturday afternoon before Christmas, Miss Pierce was interrupted. 'Your customer's here' – one of the other two young ladies prodded her elbow. '– What?' said the girl, dodging the blinding demand of eyes. 'The green handbag,' said the other, smiling with great brilliance, and diving back.

The harassed girl dodged in and out to the other side of the shop. In the dazed preoccupation that results as a kind of spiritual sunstroke from overexposure to the question and demand of a daylong crowd, she could not recall any green handbag. But then she saw the woman in the battered garden-party Leghorn standing just within the doorway, and of course! – the green handbag, £2 15s. balance, behind the writing-cases. She went forward with a quick smile.

'S'ere . . .' said the woman, handing out a pound note as if to a blank wall, "F you've sorl tha bag t'anyone . . . I pay'dfirit and you've got norite t'crooka poorwoman.' Her voice whined through the persuasive buzz of the shop. Harsh fumes surrounded her as rising incense round some image.

Miss Pierce looked at her in astonishment.

Dropping the crash bag, the woman turned to look at it, lying on the floor, as if it were some animal that had just crawled to her feet. She tried to pick it up, but could not. Half bent to the floor, she looked up at Miss Pierce with a sudden chuckle, like a naughty child.

Miss Pierce stood quite still.

'Why'd'you keepm'waiting, whydonchu giviterme,' said the woman with great dignity. There was a red poppy, the kind that charitable organizations give away on collection days, pinned on to the brim of the hat with a large safety-pin.

Miss Pierce trembled like a trapped rabbit.

'Youdonwana be'fraiduvme,' said the woman with a sudden cunning flash of understanding. 'Sorry . . .' She wagged her head, 'Sorry . . .'

Miss Pierce burned with guilt. 'I'll just get – I mean, I'll see . . .' she tried.

'Musn be'fraid uvaporeolwoman. Iwan the – the – bag' – she stopped and thought hard – 'the-the *green* bag I got f'my daughter. Y'know mydaughter?' she urged, clutching Miss Pierce's arm. ''Course y'know mydaughter –' She stopped and smiled, closing her eyes. 'S'ere,' she said, putting down the pound note.

'But that's not enough,' said Miss Pierce very loudly, as if talking to a deaf person. 'Not enough. You owe two-pounds-fifteen on the bag' – holding up two fingers – 'Two-pounds-fifteen.'

'Whas' sat?' said the woman, stupidly. Her face grew woeful, sullen. 'Don wanagiviterme. Y'don wanagiviterme.'

'But you haven't paid for it, you see,' said Miss Pierce miserably. Mr Cano was frowning at her through the crowd; she could sense his one twitching eyebrow, questioning.

'Howmuchwasit?' whispered the woman, winking at her and leaning over into her face.

'Four-pounds-fifteen. You remember.'

'Wasit?' she giggled. 'Wasit?'

'You have to pay another pound and fifteen shillings.'

The woman knelt on the floor and felt down amongst the lumps and bulges of the crash shopping bag, collapsed on its side on the floor. At last she got up again. Some anchor in the heart that even the vast swelling uncharted seas of drunkenness could not free her of, pulled at her. Underneath her stiff face, her glassed-out eyes, it was horrible to see that she was alive and struggling. The silliness of being drunk would not come up to save her.

'Iwaned to get it for her,' she said. 'I *mean* t'getit for her.'

The broken brim of the hat hid her face as she felt her way out. The whole shop was watching, each man from the pinnacle of his own self-triumph.

It had hardly turned back to its own business again when a pale girl, violently white-faced, with the thin pale hair of a slum child, swept trembling into the shop. She stood there leaning forward on her toes, shuddering with anger. Just behind her, held leashed by the terrible look of her eye, was the old woman, open-mouthed. The girl's eyes searched desperately round the shop. They seemed to draw Miss Pierce out from behind the counter: she came slowly forward. A flash of angry disgust passed from the girl to the old woman, who blinked beneath it as from a whip.

'Now what is it?' blurted the girl. 'What does she owe here?'

'She's paid some, you see,' ventured Miss Pierce. They were like doctors in discussion over the patient's prone body.

'Tell me how much, and I'll pay it,' the girl cut in violently. Under the pale spare skin of her neck, her heart flew up madly, as a bird dashing again and again at its cage.

'Oh, it's all right,' faltered Miss Pierce, avoiding looking at the old woman. 'She's not so very much behind in her payments. It's not absolutely necessary that she take the bag now.'

Hot bright tears at the recollection of some recent angry scene fevered the girl's eyes. '*Tell me how much it is*,' she whispered fiercely, crazily. She swallowed her tears. '*She* can't pay,' she said, with a look of hopeless disgust at the old woman.

'The bag was four-pounds-fifteen. She owes two-fifteen on it.'

'A bag for four-pounds-fifteen,' said the girl bitterly, so over-whelmed by a fresh welling of furious despair and irritation that her pale eyes filled with bright tears again. She turned and looked at the old woman; her hand sank leaden at her side, as if defeated in the desire to strike. 'What next. Always something. Some rubbish. Now a bag. What for –? You people give her things. She's not responsible. I've had just about enough of it. – She ought to be in a home, she should. I can't stand it any longer.' The old woman looked out at her from under her eyelids.

Trembling, the girl jerked out two pounds and fifteen shillings in silver and gave it up with a gesture of hopeless impotence to Miss Pierce. Miss Pierce handed to her the parcel containing the green handbag. The girl looked at it for a moment, with an expression of quizzical, sullen disgust. She looked as if she would have liked to hurl it away, as far as her arm could. Then she picked it up, and went out of the doorway.

'Come on,' she ordered in a low, dead voice.

And the old woman swayed after her out into the street.

La Vie Bohème

She got off the tram where she had been told, at Minos's New Tearoom, and looked around her at the streets she didn't know. Turn to the left past the tearoom and carry straight on. She crossed the road slowly and recognized in precognition the windows set with a mosaic of oranges, liquorice sticks, and chewing-gum in packets. This was it, then.

As she walked up the street, her eyes ready for the name of the building, she kept saying over and over to herself snatches of the conversation she had had with her sister yesterday. She saw her sister in her white blouse and red peasant skirt coming into the exhibition, she felt again the curious suffocating excitement of looking up hard at her and meeting her black eyes – she heard again the surprised cry 'Baby!': her sister's voice, not heard for eighteen months, so familiar, yet striking her ear afresh, showing her she had forgotten. And her sister looked just the same. Just the same. And yet in between she had left home, quarrelled with her parents, married her student *without any money at all.* – Well, how are you getting on? she had said, because she really couldn't think what would be tactful to say. And her sister laughed: Body and soul together, you know. We've got a little flat – oh very small – minute, not really a flat. – In 'Glenorin'. There's a balcony.

Live in one room. *Without any money.* – Mother said that, she remembered; kept saying it over and over, until she had felt the awfulness of what her sister was doing. *One room.* – But there, you see, it wasn't one room; it was a small flat, and it had a balcony.

I couldn't believe for a moment that it could be you, Baby. – I was still thinking of you as being at school . . .

Of course – she had been still at school, when it happened. And her sister never had thought about her much; she was so much younger, and there were a brother and another sister in between. Beside, her sister hadn't been ever a 'family' person. She felt the natural ties of affinity rather than the conventional blind ties of the blood.

Come and see me! Why don't you? Come and see my child. –
You're not afraid of the family wrath?

That was a compliment. Meeting her at an architectural exhibition,
finding that she had grown up, her sister felt perhaps they were of a
kind, after all . . .

With a balcony. Not that building over there? No – wrong side of
the street. Besides there were potted plants on the ledge – how her
sister always disliked the sword ferns in the bay window at home! It
would be something like a studio, inside, she supposed. Warmly
untidy. Lived in. God, this room! her sister used to say at home;
what a thicket of lace curtains and firescreens and knick-knackery
through which to peer out half-seeing at the world . . .

People drop in. You might meet someone who would interest you.
Anyway . . . Her sister always looked so interesting, with her black
smooth hair and her contrasting expanses of clear, bright colours;
that had always been her way of dressing: as if she had been painted
by Gauguin, or even Raoul Dufy. – But why did she persist in this
notion, this fancy of seeing her sister against a painted backdrop of
an abstract 'artist's life'. Her sister was not an artist; she was a
schoolteacher. And the young student she had married was not an
artist; he was studying medicine. Yet her sister brought to mind the
black, bright centre of a flower, set off within a corolla of the many-
coloured and curiously distinct petals each resting and overlapping in
a curve one upon the other – the pictures she had of an artist's way
of life. The simplicity of it – no lounge chairs uncovered for visitors,
no halls, no pantries; one room, and in the room, everything. The
books that start the ideas; the ideas that start the wonderful talk; the
friends who talk. She saw her sister moving amongst all this . . .
Medical student or no medical student. Hadn't her sister's friends –
whom she had refused to bring home at all after a while, because her
father asked them such banal and stupid questions at table – always
been people who wrote, acted, or painted?

The building was on the left side of the street and the name was
spelled out over the entrance in red cut-out letters, like children's
alphabetical blocks. She went in with her heart beating suddenly
hotly, looking at the names on the board and reading Mr and Mrs,
Mr and Mrs, over and over very quickly until she stopped at the

name. Second floor. There was a lift, the paint worn off its metal sides so that being inside was like standing in a biscuit tin, and when she pressed the button, it moved off with a belch that drifted into a sigh and died to a stop at the second floor.

Her sister in the red skirt and white blouse ... She suddenly felt worried and ashamed of home, of that awful stuffy 'nice' home that she was sure clung about her, left its mark imprinted on her face and clothes. And her sister would recognize it at once, and smile to herself, curl her lip. She felt very anxious to impress upon her sister that she *knew* home was awful, a kind of tomb overgrown with impenetrable mediocrity; walking along the cold high passage that leaned over the deep well of a courtyard, looking for Number 11, she calculated urgently how she might let her sister know that *she* was not taken in by home.

Number 11 was a green door, like all the others, but there was a knocker on this one, a little black mask with its tongue out. Of course!

Her smile was ready on her face as she clacked the knocker down.

The door opened to the smell of burned milk and bright warm sleepy yellow light from the wide windows; full in her face it came, making a dark outline of dazzle round her sister, standing there with a soapy hand stiff away from her face, holding back a strand of loose hair awkwardly with the knob of her bent wrist. She was wearing the same red skirt and an old pair of creaking leather sandals threaded in and out her toes. She waved her visitor in, talking, shrugging, holding out her dripping hands. On the right wall above the big divan there was a wonderful picture; her eye leaped to it, in excitement! Ah – ! An enormous picture: an Indian child, sitting fawn-coloured, cross-legged, with her arms round a great sheaf of arum lilies with their white throats lifted. There were bookshelves, sagging; a great pile of papers, gramophone records. A radio with an elongated, slit-eyed, terracotta head on it. A kind of tallboy with a human skull wearing an old military cap lopsided.

You mustn't mind all this, said her sister, urging her to the divan. I'm in a mess, the washgirl hasn't turned up for the baby's things. Of course you had to catch me like this. She looked at herself as if she wanted to draw attention to her own boldness of not caring.

Feeling rude as a fascinated child, she dragged her eyes away from the picture, vaguely. Oh there, in the corner: a door was open. The tides of light that washed continuously, in deeps of orange and shallows of pale yellow all about the room, stopped there as at the foot of a glowering little cave. Inside she could see only a confused, cellar-like gloom, whitish things hanging quite dead from the lowness of the ceiling, splashes of white, feeble flashes of nickel. If there's anything I hate doing, said her sister, clicking on a light. – There in the flare of a small globe it was a bathroom, hung with napkins sodden on criss-crossed lines of string, a bath and lavatory and washbasin fitted in one against the other, and just room enough for her sister to stand. A chipped enamel pail on the floor held unwashed napkins, and wet ones lay beneath the scum of pricking soap bubbles in the basin.

Oh, go ahead, she said. Don't worry about me.

Her sister's long hands disappeared beneath the scum; she washed and talked, vivacious as ever.

And she sat on the divan looking intensely round the room, looking, looking, whilst she pretended to talk. From point to point her eyes raced; the cushions with brick-coloured and white stalking figures like bushmen paintings; the woolly white rugs shaded with stains; the lovely green head of Pan that was a wall vase and that her sister had had at home, and that there had been an argument about because her mother didn't like the wall spoiled with the nail that held it up. There were three dead anemones hanging out of its mouth. Something was pressing into her back, and she found that she was leaning against a big book. She picked it up; whooshed the hundreds of cool pages falling back smooth and close to solidity: FORENSIC MEDICINE it said on the cover, and beneath it, his name. She looked curiously at the curves of his handwriting: realizing that some of the unknown elements of the room were also this signature.

When she just doesn't turn up like this, her sister was saying, I could wring her neck. In theory, why should another woman wash my child's napkins for me; but in practice . . . She gave a little snort of knowing better now.

Can you imagine what mother would say, she said from the divan, suddenly, easily laughing. They paused: I told you so, they called out together, laughing. Her sister held up her soapy hands; she leaned back on her elbow against a cushion, shaking her head. And their laughter faded companionably down.

Her sister had turned back to the basin, letting the water out with a gurgle. How peculiarly her sister stood, with her feet splayed out in those sandals, clinging to the floor flatly, the Achilles tendon at the back of each ankle pulled taut, strong and thin . . . The washgirl at home stood just like that, endlessly before the tub on Monday mornings . . . The recognition came like a melting inside her. She looked quickly away: sticking out beneath the cushion at her elbow she saw a baby's knitted coat. With a smile she pulled it out, tugged at the little ribbon bedraggled and chewed at the neck.

The baby's? she said, holding it up.

Oh Lord – give here, said her sister – While I'm at it –

A few minutes later, whilst her sister was drying her hands, the cushion fell off the divan, and she saw a small vest and bib, that had been hiding innocently beneath it. She picked them up; the bib smelled sour where the baby had brought up some milk on it. She put them back under the cushion.

I'll hang them out in the courtyard later, said her sister, closing the bathroom door on the napkins. She stood in the room, pleased, a little uncertainly, pushing back her cuticles.

You know, now that I look at you, I think you've got thinner, or taller or something . . . she said.

Have I? said her sister, smiling. Yes, perhaps – she smoothed her hips. Now I'll make some tea, and then we can talk.

Can't I go and see the baby? she asked. Her sister had said he was asleep on the balcony.

Oh for God's sake don't wake him *now*, said her sister. Let's have some peace. She went over to a curtained recess next to the bathroom door. Is that curtain hand-woven? she asked her sister, admiring the clay, green, and black horses on it. Mmm, said her sister, made by a girl called Ada Leghorn who ate with us – for nothing, needless to say – for five months before she went off to South America to paint. – Anyway – And she pulled it on a little two-plate stove with tin legs and a shelf piled and crammed with pots, boxes of cereal, tins, a piece of polony end-down on a saucer, two or three tomatoes, unwashed glasses misted with milk.

Can I help? she asked.

I think you could wash two cups for us, said her sister.

She got up and went to the little square sink that stood close against the stove. Out of the breakfast dishes thinly coated with the hard dry lacquer of egg, she found two cups and ran the tap over them. On the ledge at the side of the sink she found a swab, and picked it up to wipe the cups; but it was sodden; and unidentifiable bits of soggy food clung to it. She put it down again quickly, not wanting to be noticed. But her eye wandered back to the slimy rag and her sister's followed it. Her sister made an impatient noise with her tongue: Oh – look at that – she said, and quickly snatched up something the other hadn't noticed until then: a square of newspaper sandwiched over a filling of shaving soap lather, greyish with the powderings of a day's beard. *Never* remembers to throw *anything* away!

He's working so terribly hard, poor child, she said, after a moment.

Yes, I suppose so, she said, shyly, drying the cups.

You must come when he's here, her sister said gaily. It's ridiculous – not even knowing my own sister!

Yes! she said enthusiastically, and was suddenly afraid she would not like him.

Do you cook here? she asked – And then the moment she said it she heard with the sharp cringe of regret that it had come out in her mother's voice; she had said it just the way her mother spoke. I mean – all your meals . . .? she stumbled.

Yes! Yes-s! said her sister loudly against the splutter of the tap splurting water into a small pot. She planked the pot down on the little stove, taking a lid from another saucepan, much larger, with which to cover it, saying with a short snort of a laugh, Not one of those dinners of mother's at home, that are prayed over and anointed like a sacrifice being prepared for the gods – we eat. Food isn't all that important.

Of course not, she agreed, in contempt of the mother.

Her sister turned round, paused, looking at her, searching: And then we just go out for a really decent meal when we feel like it. – Naturally . . .

I always think of you when we have steak-and-kidney pie, she smiled.

My yes! exclaimed her sister. It was marvellous! The crust! ... Some day when I've got an oven I'm going to learn how to make it. I'll eat a whole one myself.

They had tea on a tray between them on the divan. Her sister tore open a packet of biscuits. Now! she said.

It's funny to think of you domesticated, she smiled at her sister.

The mechanics of life ... said her sister, watching the tea flow into a cup.

Of course, yes, you have to get *through them* to other things, she said, urging her understanding.

Getting through them's the thing, said her sister.

'... By the time I've got the house cleaned the way I want it, and put three meals on the table ...' She heard her mother. A familiar phrase of music played on a different instrument.

When he qualifies, said her sister, sitting back with her tea, we're going away ... to travel. Perhaps to Kenya for a bit. And of course, I'm still determined to go to Italy. We even started to learn Italian. She laughed. – It petered out, though. We want to go to Italy, and Switzerland ... But what we'll do with the baby, God knows ... At the thought she frowned, accusing the invisible; put the whole thing away in some part of her mind where she kept it.

Did you see the exhibition of modern Italian art last week? she asked eagerly, ready for the talk. What did you think of it?

Didn't even know there was one, said her sister. I don't know, I don't seem to get beyond the headlines of the paper, most of the time.

Oh, she said. There was an oil that reminded me of that picture of yours – she twisted her head to the Indian child and the lilies.

That's a gouache, said her sister, her eyes on the balcony. She tilted her head. Was that a grumble from the pram ...? She looked questioningly.

I didn't hear anything, she said, subsiding back.

I *hope* not, said her sister.

I rather hope he *will* cry, she laughed, I want to see him.

Her sister looked at her very attentively, her eyes held very wide, the impressive, demanding way she had looked at her when they were children, and her sister was the big sister directing the game: Look here, she said, I'm afraid you'll have to see him next time, if you don't mind. I have to go out to give a child a lesson just now, and Alan has to rush back from a ward round to be here with the baby. It's bad enough he has to interrupt his work as it is; if he's got to be here, he's got to get some swotting done at least – and he can't do that if the baby's awake. I try to get him off to sleep and then I pray he'll stay asleep till I get back. So if you don't mind – her hands were trembling a little on the teacup.

Of course not! she protested. I'll see him next time. I didn't know . . . It doesn't matter at all.

No, said her sister, smiling now, friendly, careless, you'll come often.

Did that mean she must go now?

Are you going out soon? she said.

Yes, said her sister, I must get myself tidied up . . . You can wander round behind me. Then, as soon as he comes, I can rush off.

All at once she wanted to go; she must get away before He came. It was quite ridiculous how agitated she felt lest He should come whilst she was still there. She whimpered inwardly to go, like a child in a strange place. She followed her sister distractedly around, unable to think of anything else but her impulse to go. She thought she heard a step; she thought she heard the door, every minute.

Her sister changed her sandals for shoes, went into the bathroom to smooth her hair. The bathroom was steamy with wet napkins; standing there with her sister, she felt hot and hardly able to breathe. I must hang them out before I go . . . said her sister, her mouth full of hairpins; her eyes were curiously distracted, as if all the time her attention was divided, pulled this way and that. And I should get the vegetables ready for tonight . . . Her hands fumbled with haste, remembering.

Was that the clang of the lift gate? Her heart beat up inside her . . . No. You know, I really think I should go now, she said, smiling, to her sister.

Well, all right, then, Baby, said her sister, turning with her old smile, her old slow, superior smile. Next time come in the evening, it'll be more interesting for you. Alan'll be here – that is, we'd better make it a weekend evening, when he hasn't got to work . . . But if you wait just another few minutes he'll be here – she encouraged.

No, she said, I've got to go now; I've got to get something for mother, in town. So I'd better . . .

They stood smiling at one another for a moment.

Mother . . . said her sister . . . God, always something to get for mother . . . She shook her hair freely, with a little gesture of release; then with long, sure movements, pinned it up.

– Well, I'll leave you, then, she said, dodging beneath napkins to the door. With the napkins and the vegetables and the lesson to go to, she didn't say.

And as she turned at the door she noticed something on the bathroom shelf that suddenly lifted her strong sense of depression for her sister; something that signalled out to her that all was not lost. It was quite an ordinary thing; a box of talcum powder. The special kind of talcum powder with a special light sweet perfume of honeysuckle that her sister had always used; that had always been snowed about the bathroom for mother to mop up and grumble over. You still use it! she cried with pleasure – The same old kind in the flowered box! I haven't smelled it since you left!

What? said her sister, not listening.

Your bath powder in those big messy boxes! she laughed.

Her sister's eyes wandered tolerantly to the shelf. Oh *that*! she said. She looked at it: It's just the empty box – Alan keeps his shaving things in it. Fourteen-and-six on bath powder! I didn't know what to spend money on next, in those days . . . Goodbye! she called out from the door.

Goodbye, shouted out her sister from the bathroom. Don't forget –

No, I won't, she called back, Goodbye!

The lift wasn't on that floor so she didn't wait for it but ran down the stairs and went straight out of the building and down the street and past Minos's Tearoom to the tram stop. In the tram she sat, slowly unclenching herself and thinking fool, fool, what is the matter with you? She was terribly, terribly pleased because she hadn't met Him. She was really quite foolishly pleased. When she thought how ridiculously pleased she was, she felt a strong sense of guilt toward her sister. The more pleased, the more strong the pang for her sister. As if her not wanting to meet Him made him not good enough for her sister. Oh her poor, poor sister . . .

Quite suddenly she rang, got off the tram, and went into a chemist shop. Strained and trembling so that the assistant looked at her curiously, she bought a large box of the special bath powder. She caught the next tram back to Minos's Tearoom and rushed along the street and swept into the building and into the lift. In the presence of the lift she stood stiffly, clutching the parcel. The lift seemed discreetly to ignore her nervous breathing. Out of the lift and along the passage to Number 11, and as she brought down the knocker, it came to her with a cold start – He might be there. Too late it came to her . . . As it came, the door opened.

Look, said a dark young man – Come in, won't you – just a minute – and leaving her standing, disappeared on to the balcony. She could hear a baby crying; holding its breath and then releasing all the force of its lungs in a long diminishing bellow. In a moment the young man came back. It's all right, he said, with a wave of his hand. He was holding a pair of glasses; his brown eyes were faintly red-rimmed. He looked at her inquiringly.

Good afternoon, she said foolishly.

Good afternoon! he said kindly. Did you want to see me? Or is it for my wife . . .?

I – I just wanted to leave something – she said – something . . .

He saw the parcel. You want to leave something for my wife, he said helpfully.

Yes – she said – thank you, if you will – and gave him the parcel.

She knows about it, does she? he said. I mean she knows who it's from?

She nodded her head violently. Thanks – then, she said, stepping back.

Righto, said the young man. He was in a hurry. He gave her a brief explanatory smile and closed the door.

She hadn't said it. She hadn't told Him. I'm her sister, I'm her sister. She kept saying it over and over silently inside herself, the way she should have said it to Him . . . And in between she told herself, Fool, fool . . .

Another Part of the Sky

Coming across the dark grass from the main building to his dark house at eleven o'clock on a Sunday night he stumbled against the edging of half-bricks. End up, all sunk into the earth at the same level, they formed a serrated border along every pathway and round every flower bed in the place. The young boys had laid them with all their race's peasant pleasure in simple repetitive patterns, some memory beneath their experience of rotting corrugated iron and hessian recalling to their hands the clean daub of white zigzag round a clay hut. That would come, he supposed with a smile; they would want whitewash for the bricks.

There were roses growing behind the bricks, tattering the darkness with blacker spangles of reaching foliage. The boys had planted those too. 'The man who pulled down prison walls and grew geraniums in their place' – of course the papers had got it wrong. Wrong, all wrong. Whenever things are written down they go wrong. Mistakes are the least of it; by the time they are stamped in print, words have spilt meaning and whatever of truth they have managed to scoop up. Geraniums for roses; that was nothing: but 'the man who pulled down prison walls and grew geraniums in their place' – that was a glib summing up that left everything out. As a fact it was true; in the nine years that he had been principal of the reformatory, he had taken down the six-foot walls with the broken bottles encrusted on the top, he had set the boys gardening, he had helped them build playing-fields, begged musical instruments for them. The photograph of him sitting at his desk, dipping a pen. The photograph of the boys sitting cross-legged in the garden, numbers on their khaki backs, gleams of sun on their heads cropped of wool ... When did that moment, the moment of the article, of all the articles that had been written about him, all the lectures that had been given in his honour – when did it exist?

As his feet sounded suddenly on gravel, he made a little sighing noise, casting off the bland unreality of it. It left out everything.

What had it to do with now, the sleeping darkness of the reformatory behind him, the burning starts of red and flashes of print jittering his inner sight, the quiet of the night veld darkness; the worry that filled all the spaces of his body as his breath did?

This morning he had stood amidst the voices of the boys at church service, this afternoon he had written the draft of a penal reform pamphlet, after supper he had sat with a table full of reports. His nostrils were wide with a pause of concentration, his eyes did not see. His wife sewed at some garment in her lap without looking; he was conscious now and then of the quiet wink of her glasses as she watched him.

All the day, half the night; the worry had been with him all the time. Now the surface of the day had been rolled away, and he was left with the worry, he took it with him as he went up the three steps, over the door mat made of old tyre-strips, through the door that gave to his thumb as though the latch had been waiting for his touch. For a moment the night stood in the doorway: the great hard polished winter sky that shone of itself – the nick of young moon was a minor brilliant amongst white sharp stars – without answer above the low heads of the kopjes; where in that humming space was the young boy with the neat head of a lizard? Then the door stood before night; and inside, the dry closed air of the house carried the unspoken question (Have you heard? Any news yet?), the shape of the telephone waited to ring. Here you could not escape the answer coming . . . The telephone was a nerve, ready to jump.

Somewhere the boy who had lain in the clean discipline of a dormitory and learned so quickly the ritual of the hands and the bent head that made the day pass of itself in work, lay crouched in a hovel of smoke and bright eyes and the smell of breath and beer, and stared through hours at the sluggish possibilities of idleness, rising and writhing in half-discerned murk. Saw desire melt into violence . . . wanting into having. Sat in the cave of hunched faces painted with cosy fear by the light of a paraffin-tin fire, flickered with the torn filth of old newspapers stuffed in corners (newspapers that said stupidly, crime wave . . . robbery . . . old man knifed in the street): and was free. That was the boy's freedom; that was what he had run away to, a week ago. – It was easy . . . there were geraniums, no walls. – It happened a few times every year, always with this same twinge of peculiar pain to the principal: that was what they had to run away to, these young boys; to that; that troubled dream-like existence of struggle and fear and horror which was what they knew, which to them was freedom. The governing board said consolingly: You mustn't get too discouraged when your system has occasional failures – it has justified itself magnificently in the long run, Collins. And he smiled at them, being accustomed to having patience with people whose understanding is limited to their own capabilities of feeling. Poor Collins, they said to each other – he was a dreamer, an idealist, after all – he's just like everyone else when he's proved wrong. Can't take the blow to his pride.

The boy had been gone now for a week and like others who had slipped from the cool bit of society tasting strange in their young hard mouths, he might have disappeared into the nameless faces of the native locations or he might have been brought back again to lower his head and watch himself watched. But yesterday the telephone had rung and the dutiful voice of the sergeant had said what he had been told to say: That boy that escaped from your place last week – there's been an old woman assaulted and robbed in Jeppe, and the description of the native that did it seems to fit the boy. – Yes, yes – The policeman read slowly through the description again. – Yes, that's right. – Well, that's all, we just wanted to tell you. There don't seem to be any fingerprints, unfortunately. But we should be able to get him. We just wanted to make sure we got the description right. – And the woman, is she badly hurt? – Fractured skull, ribs broken, the lot. He used an old dumb-bell that was lying around the kitchen.

The boy with the neat, small head of the lizard, the long, small deft hands. As the principal felt quietly along the passage to the bathroom, he saw again, for the thousandth time, the momentary reassurance of a flash of the boy's face, lifted from his desk as you walked in. Like a pain let go, relief came: that boy could never have done it.

He closed the bathroom door with a muted creak so that he could turn on the light without its pale square opening on the wall in the bedroom where his wife lay. The warm after-scent of a bath met him. He turned on the hot tap gently and the water was drawn like a soft skein over his hand. In the little mirror that sweated runnels of condensed steam from the bath, he saw his face with the non-recognition of weariness in his eyes. There was a moment of childish comfort, as if, having worried so much, the whole thing was accounted for, expiated. The boy could not have done the thing; not this boy, and he knew boys, had studied thousands of them, every hour of his day, for nine years. It was all right. He had not done it. The description could be anybody, was anybody. It was only that the police happened to have the description of the boy on hand because he had escaped, and so they turned to it first. Whenever they did not have anything to go upon, they fell back on something easy like this; it made it sound as if they had done something, were getting somewhere. 'The police are investigating, and have the situation well in hand.' He knew the police, too, after nine years. Thousands and thousands of faces, all brown, all brown eyes, all thick mouths. That was how the white people of the town saw the black: they were all the same, how could you tell one from another unless he had a scar, or a limp? So if a young boy escapes from a reformatory, and a young boy assaults a woman, it must be the same boy. – He washed his face under the running tap, trying not to make a noise, gasping at the water. And then he found the towel and dried his face, dried the day off his face and left his eyes burning, almost enjoying the relief of their own weariness. A muscle twitched relaxation in one lower lid.

Then he saw her stockings, washed and hung side by side on the towel rail.

As he saw them, the symbol of her routine, the orderly living out of the day which she maintained always, no matter what troubled her, what exile of worry she experienced beside him and with him – for sometimes he told her his worry, and sometimes he did not and she knew it just the same and suffered it quietly and kept her knowledge of it from him – he knew that she was awake in the bedroom. She was awake and worrying. Her hands did the things they had always done in an unconscious effort to keep one sane and for quiet reassurance, the safety of commonplace. But the very fact of the reassurance proved the existence of the worry. He could feel her eyes open in the darkness of the next room, staring at a ceiling she could not see, and at once the comfort sucked away out of him and it seemed he had to breathe hard short breaths to relieve the weightiness of his chest. He stood there for a moment with his head jerking and sagging with the intake and release of this distressed breath, and it was all back again: Where was the boy? Had he done it? He had done it. Could he have done it? Was he the kind of boy to do it? With mechanical repetition he enacted the talk with the police sergeant, over and over again. Well, that's all, we just wanted to tell you. We just wanted to make sure we got the description right. – And the woman, is she badly hurt? – He used an old dumb-bell that was lying around. We just wanted to tell you. – Yes, yes. – We just wanted to tell you. The cold of the concrete floor was hardening up through his feet as he stood dead still as though the worry were a pain that might pass if he let it, submitted to its spasm and did not give it the incentive of his own attempt to escape on which to tighten its clutch.

His feet were cold as he turned off the bathroom light before he opened the door (she would know from the very meticulousness of his care that he knew there was no sleep from which to awaken her) and felt across the passage into the bedroom. The soft slump of his clothes as he undressed moved like the darkness settling to itself; there was a pause before the long creak of his bed as he let his body down.

Across the strip of rug that separated his bed from hers he listened to her listening for him. She was so still, still with consciousness; stiller than sleep, that deepens and thins, floats and sinks, can ever be. Monday . . . Will it be tomorrow? They've found him. He did it. How can you fight against the time if it is coming, if it is to come; the time of hearing; he did it.

And though she would not let him hear her breathing, because she did not want to give it away, the answering conviction of her fear slipped silently out with her soundless breath, and reached him. He did it. Oh did he do it?

But they did not speak. They would never speak. Somewhere below the face of the boy, a pang which had never yet found the right moment to claim attention lifted feebly like an eye of lightning that opens and shuts in another part of the sky. When would there be time to speak to her, to read the face of his wife as he struggled to read the suffering faces of the nameless, the dispossessed whom God made it incumbent upon him that he should spend his life reading?

The face lifted again from the desk. Brown eyes surrounded by a milky-blue rim, the flat flush ears, the sloping temples; the neat head of a lizard . . . He studied the face, called it up again and again, searching.

The night was awake, listening to them.

They had both been asleep a short time when the knock came at the door. It dinned on sleep like thunder but at the instant of wakefulness it became a knock at the front door. The impact of dread, met at last! exploded his blood through his body like shot. His wife sat up for the light switch. The light blinded them both. His feet felt over the floor for his slippers and his arms went into his gown; the knocking was insistent but not loud, purposeful of the necessity to rouse, but considerate not to shock. His heart beat so slow and strong that every force of it seemed to swell his veins as if some painful object much too large for passage were being pushed through. He went through the house turning on light, acknowledged at last, behind him, and undid the latch of the door. It's all right, he was saying, Coming, coming. It was the voice that prisoners had heard in the condemned cell, the voice that came from somewhere, never failed him.

Ngubane, one of his assistants, stood there. With a thrill of recognition, he knew it, the lump in his blood ran fast and liquid and his heart torrented beats as drops of water fuse in the rush of a waterfall. He found his glasses in his hand and now he put them on and there was Ngubane in his neat overcoat for it had been his Sunday off and he was dressed for leisure. His own shoulders shielded the light from Ngubane's face, but he saw the man's mouth parted forward in a kind of gasp as he pressed in.

Something terrible has happened, burst Ngubane as if the opening of the door had released the words, and as the principal fell back to let the man in and the light slipped past and lifted the face out of the dark, he saw the astonishing twitch of lost control from Ngubane's nose to lip, blisters of sweat along his eyebrows. It seemed that their panic rose and met, equal. In a trance they went along the passage together, through a door; swallowed; sat down. Their eyes held one another.

I – sir, sir . . . said Ngubane.

I know, I know, he said passionately. The nostrils of his short strong nose were arched back, two cuts of sorrow held his mouth firm down the sides of his cheeks. His head was lifted in an unconscious gesture to bear. Ngubane, who had seen it before in him, flared his nostrils in sudden tears of gratitude for strength, the strength of Collins. My brother – he was shaking, shaking his head as if to rid himself of what he saw – my brother was killed on the road *now*. I was riding beside him and it happened . . . he was killed.

Your brother?

My brother who was out with me in Johannesburg. My brother Peter the teacher from Germiston. The one you knew – who came . . . The bus didn't see and he was riding on the outside. He was killed, I didn't even see how it happened, he was riding there with me and then he was gone . . .

Your brother? Collins was leaning forward with his face screwed up with the curious look of questioning closely, almost as if he were irritated with not understanding what the other was trying to say.

Two strings jerked in Ngubane's neck. He nodded till he could speak again. Peter, my brother.

He was killed on the road you say? Killed on the road . . . Collins was repeating it to himself as if it were some marvel; the room, Ngubane, his own voice rising so oddly, seemed to be sliding rapidly away from him . . . His head searched a little for air, his hand lying on its side on the table jumped, relaxed, faltered.

I'm sorry, he said, Ngubane, I'm sorry. He spoke quickly. His face was burning hot. He stood up quickly and had his hand on the man's shoulder. Tell me about it, Ngubane, he said. Speak of it.

As a child waits for permission to weep, the man put his head down on his arms and, with his nose flattened against the tweed, let his eyes, showing yellow-white as they twisted up to Collins's face, slowly fill with a man's hard sorrow.

*

When the assistant had gone (they had given him something to make him sleep, words of comfort, and the comfort of promised action in the assurance that tomorrow he must take the day off to make arrangements for the funeral) the principal and his wife sat and had a cup of tea in the kitchen. The gulp of tea down their throats was easy between them. Come on, he said, and she tried the kitchen window to see if it was locked and flattened her hands against her dressing-gown a moment in a pause before she went back to bed. He pottered about, locking up again, turning lights off, picking things up in vague question of why they should have been left where they were for the night. Then he came into the bedroom and got into bed. The two of them sighed as they moved about under their covers, settling for warmth and sleep.

Then they were still.

For a moment, you know, she said suddenly, I thought he'd come to tell us bad news about the boy.

Well so did I, he said.

She made a little sound that might have meant she was going to say something, or might have been a little sound of sleep.

He lay and the darkness came up to him, the darkness spread out to the edges of his being, the darkness washed away the edges of his being as the sea melts the edges of the sand. But just as it was about to smooth out his head and wash down the pinnacles of his features like a sandcastle, a return of consciousness rose within him and swept it away.

So did I.

It came to him suddenly and it filled him with desolation as startling and wakeful as the thump at the door. It stiffened him from head to foot with failure more bitter and complete than he could ever have imagined. *I'm sorry. I'm sorry. Tell me about it.* The boy is alive so Ngubane is dead. The boy has not done it yet, so tea can be drunk. The boy has not done it so you may lie easy in the dark. A peace can take your mind while Ngubane goes home with his brother's death. If there is room for the boy, there is no room for Ngubane. This conscience like a hunger that made him want to answer for all the faces, all the imploring of the dispossessed – what could he do with it? What had he done with it? The man who pulled down prison walls and grew geraniums. He saw himself, standing up at a meeting, the flash of attention from his glasses as they looked up to him. The silence of his wife, going about her business while he worried, nine years he worried, turned from her to this problem or that. If you search one face, you turn your back on another.

He did not know how he would live through this moment of knowledge, and he closed his lids against the bitter juice that they seemed to crush out, burning, from his eyes.

The Umbilical Cord

When he was a child there was the privilege of ownership in going behind the counter and reaching into the glass drawers full of sweets. His small hand, like a little scoop, hung over into the cool, sticky triangles he could not see; the rim of the drawer lifted hard against his underarm. And on his fingers, tiny slivers and splinters of the sugar-stuff clung in facets of pink and green, like broken glass.

But not now. This Saturday he stubbed the toe of his new suede shoes against the deeply scratched varnish of the counter whilst his eyes flickered in automatic reaction to the cars that kept going past outside the window – whhp! whhp! – whhp! – and he was seventeen and too young to remember. Now he could smell the store too; the smell of furzy woollen blankets, strong soap, cardboard and paraffin, heightened every now and then with the highly personal sweat-smell of an anxious native customer. After the whole week in the cool sweet sterile scent of the chemist shop in town, he could smell it now, and his mouth twitched down at the corner with impatience. He stayed on this side of the shop, where there were the biscuit showcase, the sweet and grocery counters, and a Coca-Cola container with the streamlined red opulence of an omnibus; on the other side his father moved about the shirts and shoes, the tin trunks and blankets, and the assistants wrapped great brown paper parcels and waited, hand on hip, for the native customers to make their choice. Every now and then the old man looked up, complainingly, the flap of grey skin stretching between his chin and collarless shirt, but he did not seem to see the boy.

Let him look for me, thought his son, let him look . . .

The cars that went by from the two towns did not stop at the country store; but Saturday was the afternoon when all the people from the small holdings round about came to give their weekly grocery order, and all the natives who worked in the brickfields and on the farms came to do their shopping. Accompanying dogs skittered out of the store before the old man; dust-powdered children planked

down their tickeys and stood gasping after drinking their bottles of
Coca-Cola at one breath.

But he stood half behind the counter, doing nothing.

His mother, with her long, great breasts that swung softly forward
under her apron to rest upon the counter as she worked, served
slowly and comfortably, kept unharassed by the habit of twenty-six
years. She made a little ceremony of delight whenever she could
supply a customer with some item in short supply. 'The very last
one!' she giggled, holding a rye loaf and waggling it as if in tantalization. And then, with a sweeping generous gesture: 'Here you are! I
only had six, and here's the last one in the store!'

He stood breaking a match in his fingers, watching her as if she were
not his mother. There was one other elderly woman amongst the
assistants; slack and heavy too, with a long time of hard work. The
other two were the young, plump country girls with bright, coarse
faces, small waists, and thick, red ankles bare above their flat shoes,
with whom he had played and attended the village school when they
were children. Then they had been together, but now with their poor
Afrikaans and poorer English, their clumsy hands weighing out
mealie meal, their crude pleasure in cheap, shiny ear-rings for their
scrubbed ears, they were shy to remember that they had once
splashed through coffee-coloured pools after rain with him. And he
was forced into patronage by their embarrassment. To think that
they had once been able to talk to each other! All these country girls
from the poor small holdings were the same; like pumpkin flowers.
Sometimes there was something about the openness of them, though,
an attraction in their not knowing about themselves, only living and
smiling and wanting a trinket or a dress, perhaps ... This roused
some faintly malicious sensuality in a young man who had played
with them as children and now, apprenticed to a chemist in a great
city, served, every day, women so different, women who were
guarded about by convictions, knowing so much about themselves,
and wrapped in their knowledge and the determination to have.

The wide, sun-coloured pumpkin flower, with its large-grained
texture.

Once or twice ... His hands gently uncurled against the counter,

88

his eyes softened with sleepiness, as after a yawn or a sigh. Beyond the window and the passing cars on the highroad he was quite suddenly back again in that day, a few weeks ago. There was a rather nice taint of sweet coloured soap − dreadful in the cake but evidently good on the skin; a special kind of live warmth in the neck and beneath the arms of Marius Coetzee's daughter. Freckles on the front of her calves, but no hairs. She had chewed a grass stalk on the way, and there were flecks of green on her teeth; she tasted of peppermint.

But he could not taste it again; as soon as he tried to, he woke to the store.

At once it annoyed him to think that he had forgotten even for a moment the resentment he fretted against this business of helping Saturday afternoon in the store. Every Saturday was worse. He wouldn't say anything, but he'd make them feel it.

His mother was smiling at him, leaning back toward a woman customer. '. . . seventeen,' she was saying. 'He's going to be a chemist.' He stared at a chaotically grubby little boy who was teasing one of the skinny store cats. But she called to him: 'Leo! Come here, son. I want you to meet some . . .' 'Fine boy,' said the woman enthusiastically. He stood there, handsome with his young face unpleasant.

'Hand me down the onion pickles for Mrs Zanter,' smiled his mother. As she filled the paper carton from the jar, she laughed down into her bosom, eyebrows lifted. 'Fancy, you remember him, eh? You couldn't trust him with the pickles then. Pickles! There used to be a big tub over near the door, and he was helping himself every time my back was turned! Mommy, he used to say, I want a "tickle". Give me a tickle, Mommy. Biscuits he didn't want . . .'

He felt the hot thrill of surliness curdle in his chest. Not even looking at the woman, he walked away; he took a bottle out of the Coca-Cola container and viciously knocked the cap off. Bubbles pricked back against his throat. Immediately three very small and dirty children whose noses had run and crusted upon their upper lips thrust a jingle of damp pennies and tickeys at him and he had to stand there, serving bottles of sweet drinks to children. A big cattle fly circled his head and kept settling on his lip. More children and natives came in and he kept handing out bottles, kept taking cold, wet, hot, dry, dusty, warm tickeys. He never looked at them; did not speak.

The old man raced past, treading heavily with his heels. 'Can't one of the girls do that?' he called, his face screwed up. 'You should be over there. They need you. Busy like anything. And you're standing here, taking tickeys!'

And now he was deadly cold, sullen; so filled from head to foot with it that it amazed him so far as he could feel anything but his disgruntledness, that nobody noticed, nobody even saw how distasteful it all was to him. They think it's all right for me, he stoked himself. They think it's quite all right for me here. 'Leo,' his father shouted, using the telegraphic curtness of comradeship in work, 'that red blanket in the window. Get it out. Near the corner there.'

To come back to this. To belong to this. He stood crouched in the window with the three-legged cooking pots round his feet, the bright pink dresses hanging on wire hangers about his head, the bottles of brilliantine, yellow celluloid combs, and tin jewellery entangled with skeins of thick purple, green, and brown wool. In the dead dry air of the window, like the air of a tomb newly opened, dead flies lay sprinkled over everything; he could scarcely move without knocking something over, and as he leaned and strained for the red blanket hooked up in the corner, he lifted his eyes to the smeary glass and met on the other side the gaping faces of native shoppers staring in and the flattened tongue of a child, pressed against the glass for coolness. He added interest to the window display; a few more came to watch him.

Looking out at them with the cold eyes of a snake, he felt he never wanted to speak, ever. He would not speak again to anyone. He did not wish to say anything at all. He saw in his mind his mother and father smiling love and talk at him, and the people whom they knew grinning liking at him, and he saw himself absolutely silent in the face of them. He did not even wish to tell them. The sensitiveness of not even wanting to speak sealed his throat like a lump of pride.

He threw the blanket out into the store and withdrew himself after it. And at once he saw with the light start of the astonishment of actuality, Marius Coetzee and his daughter. Marius Coetzee! There he stood in the store, a big farmer on whose red neck wrinkles drew a map of thirty years' work in the sun. He was half-turned out of Leo's line of vision, and the boy could see his tough hand with the big spread, horny thumb-nail, resting on the shoulder of his daughter. But Marius Coetzee was a passionate Nationalist. He neither mixed nor traded with anyone who did not believe as he did, in the Republic, or live as he did, assiduously treating all dark people as his abject servants, resenting his polyglot neighbours – Jews, Italians, Portuguese, and English – despising his brother Afrikaners who did not do the same, and never, under any circumstances, allowing a word of English to form in his mouth. Marius Coetzee drove in to shop at the big Nationalist Co-op in the town every week! Why, he wouldn't have bought a sixpence mealie meal in this store.

Then?

That brown back-of-the-head, like a curly chrysanthemum, that was his daughter with him. That was her.

Oh why had Marius Coetzee come into this store; why, when he never would, ever; when he never had, ever before? Why? Why with his daughter? Not with anyone else, but with her?

He wanted to run over to Marius Coetzee and pull at his arms and make him say why he had come. He wanted him to say: I've come because of – this or that . . .

He knew why Marius Coetzee had come. His heart, alas, no longer cool and contemptuous, remembered at once that it was only a child, and gibbering, tried to race away. His hand felt back for the door of the window and jerked and slithered it closed. He picked up the blanket.

But when he looked again, the man was still there, his hand on the girl. They did not press to the counter with the other people, but stood back, looking over the heads of the assistants.

Waiting for my father; the logic of each plain conclusion came over him in waves of helpless sickness. He was horror-stricken with the logicality with which he knew the moment was to come; the moment when the now firmly closed-down mouth of Marius Coetzee would be curving in talk like a whip and he would be saying to the uncomprehending old man, looking at him a little impatiently (what does he want of me, this OB swine), something has happened to the girl. How would he say it? Not like that. But that was what it would be. Your son, and now something has happened to Marius Coetzee's daughter.

Oh, how he feared her, leaning there on one leg, with the weight thrusting her round hip out as she waited. She didn't mind, of course. She wouldn't mind anything.

Fool, fool, fool I am — his dethroned self cried inside him — stepping out in insecurity; silly, silly, silly, thinking it's easy, on your own ... To have cut loose and found yourself dangling so frighteningly by one thread of skin from the family. To have left yourself almost nothing at all to hang on to of the safe, of the warm, the faithful. Fool, fool, flicking the days by in pictures of the moment, coming and passing, always new ones, and no time to remember.

Not even how many weeks ago it had been. Five weeks? Less?

Marius Coetzee, standing so determined and detached, had made his presence felt in the store. Now, sure enough, he moved forward to be served by the old man. The old man leaned across the counter as if he were waiting to hear: a packet of sugar or a bag of salt ...

Oh, God!

Coetzee's hard voice spoke out hard in Afrikaans to the old man; the girl was listening intently but she lifted her leg bent backward at the knee and was scratching her bare ankle.

There was nothing he could do. He did not want to be near enough to hear. But he could not go away altogether and stop trying to hear.

Now his mother had been called over. She was nibbling a little bit of cheese, as she often liked to. She smiled her good business smile. She nodded, swallowing the last of the cheese. Frowned a little, tongue reaching back into her teeth. Then, with a shrug of uncertainty, came out from behind the counter, and — she was leading the girl to the other side of the shop ... To the rack, where women's aprons and cheap cotton dresses hung together. They disappeared behind the rack. Across the shop, across his self-despair and fear, he could hear his mother's voice, up and down, exclaiming.

He tasted the salt of the sweat on his lip. And then his mother came out from behind the rack, walking before the girl who was now wearing a bright red raincoat with a hood, and giggling at the cries of praise and admiration which preceded her. 'Meneer Coetzee! Look how it fits her! I didn't think I had one left! Just this one, there was; must have been overlooked. I could have sold it over and over. Isn't it lucky, eh dear, just what you wanted. Just the one your daughter wants, Meneer Coetzee . . .' And she was laughing surprised triumph.

'I'll wrap it up for you,' the old man said. 'Lena, make a nice parcel for Mr Coetzee.'

His wife called: 'Leo! Bring me one of those paper bags – the big ones, eh?'

The old man, who could switch from business serenity to family impatience in the space of an aside, complained at her: 'Leo's getting something out of the window. Why don't you get it yourself. He's busy.'

He stood, clutching the blanket. He wanted to wrap himself in it; he clung to its thickness of folds as one sobs astonished relief on the shoulder of a friend. He stood there quite still and unseen, whilst Marius Coetzee paid for the raincoat and, hostile-jawed, went out of the store with his daughter beside him, already tearing at the package, unable to bear even momentary separation from her new red coat. Now he had forgotten her completely; there was no after-call of remembered contact with her. She had wiped herself off.

And lightly, lightly his suede brogues went across the shop; he laid the blanket upon the counter. 'What parents won't do for children,' the old man said, easing the waistband of his trousers. 'It shows you. Did you see that? Marius Coetzee hasn't been in here for twenty years. But his daughter sees a raincoat that she wants, and we've got it, and it's her birthday – so, for her, he comes here. Children! You see, even a swine like that, for his child . . .'

The warm, weak happiness that flooded him was difficult to conceal; it was as much a problem to keep it unnoticed as it had been to make his dissatisfaction noticed. He wandered over to his mother at the provision counter. She was busy. He stood just behind her, and quite suddenly he wanted to touch her, but he had not done so for so long that he couldn't.

'Mother,' he whispered in her ear. 'Pinch me a pickle. A mustard one. I feel like a pickle.'

The Talisman

How is it that no one suspects the power of clothes? How is it that human beings in the confidence of animacy cannot feel the cold inanimate standing always behind them; the things they have mastered and made for themselves, standing behind them. Just behind them, waiting: the machines and the chemicals and the gadgets . . . and the clothes.

We do not know; we cannot sense the power of things without life. Fear is only of an unknown we believe in; and this is an unknown we haven't even invented yet . . . We stir toward a discovery of it sometimes in time of war, when the missile often seems to do more and go farther than the hand that releases the button could empower, but at parades and conferences later we feel the world belongs to those who can talk, and power is safe in the human mouth again.

Chairs and tables and walls about us, and the clothes we live in; how should we think of them as existing outside of us – what can they do for us, or to us, for we ourselves have made them? . . . We are so confident of this that we sometimes even wish wistfully that it were otherwise, we even pretend it is: the advertisements in the newspaper promise that in a dress made by such-and-such a firm you will lead a new, fuller, gayer life; so-and-so's ties will make you attractive to women; if you wear Blank's coat at the interview, the prize executive job is yours . . .

I shudder when I read them.

I remember how, when I was a little girl, my sister and I used to be taken to spend Sunday with my grandmother. Grandpa was there too, of course, but he sat up in a great chair in the corner of the cold little flat, his stiff leg stretched out at an angle, and it was Grannie who basted the chicken and made the apple pie and left us with the bedroom all to ourselves to turn into a dress shop. Most of Grannie's clothes were old, they were all in the dark colours and heavy silks that could only be becoming on a pretty seventy-year-old, and she very rarely bought anything new, unless someone in the family got married. But we never grew tired of her collection, and we sold it over and over again, every Sunday. There was always the same pleasure in opening the pale, satiny walnut doors of the wardrobe and displaying the unchanging stock of limp silks and releasing the faint pleasant smell of Grannie upon the room. Some dresses would have a long white hair, curled bright against a collar or sleeve; carefully picked off and held up against the light, it would spring back into the pattern of Grannie's waved head. Certain dresses were chosen for display models, and, their wooden hangers hooked on to the swan-neck curves of the bed-posts, the skirts were spread out over the pink carpet in monkeyish imitation of the best shops.

There were favourites of course: a brown one with coffee-coloured lace that we loved (really *loved* with that softening of adoration which conquers children utterly for all sorts of odd things, seen in shopwindows or other people's houses, so that they cry out in anguish: That's mine! I saw it first! That's mine!) and a coat with fur on it that we had had to make a strict rule about, taking turns to sell it.

There was only one dress we were not allowed to sell. Now just leave that alone where it is, Grannie would say, hanging it right at the end of the rail, against the wood – play as much as you like with the others, but don't take that out.

We would not have dreamt of playing with it. I don't think we ever touched it. It was Grannie's best frock. We had seen it, of course, she had taken it out to show to us, but we had never seen her wear it and we knew that it must belong to the occasions of some other world ringed wider round our own, that we would grow up into. That dress was the stranger in the wardrobe; it had a padded silk hanger that was never borrowed or exchanged, and it had never lost its own shape and taken on the shape of Grannie.

We grew up, and the game fell away from us; so gradually, becoming less real, and then – we didn't notice quite when – stopping altogether. We were almost young ladies when my grandmother died, and my mother brought home a few things she could not pass to the hands of others. Amongst them was the dress. What could she do with it? Only keep it. It hung at the back of her wardrobe for years, then on a peg in the cupboard of the discarded and dispossessed.

One day when I was twenty, a native girl walked into our kitchen wearing my grandmother's dress. She had come to see our girl, and she stood there, smiling good afternoon at me. A sudden excitement thumped up inside me. I burned with recognition of the dress: the dress hanging aloof in my grandmother's wardrobe, and the Game. And in a dissolving flash I was myself again *as I had been* . . . Then slowly the fusion cooled, I hardened back, away, I was grown up.

The dress was there, coldly, in positive, hard assertion.

I looked and looked at it, and I felt – for the first time, as if something were beginning inside me, a kind of knowing that was fear – the power of the dress. Not just the evocative power – that, after all, had its source in me, in the deep of my own years – but the power to *be*, in a way other than human, to persist, beyond the servant girl who was wearing it and my grandmother who was dead.

That was the first time. And it happened again, I see now, at other times and places in my life: this unexpected tripping up against a trapping of some past scene, a scrap of décor from some old stage, halting me so that I must look up and find myself face to face with an old identity. I, dragged back, entangled with myself again; but the Thing, the shabby pyjamas of a dead lover, the crumpled scarf found down the back of the car seat, the borrowed shirt that was never given back – the *Thing* persisting remote from then or now.

It was a hand shown and as quickly withdrawn . . . But it was there, all the time.

When, in the sensuality of the mind that suddenly overtakes a group and sets them describing their own feelings, their confrontations with self, I sometimes spoke of the relationship between people and clothes and my own feeling about this, most of my friends protested that the experience was one they recognized in themselves. Oh yes, quite a few of us had felt that way – that most disturbing feeling! – and they laughed, misunderstanding, as probably even I did, the experience itself. For we saw it essentially as a *feeling*, something subjective, from within ourselves . . . *Feelings* were of enormous importance to us, anyway; they were our cult. We were not exactly Hedonists – we had been born too late for that; its vogue had passed when we were babies – but we had a strong home-made Blakean approach, inclining toward 'ruddy limbs and flaming hair' and any valid experience, pleasant or otherwise, rather than insulation.

The novelty of a new, strange feeling was a touch from life; who would refuse it? I, who have always played with my feelings like fireworks, wanting them to sparkle and burst into coloured light even if it's *only for a moment*, and there's a dreary smell of sulphur after that one can't escape and that I never remember about – I, certainly, would never refuse the same old beckon of fascination. And when the finger crooked at me again that day I was going to buy my wedding frock, what would I do but laugh in self-congratulation of my daring and originality of code; saying, well, at least it's something completely new for a woman to let a former lover choose the frock she will wear at her wedding to someone else!

I was going along toward the shop in my new sense of peace with myself, when out of a building he came and stopped dead in front of me. 'You?' he said.

'Well . . .!'

There was a moment. And then we fell upon one another with the noisy excitement of five years before, for he still looked like a fox with his peaked beard and bright sly eyes, and I half-hoped I was still the young ballet dancer with the Pavlova hair I had been in Cape Town then. There was a kind of thrill of revulsion in being with him again – his untidy trousers, the stains on his fingers – but our time together was so far off now, that I did not need to be afraid of it. We went to finish our exclamations over one another in a teashop, and it was there that we talked our way down to the immediate present.

All the old rather shrill and edgy impulsiveness of his way of living and talking had caught me up again by the time we left the teashop, and when he commanded, with his consciously preposterous laugh, 'Look, I'm coming along with you to choose that wedding dress. It'll be a dress if I choose it; baroque mess if you do . . .' The unfitness of the whole thing caught my fancy and my vanity and I laughed and almost clapped my hands in excitement the way a child does in the craziness of a party game.

So he chose my wedding dress; the blue crêpe dress, the blue in a peacock's tail. I wanted it, of course, I liked the sight of myself wearing it, but he, the artist, chose it for me.

What is there about the dress? I don't know. Not a distinction in the sense of fashion; nor the sleazy investiture of sentiment, the symbol taken for the reality that for a certain type of woman makes a particular dress a 'wedding dress'. I was not happy or simple enough to regard this frock as my *wedding dress*, yet when I wore it, afterwards, I was conscious of a quality in it . . . – Of course the first time I had worn it, at my wedding, I had noticed nothing, being too much absorbed in a brief metamorphosis.

I wore it quite often in the first year of my marriage; it was a useful sort of frock for many places. I even remember wearing it once after I had become pregnant and was three or four months with child. Then it became much too tight for me – or rather I became too tight for it – and I did not wear it again for a long time. My son was born a daughter, and left my body changed and rounded with milk and maternity. The dress hung at the back of my wardrobe, like my grandmother's best frock.

But after some months my body was returned to me. I went out little; I had settled down to a second-best kind of response to life that I was aware of without really understanding. I looked for the lack everywhere, even in myself, but I could not find it simply because it *was* a lack – just something not there, rather than something there, and wrong. Every experience was somehow less than one; always a little ridiculous, in the end. One afternoon I found myself walking from room to room, meeting myself in a mirror, standing about . . .

I got dressed, drove into town, and went to see an exhibition of old maps. There I began to enjoy myself *by myself* again, the way I used to. With relief, the mood that had held me lately dwindled into proportion as I walked about, interested, seeing now and then someone I knew and sometimes exchanging an opinion with a stranger in the brief intimacy, like a match struck up, of a shared impression. And then, just as I was leaving, smiling my way through the gently buzzing group round the door, whom should I see in profile, hands behind back, trowel of beard lifted up in uncertainty before an exhibit on the far wall . . .

With real friendliness and pleasure I excused myself back through the crowd. He was surprised, really glad to see me; we both laughed with that vague astonishment that comes with the unexpected meeting. I was just the person he wanted to see – he'd been going to get in touch with me, because he was trying to get suitable galleries for an exhibition of his pictures up here, and he thought I would know whom to approach. He was a man who – I am suspicious of the term – 'lived for the moment'; that is, he was always completely absorbed in the friends, the mood, the philosophy of a current stage in his development, and so it would never occur to him to trade upon a past intimacy – it was *past*, and therefore non-existent – and the suggestion that I might help him was truly naïve and merely because he knew me and my possible sphere of influence. This was a quality that made him cruel, from the viewpoint of the women in his life, and insincere from the viewpoint of men. Every time one met him, it was as if one met him for the first time. Every meeting was a fresh beginning, uninfluenced, so far as he was concerned, by previous experience of one another: if you had been his mistress last time, you might find yourself a sister this time. If you had been a friend, you might be bewildered to find yourself a lover.

Now he only wanted me to help him arrange his exhibition. I don't think he even remembered how long ago, or where, or under what circumstances we had met last time or the time before. He made the present so intense that you felt a trifle stale for remembering anything of the past. This also had the effect of putting out of mind any conscience I might have had about entering into association with him again, now that I was married. We talked exhaustively of his pictures and the exhibition, and I began at once to think, my mind pleasurably grasping at activity, where and how it could best be arranged.

I came home feeling that I had righted myself inside, that all I had needed was a change in my routine and the stimulation of strangers. Like a child who has recovered from the sulks, I felt oddly comfortable and secure at the sight of my familiar bedroom that I had left a few hours ago. I dropped my hat and bag and pulled off my dress; my old dressing-gown was good enough to get splashed whilst I bathed the baby. As I passed through the room again, carrying the child to the bath, I glanced at the things lying on my bed: and saw it was my blue dress. With a curious turn, inside my chest, a momentary beating up of my heart: how odd! And this afternoon had been the first time I'd put it on since before the child was born. And I hadn't remembered that I was wearing it, and he hadn't recognized it as the frock he'd chosen. How staid we must be getting. I gave a little snort, half-stirred, half-amused, and went with my child into the bathroom.

It is difficult for me to write now on that plane of ordinariness; now when my head aches constantly and that pain keeps alive down my left arm. Now, when I sleep so little and dream so violently with dreams so full of words, it's hard to separate what I've thought since from what I really lived.

The light of that bathroom, steamy and scented, with the cheerful noisiness of the water draining out and the gasps and grunts of the baby, the pink light of the bedroom, the tent of yellow light suspended over my chair from the lamp in the study; how strangely they come to my eyes now, like the light of a serene and beautiful afternoon shining far off and difficult to believe in, through the rift in a heavy storm cloud ... Over there, the sun must be shining, someone says ... The light of all those days, when I moved so unconsciously about, pleasing myself, I find it difficult to see. The glare of the storm in my mind flickers weirdly, lifting into significance much that I hurried carelessly over at the time, and leaving in darkness the 'events' that then filled my consciousness.

What concerned me then, what captured my imagination, was the affair that I began again with my friend the artist – yes, it was my doing. I began it; I think I always knew I had almost deliberately begun it: that was part of the fascination, the tightrope that I made of my life and set myself to walk. Keeping my balance with my husband and my baby and security that I clung to so abjectly at one end, and the man and the uncertainty that I had rejected but hankered after still, at the other. Everything else that I did, all the normal processes of living I performed without knowing. The women I spoke to, the flowers I planted, the pots and pans and sewing I touched; I experienced none of it. My whole being was centred on the tightrope, in an excitement of concentration that, in a different person and directed toward different ends, might have produced a piece of music, or an inspired painting.

And now, all that I ignored, that was unimportant background, streaming past in a blur, has taken on significance; the experience itself is the blur. What I keep seeing over and over again is the tent of yellow light suspended over my chair from the lamp; the baby screaming herself red in the bathroom; the pink light of the bedroom; the enamelled clock ticking in the sun on the kitchen window-sill. And maddening as a neon sign imposing itself against the dark at deadly regular intervals, the picture of my blue dress hanging at the back of the wardrobe. God knows I was not conscious of the blue dress at the time; I don't think I ever wore it. The 'affair' was a new thing; it did not require a talisman in the shape of the dress. I would have thought it ridiculous to wear the dress; it belonged to a joke, a friendly joke before my marriage, a time when the relationship between the artist and me bore no hint of the intensity it had since developed.

Yet whenever I try to think back over that time, the dress keeps interposing; I see it hanging there at the back of the wardrobe, all the time. I see it hanging in the exact position, in the particular disposition of folds and creases that it bore on that day much later, only six months ago, when I was to appear at the divorce court, and I went, with the listlessness of habit, to my wardrobe to see what I might wear. What did it matter what I wore? It was an occasion in my life I had not previously reckoned with; a woman never thinks, when buying a dress: now, that would be suitable to wear in court. I was so dazed and appalled that morning; like a child amazed at the pieces of a vase it has broken, looking at the bits on the floor and not believing that the thing is done . . . I kept pushing dresses along the rack one by one, incapable of sufficient concentration to make the effort of taking one out. And then there it was. Hanging on its special hanger with the belt looped up over one shoulder, and the small round bag of mothballs dangling in the neck. It hung there in the blank assertion of existence. I had forgotten it, but it had not forgotten me. I stood there looking at it, and then I felt it very slowly, examining the stitching and the pleats and tucks and the tiny glass beads, like miniature tubes, round the sleeves. And as I went over it, everything was forced back to me, I remembered myself with the disgust and fear of absolute truth, as I had been for the preceding months. All my concealed motives and self-deceptions spoke plainly back at me. I was suddenly tortured with the desire to put the dress on; yet at the same time the idea of it on my body filled me with a panic of revulsion. I could not escape from the horrible idea, like madness, almost, that the dress was *me*; that I was looking at – myself.

Six months ago. I sit here now and think: only six months back. Surely I cannot be so far from that girl on the tightrope, enjoying herself up there, not afraid she might fall? But no, I am too dizzy now, for adventure. I have been ill, and my legs are wobbly. My illness was not a serious thing, nothing out of the way, but it seems to have left something behind it. There is this pain down my arm, flashing through me so bright, it takes my breath away. But I am going to do something about it at last. I have made up my mind to see a specialist. I spoke to my doctor and he recommended a heart specialist and made an appointment for me, for this afternoon. In about half an hour's time I must go. That's the best thing to do; find out if there really is anything the matter with me, and then I can be treated, the thing can be put right.

I keep sitting here, and yet it's really time for me to go. I shall be late for my appointment if I don't go soon. I am still sitting here . . .

Shall I tell you something?

I went to my wardrobe just now to fetch my coat, and I saw the dress hanging there. My attention was drawn to it because it had slipped crooked on its hanger. So I pushed the other clothes that were pressing in upon it aside, and righted its position. As I did so, I noticed curious little marks, all over it. It has begun to rot, at last. Quite suddenly it has gone into little holes, all over, and at the seams the material has become quite thin, and pulled away, frayed . . .

The End of the Tunnel

Always midday, and always summer on the road to Lourenço Marques. All through the autumn morning, as they drove, the sun seemed a strong light from the whole sky, no shadows on the warmth but the dark of cypress beside the white light of a farmhouse or a dam bright as a piece of tin; no stone, no softness of red dust, no close grass, no bird's wing unpenetrated by the steady sun. The hood of the car was hot as a helmet; two currents of air fed them through the windows. And the road rose and fell, rose and fell, and they followed its rhythms as if they moved across the body of something that breathed deeply: hills so green and softly folded you could have passed your hand over them rather than walked them; farms spreading from the homestead set white against the slope; patterns of tilled earth, swirl of the plough setting up a wake of earth, fanwise groves of orange trees with their fruit like baubles on a child's Christmas tree. His arm was red where he leaned it on the open window; her leg, turned up under her body, numb a long time now. Once she said: Look, like a late Van Gogh. And without turning his head he pulled in his mouth in a slight grimace. It could sometimes happen that the dislike of an artist's vision of something could be transferred to the object itself, so that now his distaste for the artistic cliché of certain Van Gogh landscapes robbed him of what would certainly have been his pleasure in the sight of three cypress, changing places gracefully as the road altered the perspective. They were aware of this, of course, as they were aware of so much that they might have left unanalysed, and valued in one another only what came from the innocent eye. Out of the human silence – the car filled the ears soothingly with speed – he lifted his hand with the watch on the wrist and traced out something along the horizon. She knew it was not for her, it was for himself, and she smiled, also for herself.

When the road lowered itself gently down between the hills and there was a bridge over noisy water and trees that hung, transfixed, above it, she sat up suddenly and he stopped the car. Their senses pricked up like the ears of animals at the scent of water. He got out and she slid across the seat after him and they walked in the sun to the edge of the bridge, stiffly, a faint ringing in their heads, then pleasure in the flex and pull of muscles making them conscious of the unconscious effort of walking. They hung over and looked. He was not the kind of man impelled to throw a stone. She looked for a place to climb down, began to feel along the bank for the foothold of rock, but he caught her guilty smile like an adult interpreting the ingratiating wile of a child about to do the forbidden, and said: Not now. As much as you like later, but now's not the time to stop. And very conscious that she was not a child, in the fact that she could resist the impulse with the adult's knowledge of its unimportance instead of the child's urgent certainty that it will never come again, she came slowly back to the car.

Tiredness settled down upon them again; a physical weariness that ached in the bones of her instep, a spiritual exhaustion that made him want to close his eyes. He hoped she would not speak, troubled with the fear, ever present simply because it was foolish, that something had gone wrong, looking for reassurance from herself rather than from him. But her mind had taken refuge in her body; its bruises had come out through the flesh: she only knew that her feet ached – she pressed her instep with her palm – and her stomach, empty and yet pressing so close to her throat, gagged her. He said, rousing himself: I'll get us to Nelspruit by one. Then we'll go to a hotel and have something to eat and a bit of a break.

I feel sick, she said.

He smiled, he wanted to touch her, to uphold her, but there is a point beyond which it is humanly impossible to draw upon oneself. Love can only signal with earnest eyes behind the hand of depleted nervous energy clapped over its mouth. He drove faster, watching the road, tensing and relaxing his thigh muscle as if the small ease and unease reassured him of the continuance of everyday living, of a time unwinding simply beyond now.

The streets of a pleasant town you do not know create the artificial calm of impersonality; you accept the wide level stretch, a country-town street – filled with sun, like a hard beach with the tide retreated and only the sun flowing over the emptiness – a small figure in red scuttling across beside an adult, bicycles twinkling on the edges, the kerbstones painted white. Nothing has ever happened at that street corner, no one has ever confronted you, coming out of that shop. A town, abstract, made of low white buildings with people made of faces and clothes, as far from lovers, friends, enemies, as the hypothetical family illustrating an advertisement, or the exclamation marks of paint representing distant figures in a landscape. For the time, *people* exist in an easy moment of oversimplification.

And the town accepted them; a man and a woman, young, with the strained vacant eyes of travellers, with the clothes and the air of strangers. She had suddenly remembered the name of a hotel that someone had once mentioned to her and they drove hesitantly down the street, looking for it. There it was; and because it was white and built round the three sides of a small bright garden where red hibiscus bloomed floridly before shiny uncut grass, they felt it was pleasant.

He jumped out of the car – he had a way of recovering his spirits with a bound, like a dog shaking itself from a sleep. His hair stuck up, thick and almost visibly alive, as growing grass is. To her, who watched herself and him as one might watch the weather in the sky, taking the slightest sign for portent, deciding the hurricane from the quick darkening cloud momentarily covering the sun, it was the complete justification for herself, for him, irrational and therefore certain as no conviction of reason could ever be.

Inside the hotel there was no one about. The reception office was empty; the lounge dim above grass chairs grouped in fours around glass-topped tables. There was the smell of floor polish, the air of a waiting-room. She read the notices, CHILDREN NOT ALLOWED IN THE LOUNGE, A DANCE WILL BE HELD IN THE PALM COURT EVERY THIRD SATURDAY AT 8 PM. ADMISSION: 10/6. HOTEL GUESTS: 5/- Above double glass doors curtained in net there was another: DINING-ROOM. He had been touching the pollen-thick stamens deep inside some unfamiliar lilies that stood in a florist's silvered basket, and now he went over to the doors and rattled at them inquiringly. At once an Indian with tired obliging lines appeared, his serving jacket half buttoned in sign of off-duty, and told them that lunch could not be served before one o'clock; the electric clock on the wall gave a little jerk to twelve fifteen.

They were rather put out. She seemed to feel herself swaying slightly, with the motion of the car, where she stood. 'It doesn't matter really. I want to go to the chemist and get some aspirin. And I must tidy up –'

'The cloakroom is along the veranda to the left, madam.'

They went out again into the sun and crossed the street to the chemist. Seeing herself in the mirror behind the counter her tiredness seemed intensified to nausea again; it was impossible to think or feel beyond such tiredness. And the thought made her anxious: this was not the way it should be . . . but even the thought slipped through the slack of tiredness. The assistant looked to him to pay, seeing men and women as husbands and wives, and husbands responsible for their wives' purchases. And he already had his hand in his baggy trouser pocket, dredging up silver from notes with the suggestion of uncertainty and surprise, as if he were not sure whether there would be money there or not. Of course they had been into shops together many times before (where had they talked but in teashops and along the streets amongst the press of other people, remembering just before it was time for her to go that there was some purchase in the surface conduct of her life that she had forgotten, soap for the house or shoe polish for her husband) but now the small act was significant, it was the translation of the private, the personal into the language of the world. It was at the same time an achievement and a surrender, the sweet spurious comfort of acceptance, and the exchange of the reality for the symbol.

'What do you want to buy?' he was saying. 'Do you want something else?' But there was nothing she wanted, even to please him. She was conscious of her hair rubbed into tangles against the car seat, her paleness.

In the cloakroom at the hotel (it was obviously the one meant for casual guests at dances, there was a little shelf beneath the one mirror – wan as a pond on a grey day – round which the paint was stippled with fingerprints in lipstick) her consciousness of her face was confirmed. She looked unfamiliar and rather plain. She washed in cold water without soap and dried her face as best she could on a handkerchief. She put on her cream and powder and painted her lips and her face emerged like the pale blur of a print turning clear and definite in developer solution. When it was done she realized suddenly how she had concentrated on it; how important could it be, weighed against all he knew of her, all he saw when he looked at her, the hardness of her face in obstinacy, the calm secret sleeping face the morning after love, the steady, seeking face of a child, more constant than any, always there, behind them all, beginning of them all? – That is how love is blind, not the way the platitude would have it: blind to the attractive smooth surface that does for others. Knowing this, she marvelled, humouring herself ironically, in what small busynesses her insight was swept aside by a quasi-magical ritual in which, for the duration of its performance, she could be as believing and absorbed as any seventeen-year-old factory hand.

When she got back to the lounge he was sitting near the basket of flowers with his arms resting curved along the chair arms. He said: I've combed my hair – as if he had just performed some great service for her. He had the sincerity which can be perfectly naïve without appearing incongruous coexistent with intellect. It irritated some people, charmed some, was on the roster of reasons friends had used to try and dissuade her. Now for this once and by this one woman he was loved for it, because for her it was also a little saddening, as of an innocence of the heart that surely cannot last. His deep joy in her being there that suddenly broke through in his face was about to release both of them, to give them back to one another as they had been, beyond guilt or reproaches, before the explanations and the legal quibble and the practical arrangements; – they were about to speak, it was coming – when a man came in through the reception office and looked at them as he passed to a door on their right.

He was in the room and yet he was not. They could hear him moving about, and some unidentified sounds rather like a finger-nail being run over moiré silk. Almost at once he came out again, and, like a fanfare in his wake, a popular song opened in nasal blare. It filled the empty room peopled by chairs with a kind of shock, as if voices had spouted out of a dreaming sea, or a drunk man had started shouting in a hushed theatre.

The man stood a little way off, waiting for some effect.

'That's more like it, isn't it? We're not really so dead around here.' With his hands on his hips, he came smiling to them. He stood there certain of their pleasure, a man with the young-old face of a film star, the tanned face lined very slightly – it might be the sun, it might be laughter, marking round the eyes – the clipped moustache, the good teeth a little yellowed, again perhaps nicotine rather than years, the loose silk shirt and tropical trousers slung flatly round his hips to emphasize a lack of paunch. He carried his youth with the conscious air of someone who has already lost it.

For an impossible moment all three of them were listening to the song.

It seemed to hold them down in their chairs listening to it. He stood with his head a little on one side, his eyes cocked sideways. The girl smiled with nervous compulsion. There would be no help from the young man, who had no notion of appropriate social formulae, who, when he could not be himself, lapsed into selfish and unrepentant silence.

'You hear a lot of this one up your way? – Jo'burg?' said the proprietor.

'Yes!' she said, with the ridiculous lying enthusiasm with which one answers a child who has asked whether one drinks milk, or believes in Santa Claus. She could have managed quite well had she been on her own, for she had a gentle dishonest facility with people, but in his presence she embarrassed herself, with his eyes she saw herself capering.

'They do them to death, don't they? But this is a catchy thing, all right. Soon as people come in of an evening, it's on. I'll have to send up to Johannesburg for another record of it, soon, it'll be just about worn through.' He had let himself down on to the edge of the adjoining table, resting on the palms of his hands. He paused a moment, regarding them with a half-smile, easily. 'You've been fixed up?' The question was man-to-man rather than in the way of business, and addressed to the young man in the unquestionably accepted code that practical matters are for men. He could not escape answering. He said coldly, in his beautiful voice: 'Thank you. We are waiting for lunch.'

The voice was apparently unexpected; she saw the older man looking at him, as if for the first time, probably indeed for the first time, for this man with his slightly tarnished air of sexual gallantry would think it unmanly to notice another man. Now he looked with a faint growing air of distrust at the unimportant clothes, the intense face; perhaps here was one of those curious beings, a man who wouldn't play snooker, who wouldn't care about golf, who wouldn't be one of the boys in the bar, and yet they are men all right, when it comes to women . . . But the record had ended; he listened for the click of the change mechanism; heard it with a slight nod.

'This one's my wife's favourite.' He grinned intimately to himself. 'Whenever she goes up to Jo'burg, she buys what she likes, and whenever I go, I get what I like; always remember which ones I've bought, even a year or so afterwards. She's just been up, a week ago. Only came back on Friday. Every time she comes back she's got herself a new hair-do and I have to guess what to look for when the train comes in. This time she went up in the car, though, it gives you more of a chance to get about. Do you help your husband with the driving?'

'I like to look out the window in peace.' She was even a little strainedly playful, keeping it up.

'The bell's behind you,' said the young man to her suddenly, as if he had just entered the room. 'I should like something to drink.'

'Sure thing – you get dry on the road. Where you going? Lourenço? Good place –' He leaned gracefully to the bell before she could reach it, then, as if without thinking, pulled out a chair and sat down with them.

An Indian with his little round tray came in for the order.

'Sherry. I'll have a sherry,' she said. The young man nodded: 'And a beer.'

'What about you – you'll have something with us –' she said.

The man smiled, carefully charming, impressing his regret at the loss of such a pleasure: 'No – I never do with guests, you know – a matter of policy. You mustn't be offended. If you start it with one, you've got to do it with all. Like when we have dances here, you know, I never see my wife, she dances with one, she's got to dance with the lot' – he laughed and she laughed with him – then he shrugged it off with a lift of the eyebrows – 'I don't mind. I like to see other people admiring her, as a matter of fact. I like her to dress well and keep herself attractive. And though I say it myself – well . . .' He sat back and drummed his fingers on the chair a moment, sizing up whether they were worthy of such a confidence or not. Then he leant forward and opened his mouth with a short indrawn breath before he spoke: 'Do you know that we've been married eighteen years in April and we've never had a word? We've always been able to *talk* to each other; so many married couples got nothing to say after the first six months. Sometimes we wake up at night and lie there talking for hours. We can tell each other anything. Anything.' He was looking straight at them, triumphant.

'Unusual,' she repeated stupidly. 'It's unusual.'

'That's the trouble. Most people can't. We don't live in one another's pockets, we each go our own way, but it's all open. I know she goes out with fellows when she's up in town, and why not? There's nothing in it, it's all above board. It's simply a matter of . . . trust, that's it . . .'

'Confidence,' she supplied, out of a habit of offering the right word when someone hesitated. She knew that was the right word. Confidence; it was what her husband in his fatherly endless understanding had had in her. For some people it meant dances, parties, for others, concerts, exhibitions; but really it was all the same thing. She and the hotel keeper's wife, who went out with fellows, on the parole of confidence, confidence at first so loyally and gratefully used (she would say she likes a good time, I would say civilized people must have individual liberty) and in the end thankfully snatched as pure opportunity. She struggled against this picture of herself, ranged beside the hotel keeper's wife. It seemed that they stood grouped together and the woman turned to her with a smile of complicity and she stiffened, fought against it, but some other part of her, unemotional, insistent, and unmoved by pleading, tears, and indignation, held her to it. She looked across at her lover. Head down, the stain of the sun beginning to show along the ridge of his nose, his was the tempered flesh of the *religieux*, who does not feel gibes, jeers, or the silent mocking of commonplace because he has too much faith to see even momentarily, his belief as others see it:

simply one of a thousand crackpot cults from Jesus to Yogi. But he had known it would not be so for her. She would doubt herself with every doubt levelled at her, she would have misgivings with every misgiving of an old, hard, jealous world, scratching and whining over what it has never had for itself. You must understand, he had told her, that everyone, everything will be against you, in principle if not in person. The face of an unknown woman taking her child to school will be a reproach to you. And another time: ... hurt everywhere, because you're running counter to laws to which your own moral nature subscribes. People will try to punish you, you'll try to punish yourself – you understand? If we're to get out of this, it'll have to be backwards, against the light, on our hands and knees, through a long dark tunnel.

'Love,' the man was saying, 'so long as you love each other, that's what I always say. Keep on loving each other and everything's OK. He sank back in his chair with a furtive, admiring air, his hand lifted in a staying gesture. His voice had dropped, as if to avoid frightening the approach of some pet animal. 'There she is,' he said slowly. 'That's her, there –' The flap door of the reception desk rose and snapped down again behind a tall bold-bodied redhead who walked across the foyer and out of the front entrance, looking straight before her and smoothing her blouse down into the waist of her skirt. As she pushed the silk in, she held a breath high in her chest to make room, and her breasts rose in their shape and fullness. Her heels chattered down the steps, her red hair swung.

'We've got a daughter of sixteen.' It was pronounced in smiling anticipation of astonishment.

She said it. 'You simply wouldn't credit it.'

The man accepted it as his due in the right coinage. Like the softening influence of a paid bill, it expanded his interest toward them. He looked at them a moment, the young man with his unfathomable face, drinking beer with the concentration of a bird, the girl who had put down her glass and paused with her hands on her knees, as if she was about to say something that she would never say, ask herself some question she could never answer.

He stood up. 'You two haven't been married very long, I don't suppose.'

She looked as if she had not understood what he had said, and then her eyes went slowly to the wedding-ring on her finger. She wore it still, out of superstition of, rather than respect for, the law. She had put it on because she was not yet finally legally freed of her marriage, and there was the feeling that she must not damage, by anticipating its accomplishment, the life beyond it which was to come. She was fully aware of the hypocrisy of this reasoning, but that did not release her of its compulsion. She saw her lover looking at the ring, too. The ring had been a sign, signifying quite the opposite to what one might expect. When she had worn it at their meetings it had come to mean that he had nothing to fear; she was free of the marriage in herself, and was conscious of only the legal semblance of the bond. But when she had come without it, he knew by the unadorned hand that the old ties seemed to her to have reasserted their validity, and because the marriage was still alive to her in her heart she did not need its symbol on her finger. And on the presence or absence of this small ring had hung the balance between so much hope and pain.

A slow expression of delight came over the man's face as he interpreted the pause. It seemed that already, in the quirk of his mouth, he was telling yet another 'honeymoon couple' story to the men in the bar, to the red-haired wife who would laugh in the superiority of her full-blown sex.

'Well never mind. You just remember' – his hand rested a moment on the young man's chair in a masculine hint – 'so long as you love each other, it's OK. I'm talking from experience.' With a backward smile, he was gone into the dining-room.

At lunch he said: 'You're droopy, Theresa.' It was characteristic; his word, his snorting accusation. He had never treated her as she was used to being treated, as the creature whose mood must be accepted as the key to which the moods of others must be pitched in hushed respect. As she looked at him, firmly buttering his bread – he did not care what he ate or when but always ate with concentration – she felt again that awful rush of pleasure, possession, and unbelief, the divine unbidden lunacy that came to her in spite of the fact that she didn't believe in it; that she knew must wear out; that she knew nothing in life, nothing in the cherished resources of the mind, could equal. She loved him so much that love carved him out in relief from the room of human and knife-and-fork chatter, the past when he had been different and the future when he would be changed, and he became the whole world lifted clear of time. Out of weakness and incongruity, she, who never cried unless there was not even the witness of a mirror, saw the outlines of the crockery turn wobbly with tears. As he tucked a piece of roll into his cheek he looked up and saw her, unable to eat, looking before her with big glassy eyes. He saw not so much the tears as the pathetic attitude of her shoulders, as if, by keeping quite still, they were trying to excuse her.

Suddenly he became very gentle to her, he almost fed her, he helped her through the meal and through the faces of other people with a special kind of restraint and sanity. He had always shown great tenderness toward her, but this was something different, something she had never known in him before. When they were in the car again and the town was behind them she told him – it was an unburdening almost in the physical sense, she wanted him to lift it from her mind, to carry it for her – the humiliation she suffered so idiotically, since her intelligence accepted it as merely superficially true and quite unimportant, at the slightest evidence that her behaviour in their relationship could be casually bracketed with that of other women. Even as it all came out – the hotel keeper's wife and 'confidence', the sham, the vulgarity – above all the vulgarity – she knew the answers that were there for her. There was that unmoved, unvanquished part of herself that knew the answers: you have had the courage to take what you want, but now you want to be a good girl into the bargain. And there's a snobbery in you that doesn't like the thought that a woman who doesn't know anything above the level of her breasts might have exactly the same emotions as a woman who holds all the beauty of the world in her head.

But he didn't say them. He didn't say any of them. She sat there with her eyes fixed on him dog-like for comfort, asking for comfort, and he gave it to her. In her downcast insistence she was demanding it of him, and he was giving it to her. None of his penetrating intuition, none of his sharp logic; only comfort, soothing. Soothing. That was what he was that he had never ever been before. And yet it was familiar to her, she clasped it to her with the closed eyes and the wriggling sigh of a child handed a familiar toy. She watched the fields go by with half-interest and the tension in her chest dissolved like a physical melting.

She leaned slightly against his arm. It's all over, she thought, we're out, we're free, it's really happened.

And then suddenly her mind turned on her. Soothing. That was how her husband had been to her, gentle, comforting, like a father . . . Dismay threatened her with panic.

I'm going to make him just the same, she thought, *I shall change him into just what I've always had.*

Protest and dismay tingled through all her veins as though she had just taken some fiery drink. She threshed about wildly within herself for an escape, but there was no way out of this prison walled by her own skin and guarded by the alarm of her own nerves. With the sharp breath of confession already drawn into her mouth, she turned to him, appealing – and stopped herself, and in time, and sank back against the seat slowly and began pleating, fold on fold, the material of her dress.

Monday is Better than Sunday

The smell of kippers browning in butter brought morning to the flat. The young ones lay late in bed on Sundays but the old master was about the bathroom already, stropping his razor with the slap! slop! slap! of a horse trotting sharply in the street below. 'Lizabeth!' he bellowed. 'Get my breakfast! Have it ready.' His slippers thumped up and down the passage. He stood in the kitchen doorway, pinkly shaven, stomach protruding in his white bowling trousers: 'Where's my breakfast?'

Elizabeth carried into the dining-room – that, closed against the morning, held last night's liver and cigar smell – the butter-and-sea scent of kipper, the orange juice, cold and bright in its glass, and the two large squares of brown toast. Out she went again, walking quietly in someone else's shoes, her sullen head in its blue knitted cap.

'Lizabeth!' the voice choked with impatience. 'Where's the tea?' She took the teapot off the stove and brought it to the table. He grunted.

'Why don't you see that the milk's hot? Why do I always have to tell you.'

She felt the jug and then went out.

Soon she heard him, bustling and aggressive in the bedroom, his wife's voice coming up from the pillow: 'What's it, Daddie?'– 'Blooming girl – does not listen. If I've told her once –'

On his way out, she heard him at the flowers in the lounge; a rustle of red gladiolus petals curled like tongues for want of fresh water, snap of the smooth, crisp straight stem. 'Elizabeth!' he said as he passed to the front door. 'Put water in the flowers, eh?'

'What, *baas*?'

'You must put water in the flowers. You don't do it. Give them all fresh water.' He stood looking at her out of his small, restless eyes like the little eyes of a big animal, bison or rhinoceros, always uncertain whether or not to charge; but he could think of nothing else. He grunted and left.

Elizabeth took the fowl out of the refrigerator and began to clean it. Out of the cold white corpse – the skin puckered in a pattern, as if stitched where the feathers had been plucked – came the red guts in her brown hand. Blood flowed, alive and cold from the refrigerator, over her fingers, over the old wide yellow wedding-ring that had grown its place into her finger as a hoop of wire, tied round the trunk, makes itself part of the tree.

There was the long-drawn sigh of the lavatory being flushed, and then the missus appeared in the kitchen doorway, blinking in her checked dressing-gown. She was a fair woman with thin hair slipping the curlers on her pink scalp, and as she was much alone and no one talked to her very much, her mouth always moved a little, soundlessly, around the things she might have said. She looked slowly round the kitchen and then went back to the bathroom.

Elizabeth shook the pan in which the crumbly butter from the kipper had coiled into a surface like thin ice over the liquid beneath, and taking two more of the plump fish from their grocer's wrapping, dropped them in.

The sizzling brought the missus back. Yet she did not like to say what she had come for. She opened the refrigerator, moved something inside it, and then shut it again. She wandered over to the stove. 'Who're these for, Elizabeth?' she whispered; her voice was always the quietest, softest possible.

'It's for the young *baas* and the little missus,' explained Elizabeth boldly, letting the volume of water from the tap run through the fowl.

'But they're not ready yet,' said the missus, wanting to have it explained. 'They're not up yet.'

'I did think they were,' said Elizabeth, tucking the fowl's wings into position.

There was a moment's silence.

'They're still asleep,' said the mistress, sibilant with concern. 'Still in bed . . .'

There was no answer but a spurt from the pan. She turned and left. She went to knock timidly on her son's door, and when there was no answer, timidly entered. But the bed was empty of him, sagging empty of his shape as a glove from the hand that has filled it.

She found him in the bathroom. 'The girl's made your breakfast, son,' she said. 'Tell Adelaide to hurry up. Everything's cooked and ready.'

'But good God, what for?' he said, the faded animation of the night before lying like the shadow of his beard upon his face. Toothpaste foamed at his mouth. He spat. 'Del,' he called, 'you can have your bath afterwards – we've got to have breakfast now.'

Her hair hung heavily on her shoulders, her thickly white hand hung heavily on the porridge spoon; it was too early for her to talk, and he held the Sunday paper in one hand and fed himself dabs of porridge with the other.

Elizabeth came in and took away the porridge plates.

'She doesn't say good morning,' said the girl.

'Fool she is,' he said, reading. 'Just goes and makes breakfast whether anyone's ready for it or not.' The more he spoke of it, the more it irritated him. 'Doesn't bother to ask; just goes ahead and does it.'

The girl, who wanted to be liberal and to recognize her personal conception of the equality of servants and masters, but didn't quite know how to convey this expansion of the spirit, tried to think of some explanation, but couldn't.

In came Elizabeth.

'But I don't eat kipper,' cried the girl, prodding the beige fat fish steaming tenderly beside the egg on her plate.

'Go on. – It's nice for a change,' he said, still reading.

'I never eat kipper,' she said, looking at it on her plate.

Elizabeth stood there with her tray, offering no solution, giving no reaction; merely waiting to see what was to be done.

'Here,' he said, 'I'll take it.' He flipped it on to his plate, then said with dismay, 'No, I can't eat all that. – You can have it, Elizabeth. I'll leave it for you, eh?' And he put it aside.

'Thank you, Elizabeth,' said the girl, when the tea was brought in. She felt beholden to her. But Elizabeth's dull-black face accepted nothing.

After breakfast the bath water ran, the young people went in and out, the girl carried her pots of cosmetics, her hair nets and pins and combs from mirror to mirror. In the room she had left, shoes met in social groups on the floor, stockings snagged on Elizabeth's hard hands as she lifted discarded clothes from the bed in order to make it. Down at the bottom a hot-water bottle, now cold as a jellyfish, wore a knitted cover of orange wool. Elizabeth threw it out, made the bed, folded the pyjamas. She was screwing back the lids on cream jars and lotion bottles so that she could clear the table to dust, when the young one came in, dressed and emerged into her day-time self now. 'Oh!' she murmured self-reproachfully; but it seemed too late to do any tidying up herself – she only got under Elizabeth's feet. Picking up her book, and taking a bottle of nail varnish as an afterthought, she fled.

In the dining-room the table was still laid and the missus sat quietly in her dressing-gown, drinking a cup of tea.

Elizabeth went from bedroom to bedroom, stretching, bending, sighing; lifting each crazy, sprawling bed by the scruff of its neck and sobering it to square neatness.

The young girl passed along the passage and heard her talking to herself as she scrubbed out the bath; 'D'you know what?' she laughed, coming to kneel beside the young man on the sofa, like a child bringing some treasure to be shown. 'That girl's a bit queer. She's saying Oh Jesus! Oh Jesus! all the time she's doing the bath.'

They went out on to the balcony and sat with their feet up in the sun whilst the paper blew and crackled in their hands. The visitors came; there were cries, laughter, the front door opened and closed, children, full of the excitement of being newly arrived, skated the rugs. The voice of dinner began to rise in the kitchen, too; a blare of hissings when Elizabeth opened the oven to baste the chicken, the mumble of gently boiling water waiting for the vegetables.

'Elizabeth? Would you make some tea for Boss Albert and Miss Nellie, please,' stated the young girl politely.

There was another knock at the front door. Adelaide answered it, and when she came back to the balcony again: 'Who's that?' asked the young man. 'Someone to see Elizabeth,' she said. 'No other time, of course, but now, when she's cooking.'

The young man and the girl ran in and out, busily hospitable, for clean glasses, the lemonade opener, some ice. Elizabeth was bulky; they dodged round her, bumped one another. 'Oops!' said the young girl, with a sudden smile. Elizabeth opened her mouth a little, showing three big teeth alone in an empty gum.

Shouts of laughter washed up from the lounge and balcony. Smoke wandered through the air; ash speckled the carpets. In the kitchen the sound of cooking rose to a crescendo, and Elizabeth whipped cream. With the bang of the door and the thump of his woods dropped in the hall, the old man was home. His big face tucked with pleasure, he swung the children into the air, went into the lounge like the ringmaster entering his circus. 'Stuffy,' he frowned. 'What's the matter here? Why don't you open the windows?' A woman smiled beautifully and wrinkled her nose: 'It's kipper,' she said. 'I could smell it as soon as I came in.'

The old man went from window to window, swung them open, grumbling briskly. When he had finished he stood a moment; 'The flowers' – he clapped his hand to his ear – 'Oh, my God, those flowers!'

'I thought I told you to do the flowers?' he accused Elizabeth over the cooking pots. She did not answer; went on stirring the white sauce. 'Why didn't you do it?' he demanded. Again she did not answer for a moment, pouting down into the steam from the pot. 'I was busy,' she said at last, non-committally. – 'Well, she *was* busy,' said the girl Adelaide, coming in at that moment with the empty ice dish. And again she saw Elizabeth's face, turned steadfastly away from her, and felt again that ridiculous sense of rebuff.

Elizabeth took another look at the chicken, almost done now, pushed the vegetable pots aside to keep warm, and took the extra leaf for the dining-table from behind the kitchen door. Whilst she was laying the table the old missus came tentatively in and, trying not to look at the old blue skirt and man's pullover, whispered: 'Don't forget your white cap and apron, eh, Elizabeth? You know the master likes you to wear your apron . . .'

The radio was on now, above the voices. The old man turned it up for the news. Sshhh . . . The voice blared through the flat. Elizabeth turned and bent, came and went in a breathless routine; stove; sink; table; refrigerator; assembling the dinner. Gravy sizzled; cauliflower slithered on to its dish; Elizabeth went into the dining-room and shook into life the silly little laugh of the cut-glass bell.

And they all came in to dinner. The chairs scraped in and out, the children changed places three times; they talked and laughed and no one had remembered to turn the radio down. The old man carved, the knife squeaking through juicy chicken flesh – and a potato shot off the dish and made a greasy patch on the tablecloth.

Elizabeth, you haven't given Master Peter a serviette.

Elizabeth, slice a lemon and bring it.

Elizabeth, another spoon.

The cheese that's wrapped in paper at the back of the refrigerator.

Bring some ice, please.

Elizabeth, why did you let the sauce go lumpy?

Bring a fresh tomato for Miss Vera.

When they had left the litter of the table Elizabeth put the drumstick and the pile of potatoes and the stump of cauliflower that was her dinner into the left-over warmth of the oven, to share later with her husband, and plunged to her elbows in the washing-up. The old man went to lie down, the others sat about in the blue haze of the lounge, smoking and talking. And by the time Elizabeth had put away the dishes and cleaned the rim of grease and food from the sink, they were waiting for tea. Once again the kitchen added its voice to the voices, and the kettle hissed and frothed at the lid for attention whilst Elizabeth filled tarts with jam and buttered the scones.

And when tea was over they sat around amidst the flagging talk and the forgotten cigarettes and realized that Sunday was almost gone again, ebbing with the heaviness in their stomachs and the red sun cut into red-hot bars by the railings of the balcony. Monday was coming. The freedom of Sunday wasn't freedom after all, but only a routine-dictated time of inactivity. They were waiting for Monday, that they hated; and that was the distaste, and the disappointment of it: Monday was better than Sunday.

No one remembered to call Elizabeth to clear away the tea-things. She stood in the passage a moment, her thick, set lips slightly open. Then, swiftly and quietly, she closed the front door behind her so that it only clicked faintly, as a person clicks his tongue in a sleep, in response. The cold clear breath breathed out through the cement lungs of the city met her on the open corridor, seven layers above the tiny cement courtyard buried away below like the smallest of the Chinese boxes. Up she went, on the spiral back stair clinging like a steel creeper up the side of the building. And at the top, there was the roof, with something of the remoteness, the finality of all mountain-tops. All around the sky was pink, streaky, and farther away than ever. A thin shadow of smoke aspiring like a kite from the chimney of the boiler room asserted this. The grey row of servants' rooms, one-eyed each with its small square window, looked down at the grey pebbles that covered the roof.

There was no one about. Bits of torn paper and empty lemonade bottles huddled against the balustrade. Elizabeth drew her foot out of her shoe and scratched the sole, hard and cracked with all her childhood of walking on hot bare earth, against her ankle. Beneath and around, as far as she could see, there was block after block of the city, nothing but spires and jutting rectangles of cement, deeply cleaved by black streets, and faintly smoking. Here and there, like a memory stirring, the fleck of a green tree.

Elizabeth stood looking down over it for a minute, and was lonely.

In the Beginning

'And what's the old girl like?' he said, thinking.

'What a hag,' said Marks.

'Bad?' He leaned against the washstand, his eyes following the other from the bed to the suitcase, from the suitcase to the bed: like watching a game of tennis.

'Ah-h man.' Marks stopped, drew up his face as if to cry. He stuffed in a pair of dirty socks; pushed down a hanger that kept elbowing out.

'That's good news,' he said.

'A hag,' said Marks, 'I'm telling you.'

'So the old girl's a terror,' he said, without moving from the washstand, as a young man with a red, nubbly face came in, carrying a portable radio.

'Who's that?' Badenhorst asked with an intense grin of curiosity.

'Who do you think?' He looked at him with the level appraisement of the long suffering.

'Sister Dingwall?' asked Badenhorst innocently. Communication with him must always be preceded by a restatement of facts already assumed, and as well known to him as to everyone else. It was a kind of ritual one must go through with him.

'No,' he said. 'The other one.'

'You look out with her, I'm telling you,' said Marks happily.

'Well, if that's the case, I wish I were you, and finished, instead of beginning. How many did you get, anyway?'

'Fifteen.' Marks was having a last look in the wardrobe drawer; he banged it back.

Badenhorst said from where he crouched half under a bed, trying to plug the radio in: 'Did you get a lot of babies, Marks?'

'I just said. Fifteen.'

'Hell! We've got a long way to go, eh? Once the first one's over I won't mind so much – what do you say?'

He said from the washstand, 'I'll tell you when the first one's over.'

'Don't forget, you must be there when the head's born; if you're not, it's not your catch and you don't get any credit for it. She'll tell you there's plenty of time – she'll always tell you that – and then the moment your back's turned, the kid pops – and there, you've missed it. – Look, I'll leave these for you chaps' – passing the rickety wicker table on his way out, Marks picked up a pack of cards – 'But look, bring them back with you . . .? You can give them to me at Medical School.' And he stood a moment, raincoat over his arm, suitcase pulling down one shoulder, looking back at the big bare room with the four well-kneaded beds like grown-up candles beneath their canopies of dirty mosquito netting; the wardrobe with the spotted mirror; the rain-stained ceiling, the unopened suitcase, the bleary window; the young man with the pimple-scarred neck squatting on the floor; and the other, leaning back against the washstand with the broken door. Marks smiled to be leaving them to it.

In the morning, coming out of the hotel on the way to the hospital he passed the only painted portion of the hotel – a white, square room with a door marked BAR and a smaller door marked OFF-SALES DEPT – and came out on to the road and saw the sea, lying away down there below and the flying-boats resting on it like dragonflies. Climbing the slope between the sea and himself was a confusion of waving cranes, ships, warehouses, and rail tracks that was the docks. The flying-boats glittered at him for attention. But it was all a long way off, like seeing someone's mouth opening and shutting urgently, but not being able to hear. He trudged on up the hill to the hospital.

There was the red-brick, institution gateway, staying and support-ing the usual institution waiters: the people who are always there, outside prisons, hospitals, and public homes, waiting for news or for visiting hours. Two Indian women sat bundled up against the wall, their black hair steely in the sun, and an ancient couple, dried and creased as only Indians and mummies can be, squatted with their knees up to their chins in the gutter. Two little Indian girls in yellow silk fluttered about, very shy, uttering decorous, suppressed cries when they caught one another, and a native baby, resting his paunch on the ground between his outstretched legs, watched them in silence. The Zulu watchboy, cotton reels pushed through his ears, sat on a small soap box, straining at his serge uniform. Seeing the white coat, he wheezed respectfully and tipped his cap.

The hospital was red-brick, old and new, wings and separate buildings, double and single storey, this way and that on top of the hill. Round the corners the wind whirled grittily into his face; he found the Maternity Section, fly-screened like a big meat-safe, and going inside, walked through a long ward full of surpriseless eyes, laconically watching, or not seeing him from the rows of humps beneath brown blankets.

The little plump brown nurse led him along the corridor. She called him 'doctor'; he smiled to hear it, and began to get himself ready. Outside the door he knocked at once and went in.

Sister Dingwall was looking up straight at him and he could see that so far as she was concerned she had seen him hundreds of times before; she was sent two new medical students every fortnight. He introduced and explained himself, relieved and surprised, as usual, to hear how respectful and quiet he came out in the presence of authority. She asked questions and told him what was expected of him in a plain, cold Scots voice, looking into his face with what would have been insolence, curiosity, or interest on the part of another person, but was in her so entirely disinterested that it could be taken for nothing but what it was: a desire to make herself plainly understood. When she looked down at her report, her mouth locked in at the sides and she tightened her nostrils; when she lifted her head her eyes stared straight back, dark and deep-set, not by beauty, but by time and a masculine sensibleness, from beneath rough and shaggy eyebrows whose long hairs swept in a kind of wavering grandeur of line from the frown-niche above her nose. She had no lips and her false teeth were ugly and too regular, like a row of mealies.

He followed her to the delivery-room, the theatre, the nursery, and when she left him in the cubicle of the student doctors' duty-room, he stood twirling and untwirling an end of cotton round the button of his white coat, wondering what he had expected. Something more positive, certainly; something he could have related. She was too impersonal even to make herself unpleasant.

Badenhorst's *Manual of Obstetrics* was lying on the table. What had she said as she went out? 'Now's the time when you want to use your eyes and ears and common sense.' But she said it neither as encouragement nor warning: it was merely a statement of disbelief in the existence of such qualities. He thought of this with a mild flash of irritation.

– And her face, disappearing round the door, with that peculiar loop of hair, streaky black and grey, pulled out under her veil on to her forehead, yearning toward those eyebrows, like the pictures of his mother in the twenties!

After three days it had replaced all aspects of living, for them. From eight in the morning until twelve at night they moved between the labour wards, the delivery-room, and the nursery: the door opening on women crouched on their haunches in the concentration of birth pains; on the steam and warm bloodiness cut by the flash of steel instruments lifting wicked crocodile mouths out of the sterilizers; on the squirming surface of the new-born – real people lying row upon row in canvas hammocks, with live red mouths squared for continuous demand. In between times they sat waiting in the duty-room, with cockroaches and the cups of tea and chunks of sugary 'shop' cake. Even when they trudged back down the hill to the hotel to sleep, the extension telephone on the wicker table tied them to the smell and sight and sound of birth. They talked of nothing else; their ears shut out all temporal sound, attuned to the delicate drum of the foetal heartbeat approaching from the other world. Their jokes were of birth; 'position is everything in life' they laughed, discussing, discussing. Where was the head? Was that the knee? How was the child lying? And the riddle of the world was the mother's belly – all the day and night-long succession of bellies – over which their hands passed and the concentrate culled from the *Manual of Obstetrics* pondered: half-knowledge, half-instinct, like the hands of the water diviner.

The mental and muscular concentration of the women giving birth magnetized them; they were part of it, too. What else was there? What did other people do, who were not busy with this business of birth? It did not seem that other things could be happening at the same time.

When the first one was over, he felt emotional, as if he could have cried, or grinned foolishly. It was a most beautiful child he held, more beautiful because it was brown, and in a newly made creature, not two minutes old, the scrolled, wide native nostrils were marvels of intricate craftsmanship, so much more skilful than the smudgy nub of a white baby's nose, and the half-inch long black curls, sudsy with *vernix caseosa*, made the baby look as if it had been interrupted in the midst of a shampoo, and made him want to laugh with pleasure at the cheek of it! He bathed it and cleaned up the mess; Sister Dingwall walked in and out. He wanted someone to say: there, it wasn't so bad was it? – so he smiled at her, in a kind of self-deprecation.

'It won't always be as easy as that,' she said, staring straight back at him. 'Don't go thinking yourself an obstetrician on the strength of that.'

True, it had been a multipara who gave birth with the practised confidence of experience; it had been a normal vertex presentation. But others that followed were nearly all complicated in some way, and the effort and fear of his own inept hands which they involved made the reconstruction of them in memory as separate experiences impossible; they soon became merely different aspects of the one thing: birth – and even the first lost its emotive significance.

'Did you tear her?' became Badenhorst's obsession. – It was a point of medical honour, and also, between them, a rivalry, to try and deliver a primapara of her first child without tearing the inflexible and narrow passage of her body. Badenhorst had torn three badly. He had torn one. What added to the pre-existent difficulties of both their and the patient's inexperience in these cases, was the rule that no anaesthetics might be given in any but operable emergencies. The pain of the women was flustering, hard to bear with. 'At home in their kraals or their dirty shacks they'd have it a lot harder,' said Dingwall, always standing by. She would walk over to the woman, and bending her stiff, rooster-breasted body, take the brown naked shoulder in the grip of her hand with the nurse's big, leather-strapped watch turned face-inwards authorizing it, and shout into the woman's face: 'Come along now! That's enough of that! That's enough noise. Quiet now, d'you hear me?'

'If she keeps on with that, slap her face,' she said once, noting on her watch that it was tea-time, and opening the door.

'– Well, did you tear that kid?' Badenhorst looked up from the cake crumbs on the duty-room table.

'No. She's all right. – Miserable little baby.' He sat down in his birth-smeared mackintosh apron, looked for a cigarette.

'What do you expect? Did you see her age? Fifteen years old.'

'Babies for babies.'

'I'm surprised you didn't tear her,' said Badenhorst.

'No, I managed,' he said. He knew that Badenhorst would go out presently to ask the native staff nurse if he had.

'My God, she is a hag,' he said, sickened.

'Dingwall?' asked Badenhorst. 'I was talking to her last night.'

'I didn't know she could talk.'

'Neither did I. She's been a midwife for twenty-seven years.'

'That doesn't make her any the sweeter, I'm afraid.'

'Imagine how many kids she's seen pop! Imagine how many she's bathed.'

'She should have tried having one herself. It might have made her a bit more human.'

'She never got married,' said Badenhorst with a shrug.

'Who would marry her, for God's sake . . .'

'Oh, she mightn't have been so bad, twenty years ago.'

They looked at one another and laughed.

'That bit of hair,' he said, laughing. 'That bit of hair. How I'd like to stuff it back under her veil.'

'I'll go and make tea,' said Badenhorst, taking his feet off the table, and went out to ask the staff nurse whether the Indian girl had been torn.

Little touches of antiquity; the juxtaposition of her acquired scientific knowledge to the instinctive creative knowledge of the peasant women patients; her official authority in a domain where woman's is the natural authority of birth: these things turned their reaction to Sister Dingwall's snubs, the human rebuff of her coldness, the draining of their confidence through her expecting nothing of them, toward ridicule. There were only two ways to turn: one was into dislike, the way Marks had gone, the other was into ridicule.

She became 'Ding-Dong' to them; when they heard her insistent voice in a long monologue of blame against one of the native staff nurses, they lifted their heads and smiled. 'Ask not for whom the bell tolls . . .'

They discovered that she collected stamps – for her father in Scotland – in her off-duty time. 'Twenty-seven years of multicoloured babies; lording it over young nurses; sneering at medical students; and stamp collecting for fun: no wonder she's turned into a starched despot.' They could hear her particular stiff, measured stalk down the corridor. 'There she patrols' – Badenhorst jerked his head toward the door.

She was a little deaf, but like that of so many people, hers was a selective deafness, and she heard what she chose. Yet she had the stare of deafness; that look coming up straight at you, as you stood palpating or examining – or was it merely the look that told you that you didn't know, flatly and plainly . . . When you asked her advice or help on a case, she gave you that look again, and always, without a word, went ahead with the appropriate manipulation. She always *knew* when you would be coming to her; it was in the set of her mouth, when you did come.

'Every time I deliver a baby for the rest of my life, I'll see that face of hers with the mouth pulled in with self-control at my idiocy and that bit of hair straggling out,' he exaggerated. 'She's an irritating old cow,' sulked Badenhorst. – She had a way of catching the corner of her underlip in her teeth, and pursing out the top one like a horse, whilst she swivelled her foot on the old-fashioned waisted heel of her white shoe and looked away, each time he tore a case.

In the evening he went to Sister Dingwall and said: 'Do you think it's all right if I leave the case that's just come in, whilst I go for supper? I don't want to miss her, though.'

'You should know by now,' she said, lifting her eyebrows and looking down at her accounts.

'– Don't go, Doctor,' the little staff nurse took him aside in conspiracy. 'The baby, it'll come when you're gone.'

He went back and examined the woman again. She smiled at him, said something in Zulu that he didn't understand.

Badenhorst was having his first evening off, so he couldn't call him. He went back to Sister Dingwall. 'Sister, there's a possibility that the woman's going to have twins.'

'Who says so?' She was counting out soap into a box held by one of the staff nurses. The little brown nurse turned her eyes, white, in fearful appreciation, wanting to smile.

'Well, I think so,' he said.

He stood there.

'All right,' she said, dismissing him.

A few minutes later she came into the ward. He was persuading the patient who, like many native women, wanted to get out and squat on the floor, to remain in bed. A pain came on, strong and pulling, and Dingwall stood waiting for it to pass before doing her examination.

As soon as the woman had struggled out of the current to rest again, he became full of the excitement of explanation; did not know what to show the sister first. 'Listen,' he said quickly. 'Two hearts, I'm certain. It's plain, isn't it? It's unmistakable – I think. And then here – if you get your hand here – that's one head, eh? And then feel down here – that's another, I'm sure that's another.' He watched her face as she examined, waiting.

'Yes,' she said. 'You're going to have twins.' It was the first time she had ever made anything approaching a joking remark. He wanted to laugh, was afraid to, lest after all, in the distortion of his excitement, he had mistaken the tone.

The woman had borne four children, and the rhythm of birth developed quickly in her. Soon the first child was born, lying small and glistening wet, a very light yellow-brown in his gloved hand.

'Fine child,' said Dingwall, showing her mealie-cob teeth.

'Not bad,' he said admiringly. He felt he must do whatever she told him. He thought of Badenhorst, sitting in a cinema, not knowing about his twins.

'Well, what are you waiting for now?' she said.

He twitched his cheek to work his mask into a more comfortable position: 'I don't quite know . . .' he said, but felt confident.

'Well you're not going to stand there and let her relax and have labour start all over again from the first stage, are you?'

'No,' he said. 'Now for the other one, I suppose.' The woman's body still gaped, unlike the aftermath of a single birth. 'But I can't see the head at all,' he said, looking up from examination.

'You can't see anything,' said Dingwall. 'If you're going to wait to see the head come down then you're going to have her in labour again, right from the beginning.'

'Oh, of course,' he reproved himself.

'Here,' she said, handing him a pair of forceps. 'Give the bag of waters a nip – one little pull will be enough to break it. Just go carefully – guide the forceps along your hand: put your hand in first.'

Of course he knew that was what he had to do. He had read about it time and again. After the birth of the one twin, remove the bag of waters and the second child will follow at once, in the path opened for it by the first, without further labour.

He turned back to the woman, waiting, like a cave; forceps in his hand. Slowly he inserted the forceps. But where was he? Inside the woman's body he felt only darkness, softness, and did not know. His hand crept along, but what? Where? The forceps were so hard he was afraid of them. It seemed that his hand could recognize nothing, nothing that he knew in his mind as a landmark of anatomy. He felt distressed, and a yellow dancing spot of concentration went in and out in front of his eyes. He was holding his breath.

He struggled on and said nothing, and Dingwall said nothing: he knew she must be thinking that he was getting on with it. The idea agitated him feverishly, made it impossible for him even to think what he was doing; like running and knowing that there is someone just behind you and yet being afraid to look and see how near, lest you give yourself away. At that moment he felt something, with the steel tip of the forceps; the start went right through him, the way he started sometimes in bed, just as he was going off to sleep. Not wanting to, not wanting to, he opened the forceps a very little and closed them on the object, the bag of waters.

But what if it was the uterus?

What if he pulled down the whole uterus?

It couldn't be. It must be the bag of waters.

Water ran through his whole body, flooded all his arteries and made him light, light all through. His hand opened of itself; with the obedience of the lifeless, the forceps let go. He drew out his hand

and the forceps, straightened his back, and felt that he was smiling at Sister Dingwall, felt his face smiling at her in he could not imagine what way, but unable to do anything else with it. 'No,' he said, still smiling, and shrugged his mouth.

He knew that he stood there, unable to stop the smile.

She came, bent her starched rooster-breast over the woman, took the forceps from him and inserted them, along her hand. Through her face, concentrated under the stiff loop of hair, the mouth locked in, he watched her searching. Then he saw her mouth unlock, it was half-parted, in chance, catching at a breathless moment of uncertainty; and she shut her eyes – shut her eyes tight, and tugged.

It was astonishing, the sight of her; the set, preserved body, the face that had decided its expression long ago in 1920, the neck that always knew and never hoped or feared: all screwed up, trusting to luck like a child wishing hard at a lucky-dip bin . . .

In a moment she held the child; born into her hands.

Coming out into the late night and walking round the building with the secretive grating roll of the stony path beneath his steps, the evening throbbed back through him as blood thumps slowly, reliving effort, after exertion. Mechanically, he lowered his eyes ready for the wind; it came, in a gritty burst at the corner, blurring the light from the sea. He smelled dust, then the sea. The boat lamps bobbed and swung, far down. Out the hospital gates and down the hill, the wind pushing him from behind, his feet striking the road jogged him pleasantly, making him go faster.

In the big empty room at the hotel, he slowly took off his coat and emptied his cigarettes, matches, and keys out of his pockets. He kept thinking about her all the time, seeing her. He saw her looking up at him with that look, with her mouth down. He saw her back disappearing authoritatively down the corridor. He remembered the stamp collection, the old father, sitting under a plaid rug somewhere in Scotland. He saw her smiling, the mealie false teeth holding your attention, the loop of hair carefully arranged. Twenty-seven years in that place! Never anything else! Days and years of other people's babies. The stamp collection and the old father, for fun.

He was sitting on his bed, shoes off, and he looked up and saw himself in the narrow wardrobe mirror opposite. He was alone in the room with himself, with himself looking at him. He looked back, shoe in hand. Red, crinkly hair, that very pale skin of the red-headed, and the ugly shadows that freckly people get beneath their eyes. The eyes were light, on guard with an expression he did not feel. And the mouth, the glum mouth, set in the line of a disappointment he did not even remember.

Why, *I* look different from what I am, he thought suddenly, that is me, but I don't know it. And also that is not me, and other people don't know it.

And he lay back on the bed, wanting to be still with the novelty of understanding.

From

Livingstone's Companions
(1972)

A Third Presence

When Rose and Naomi, daughters of poor Rasovsky the tailor, left school in the same year there was no discussion about what they should do, because there was no question about the necessity to do it. The old Rasovskys had got the naming of the daughters all wrong. Naomi was everything 'Rose' suggested, Naomi was pretty and must marry the scrap-metal dealer who would give a home to the old Rasovskys and the girls' brother; Rose, who cruelly bore her name along with the sad Jewish ugliness of her face, was clever and must get a job to help support the family. The boys who flocked around Naomi and with one of whom she might have fallen in love didn't come into the decision any more than the university scholarship Rose had won. Certainly, necessity being what it was, Naomi was the one who came off best: the husband built her a red-brick house in the new suburb marked out in the veld of the small South African town, she enjoyed the fun of choosing furniture and the status of being called 'Mrs', and soon she had the importance of having produced a baby, and a son at that. Rose, on a Sunday afternoon, came to see the baby for the first time and at the bedside, where Naomi was surrounded by frilly jackets, shawls and flowers as by a panoply of a throne, said with wonder, 'Was it very painful?' Naomi, full of secret knowledge, said, 'Oh no, I wouldn't say painful.'

Rose had brought a beautiful little garment for the baby, something exquisite and expensive; she supplemented her salary as a junior typist in a lawyer's office in Johannesburg by doing bookkeeping for a small import agency, at night. She became quite famous for her presents, and Naomi's children used to look forward to the visits of Auntie Rose with special anticipation. These delicate and lovely offerings, unlike anything they saw about them in their own home, were discovered only by Rose; it was she, too, who found that there was a vocational centre to which Raymond, the sisters' younger brother who had had some damage to his brain at birth and had not developed mentally beyond the age of eleven, could go. He should, of course, have been sent to a special school when he was little, but the Rasovskys had been too poor and ignorant to arrange that.

The centre's fees were high and Ben, Naomi's husband, with a growing family to support, could not be expected to be responsible. Rose looked for a better-paid job and hired herself out to a political party as election agent, in addition to her bookkeeping. Every month she asked her employer to give her two cheques: one was made payable directly to the vocational centre, the other was hers to live on. She never quite gave up the idea of studying by correspondence for the university degree for which she had forgone the scholarship, but the books lay about in the back room where she lived alone in the city and served only to fill her with sudden realization of time passing and a preoccupation with her many jobs from which she rarely, in the sense of personal liberation, looked up. There would be time next year, perhaps, to study for a Bachelor of Arts degree; and next year ... And then the time came when she knew: what should she do with a BA if she got it? She could not afford to take a junior lecturer's job at a university. And anyway, what a degree had stood for – sharing the world of ideas with other young minds, and so on – she was nearly thirty and surely had bypassed all that. It was too late to splash around in the shallows; so far as the world of ideas was concerned she had had to enter dark water breast-deep.

For there had been Dr Ferovec, by then, the Hungarian Catholic philosopher who had come to South Africa as a refugee in 1956. His English was too poor for him to be given a professorship, and his temperament too difficult for him to keep a lesser post at a university, so he had ended up teaching in a crammers' 'college' in Johannesburg. Because she needed the money, Rose was expected to charge less for her work than others, and she was always being recommended to people like Dr Ferovec who wanted typing cheaply done. She went to take dictation in his room on Sundays, and there, at last, in this stranger of strangers, talking to himself in an unrecognizable tongue, his grey hair full of bald patches due to a nervous disease, she found her first lover. He lost his job but she believed in him and cooked for him each night before she settled down to type his philosophical treatise, which they had decided they must translate together if he were ever to get the recognition he deserved. He said to her, 'You know nothing, nothing,' and it was true that the Jewish tailor's daughter had never seen Budapest in the good days, nor the beautiful woman who had been Ferovec's mistress, nor lived through revolution and counter-revolution. All she had were the back-room tasks of petty business – the drawing up of balance sheets, the analysis of some merchant's brand of profit and loss – and the absolutely private and incommunicable matter of her face. But in their distance from one another he and she were nearer than in their distance from others; she was there when he put out his hand for all he had lost.

Rose took him home, once, to Naomi's house, presenting him, with timid assurance, as her 'friend'. The shrill atmosphere of Sunday lunch among bright children and trite family exchanges repelled his intellectual qualities, antennae-like, into the shell of a beaten, sickly, shabby man. Naomi's husband was not really young, either, but his fleshy chest in a striped towelling shirt as he cavorted round the lawn with the children, and his big face with the cleft chin as he insisted, taking another piece of cake, 'So if I put on another pound? So what's the difference, I'll only live once?' looked full-blooded in comparison. If you couldn't *talk* to Ferovec – or rather if he saw he couldn't talk to you – you simply couldn't understand what he was. Rose could see that they felt a family shame and pity for her. She could hear her old mother, when they had gone, taking advantage of her poor sight to say to Naomi, 'What sort of a man is that friend of Rose's? What does he do for a living?' And Naomi saying, 'Well, Rose lives a life of her own, Ma. She knows all sorts of people. I don't know, perhaps he's someone she works for.'

But of course Naomi knew that, at last, her sister had a man, this elderly man with the patches on his head. Out of a need to be kind she would say on the telephone, 'And how's your friend, the one who came that day . . . Oh, I'm glad . . .' Face to face with Rose, she did not mention him, and they confined their communication, as usual, to discussions about the welfare of the parents, the problem of Raymond (who was now thought to be capable of taking sheltered employment), and Rose's reception of the exploits of the children, the new curtains, the sun-porch that was being built on, and Naomi's latest dress. Naomi had never looked better than she did at this time. Her three children were all at the indiscriminately charming puppy stage between two and seven, and, seen among them, although no longer the appealing child-mother she had been, her wonderful complexion suggested at once to all sorts of men the simplest desire to sink one's teeth into her, and brought her the simplest pleasure of acknowledging this without ever having the urge to gratify it. Like many sexually unawakened women, Naomi was a born tease. Rose gave surcease and even joy to Ferovec but no man ever glanced twice at her as she went about her work in her quiet clothes, making the best of herself.

After Ferovec (the translation of his treatise had caught the attention of an Oxford don who had quoted from it extensively in his own paperback popularization of a related subject, and Ferovec was suddenly offered a chair at one of the new English universities) there was Dirk Mosbacher. The family never saw Dirk Mosbacher but no doubt they got to hear about him, remote as they were from the life Rose was living now. They certainly would have heard that poor Rose was being sponged on by another misfit – at least ten years younger than herself, this time, and an Afrikaner, into the bargain. Naomi was not aware of it, but she felt guilty about Rose, and she even tried to bring her together with a distant relative of her husband – shame-facedly, because the man was the owner of a mineral-water factory whose only pretension to interests outside business was Freemasonry, and, after all, Rose was a clever girl. But at least he was a decent Jew. Rose was polite, as always, when she found him in Naomi's house, and, as always, seemed to have no idea how to attract a man. The mineral-water factory owner badly wanted to get married, but it was clear that he couldn't have brought himself to consider a girl like that, unless there happened to be money as well.

Rose had a lot of trouble with herself over Dirk Mosbacher. Through him she fought and discarded once and for all the standards and ambitions by which she had been disqualified, all her life. She had always thought of herself as the one who stood outside the warm-lit house where the faithful husband and the desirable wife created the future in their children. Because she knew no other, in this image she made every private compact she got herself into, however absurdly unsuitable the facts were. When Dirk slept with other women and never thought to conceal this from her, she felt the double affrontation of the wife neither preferred nor sufficiently feared to command deceit. Yet why had Ferovec been 'faithful' to her? Because he knew few other women and was not at a stage in his life when he was attractive to them; not because he was a 'husband'. And why should Dirk, who shared, as she well knew, a number of strange dependencies and loyalties with different people, keep this one form of human intimacy exclusive to her? Would she have expected him to talk to no one but her of his ideas about the relation of man to shelter (he was an architect who had never quite finished his course) or about politics? Yet these were as important to him as sex. There were women and even men, occasionally, with whom, in sex, he had certain things in common, just as there were people with whom he had ideas in common. He was not a 'husband' who left his plain, older 'wife' for a pretty face; he was a man, free and answerable to the whole world. He lived with her, he told her, because she was the only honest person he knew; and she could believe him, although he took money from her. She threw away the strange structure, semblance of the nest, that she had patiently stuck together again and again out of the torn-up bits and pieces of incongruous instincts.

Often when Rose went home to Naomi's for Sunday lunch it was after one of those Saturday nights that seemed to blow up atmospherically round Dirk. Painter friends, political friends, jazz friends crowded into the flat. They all drank a lot and Rose provided food, though this was not expected. Dirk Mosbacher disliked what he called polite sterility in human contact, and would sit up all night among people who struck sparks off one another, no matter how aggressive the atmosphere might become. His little, yellow face with the thin black beard outlining the mouth perpetually contorted in talk was the curious Mandarin face of many intellectual Afrikaners – a bulky, blue-eyed people in the mass. He was tender to those who did not survive the evening, and would give up his bed and blankets to let them sleep it off until morning. He also gave asylum in Rose's flat to various Africans whose talents or political ideas interested him.

Rose would creep out of the sleeping flat on Sunday morning and take the train home. There was always some occasion in Naomi's house; Naomi was like a child, for whom time is spaced by small personal events. On her tenth wedding anniversary there was her diamond engagement ring, reset, to show on her thrust-out hand. At one time she tinted her hair, and was waiting in the doorway with an air of sensation when Rose appeared, while the old mother looked on indulgently – 'Meshuggah, what can you do with them today?' – and then brought her eyes to rest on the other one, a good girl, the image of her father, with her thick glasses and sad, heavy nose. Rose was the perfect audience. 'It looks fine on you,' she would say without a trace of bitterness, of some hat Naomi was displaying. 'You put it on, Auntie Rose, you put it on!' And to please her niece, Rose would consent unembarrassedly to the spectacle of herself, looking back from the mirror with silk petals pressed down over the face of some old Talmudic scholar from Eastern Europe. Her family did not ask her about her life because they feared that it was empty. She did not speak about it because she did not want them to know how pathetically limited and meagre the preoccupations of Naomi's household were.

Dirk Mosbacher was derisive about Rose's former association with 'that posthumous old Popish pundit' Dr Ferovec, but his very derision, displayed among friends, partook of the distinction Johannesburg people feel in anyone who has a connection with the intellectual centres of Europe. Ferovec had become one of the popular protagonists in the fashionable newspaper and pamphlet debates on religion and authority then current in England; even if the group who frequented the flat were not interested in the whole business, they still saw in Rose, quiet Rose, the woman who had been close to one of the 'new philosophers' they read about in the English papers. It gave her the certain quality of an unknown quantity; one of the painters' girls decided that her looks were immensely interesting, and that she ought to dress to match: Rose slowly gave way to severe, strong-coloured, robe-like dresses in place of the neat suits that had been her protective colouring for years. With the rigid self-discipline of those who know they cannot rely on any obvious pleasing qualities to excuse their deficiencies, she had never dared allow the emotional strains and private trials of her personal life to show in the office, and – a marvel without sickness or tears – had become the most invaluable person in a big import agency (she had been with the boss from the beginning, in the days when he rented a tiny office and she worked for him in her spare time). The firm had twice sent her overseas on business. She drove a small car, and did not have time to visit her family more than once a month, now.

One of the black men with whom Dirk had argued and drunk and for whom Rose had bought shirts and typed letters made his way to England to study, and wrote a book. It was a bitter book, one of the first of its kind, and it created a small stir; the English papers called it a 'scathing indictment of white South Africa' and the South African papers called it an 'anti-White tirade', but it was prominently dedicated, in flowery language, to two white people, Dirk Mosbacher and Rose Rasovsky, but for whom the author would have 'succumbed fatally to the hate in my heart'. It was not the sort of book that Naomi's ladies' book circle would buy, but the story of the dedication was the sort of thing that makes news for the Sunday papers. Naomi's eldest daughter, Carolyn, saw it. 'Don't read it to granny,' said Naomi. She decided not to mention it to Rose, next time they saw her, either; poor Rose, now that Naomi was old enough to look back, what a terrible thing it was to have pushed Rose out into Johannesburg, a little girl of seventeen alone in some miserable room. What sort of chance had Rose been given? What had their parents had to offer them when they were girls? Papa Rasovsky, dead many years now, and the old lady, still going strong although she couldn't see more than blurred shapes – they had a lot to answer for. Naomi felt suddenly sad and heavy; it was true that she had begun to put on flesh and when she sat back in a chair she saw the solid weight of herself.

But Miss Carolyn was a cocky girl, in her first year at the university and full of the superior social status of higher education if not of a love of learning, and she twitted Aunt Rose, 'I see you've been getting yourself in the papers, eh? Couldn't they have taken a better picture – honestly, I hardly recognized you!'

Poor Naomi! Rose had lately often seen her face exasperated and bewildered by that girl. The children were so charming when they were little; the boys had grown into louts who looked up from comic books only to growl, 'Man, leave me alone.' Naomi complained about them in their presence: a sign of helplessness. But what could

Naomi know of the delicate business, the pain and rebuff, the unexpected acceptance and unexplained rejection of approaching the mystery of the individual? Since she was a child she had known nothing but extensions of herself and her own interest, with her parents and her husband she shared the blood of her children, and the milk the children imbibed from her body was assumed as a guarantee of their identity with her. Naomi had not dreamed of the strange reassurance one could experience, seventeen and alone in the back-room of a lodging house in an unfamiliar city, in the daily contact with the black woman who came to clean. Naomi had had no chance to learn that a man who had lived a whole life in another continent, another age, another tongue, could be patiently reached through the body. Naomi had no way of knowing the moments of rest in understanding that come, outside sex, outside intellectual compatibility, outside dependency, between people more than strangers: Rose herself when she was unofficial 'teacher', years ago, and Dirk's ambitious, half-literate young black friends.

Dirk Mosbacher left the country and perhaps it was unlikely that he would come back. He had given evidence to the Anti-Apartheid Committee at the United Nations and had been offered the opportunity of setting up a cultural centre in one of the new African states. It was exactly the sort of thing that suited him; he would have a jazz group working in one room while a play was being improvised in another, and an adults' summer school was painting in the yard. He wrote long, critical letters to Rose, which she read out to friends at the flat. The flat was as full as ever, though the composition of people was changing somewhat; Rose was living with the correspondent of an overseas newspaper, now, and he brought along numbers of journalists. She accompanied him to press dinners and other social events to which a newspaperman of standing was invited. Naomi had seen a picture of him in a group with Rose on the social page. He was a tall, stooping Englishman, with a moustache and an expression of private amusement. No one would have expected Rose to bring him home to the family; what on earth would they have to say to Rose's friends? Yet Rose continued to come home, regularly, dutifully, and as soon as she was there the old relationship of the situation that underlay their lives came into existence in silence between the sisters as if nothing had happened since: they were the two girls of seventeen and eighteen who had not discussed what had to be done.

But when, on her fortieth birthday, Naomi opened the door to her sister Rose there was a difference about their being together. It was as if someone else were also in the room. After Rose had put down the flowers and the box of peaches bought on the road, and they were sitting in the living-room, Naomi looked at Rose gazing out into the garden. The third presence, like a phenomenon of double vision, slid into the single outline of focus: 'Something's been done to your nose.'

Rose kept her head steady so that it could be looked at, moving only her eyes. 'Yes. I was wondering when you would notice.'

'As soon as you came in. I didn't know what it was.'

Rose still kept her head on display, the habit of obedience of the younger sister, but Naomi was not looking at the nose.

She said, 'Was it painful?'

And Rose answered, 'No, not at all, really.'

Naomi sat with her mouth parted, patting the arm of her chair. The children didn't like the Jacobean style she had chosen for the room when she got married, but it had been the very latest, then; now Ben said they couldn't afford to throw good furniture away.

Rose said, 'People think it's a great improvement.'

Her sister gave a consenting shrug, as if conscious of the obligation to doubt the need for improvement.

'I hated my nose more than anything,' said Rose. But because they had never talked about such things her tone was the one in which, on her visits, she would praise the soup at lunch or remark on the traffic that had delayed her.

'What's it all matter, in the end. It's not the face that counts, it's what's behind it.' Naomi's polite platitudes hung in the air, and, confronted with the honesty with which her sister sat before her, she added, 'It's nicely done.'

Rose mentioned the name of the plastic surgeon: a very expensive one. Rose's little car was new, too. Naomi had never had a car of her own, though it was the fashionable thing in the small town for wives to have their own runabouts; it was the same with the house that had been built for her – what had seemed status and luxury to her then, was now ordinary and almost humble: people going up in the world had left the suburb and gone to a newer one, where they had patios and swimming pools instead of red-brick stoeps.

Fortunately it was a weekday and at lunch there were only Rose, Naomi, the old mother, and their brother, so there was no one to pass remarks. The old lady could not see well enough to distinguish any change in Rose, and Raymond, in the downcast timidity of his slow mind, had always been afraid to look directly at anybody. He had been back living with Naomi for some years, since the only kind of sheltered employment he didn't run away from was being allowed to potter around among the mounds of twisted metal in Ben's scrap yard. Although old Mrs Rasovsky could scarcely make out Rose's shape, she kept putting out her hand to touch her, with sentimental tears in her eyes that embarrassed her daughters.

'Let Rose have her food, Ma,' said Naomi.

'You're all right, thank God, you're keeping well?' the old lady kept saying, in Yiddish. It was all she had ever said; it was the formula with which she had disposed of their lives, helpless to ask further or do more.

When Naomi said goodbye to Rose at the car she felt the necessity to make some final reference to the new nose. She wanted to say something nice about it, but she suddenly said: 'Now the next thing is contact lenses.'

Rose looked terribly uncertain, the smile went out of her eyes though her lips still held it, she had none of the calm self-acceptance with which she used to try on Naomi's pretty hats. She said, with an effort at deprecation, 'Do you think so?' And the little car drove away.

Naomi walked back along the gravel path between the yellow privets. She went into the room where the old woman sat, legs apart, in her corner, and said, 'The next thing is contact lenses. And then she could have married Ben Sharman instead of me.' But the old woman was deaf now, as well as nearly blind.

The Credibility Gap

'You go.'
  'No, it'll be for you.'
  The timid ring of the front door bell or the two-syllable call of the telephone produced the same moment of obstinacy: everyone appeared to be going on with what he was doing. The young brother continued to hammer away somewhere. The elder, if it so happened that he was in the house, absolved himself because he now had his own flat with his own front door and telephone. A house-guest – there was usually someone who had nowhere else to live – didn't feel it was his or her place to get up. The mother knew it wouldn't be for her. It was for the daughter, inevitably, since she was in one of the expanding periods of life when one moves through and with the zest and restlessness of the shoal. But often there were reasons why she did not want to respond without an intermediary: the complex social pattern meant that she was supposed to be out when she was in, or in when she was out.

You go. It'll be for you.
  The schoolboy Rob took no notice, anyway. The cats were disturbed by anyone leaving a room or entering; they lifted back their heads from bodies relaxed to tiger-skin flatness before the fire, and opened their eyes. Pattie's casual, large-footed friends trod into flowered saucers scummed with disdained milk that stood about all over the place. Cats and saucers were the mother's – old-maidish possessions that could be allowed a woman who, if she had no husband by now, had among other things the contrary testimony of children grown and half-grown who were half-brother and -sister. Pattie never thought of her mother when she was alone with friends her own age, but sometimes when she and the friends and her mother were drinking beer and arguing in the living-room at home she would have an impulse the converse of that of the parent to show off its child. 'Don't tease her about her cats. It's her passion for

147

cats that got her out of solitary confinement when she was in jug. Honestly. She was supposed to be in solitary for leading a hunger strike among the political prisoners, but the chief wardress was as dotty about cats as she is, and they were such buddies discussing their dear little kitties, the old girl used to let her out secretly to sit in the prison yard. It's true.'

Yes, there once had been a ring at the door in the dark early hours of the morning that was for Mrs Doris Aucamp. Years ago, when the children really were still children, and there still were real political opposition movements in South Africa. The two elder children – Andrew and Pattie – at least, remembered something of that time; someone had moved into the house to take care of them, and they had been set up on the Johannesburg City Hall steps one Saturday among the families of other political prisoners, wearing placards round their necks: WE WANT OUR MUMMY BACK. Most of the friends drinking beer in the living-room and discussing the authoritarianism of the university system or the authenticity of the sense-experience known as getting stoned had heard about the massacre of Sharpeville – if from no other source, then from references to it that came up in overseas magazines; one of the boys, studying abroad, had even discovered that in New York there was a commemorative rally at Carnegie Hall on the anniversary of 'Sharpeville Day', held by South Africans in exile. It was with quite a momentary thrill of admiring curiosity that they realised that this woman – somebody's mother – had actually served a prison sentence for what she believed (of course, what they *all* believed) about the idiocy of the colour bar. It both added to and detracted from the aura of those among them who now and then were moved to defy minor-sounding laws against marching the streets or assembling for protest: so these 'activists' were not the discoverers that danger, in some times and places, is the only form of freedom? They had only dug up, afresh, to offend the docile snouts of the population, what the major punishments of those minor-sounding transgressions had forced people to bury, and forget where.

– This woman wasn't bad, either, in spite of her age, not bad at all. There was at least one of the young men who wouldn't have minded indulging a kind of romantic lust in response to that mature sexuality, confidently lived with for a lifetime, vested in her blunt, nicotine-tanned hands as she stirred her tea, and the turn towards the table of those rather big breasts, sloping away from each other a bit like an African woman's bubs – she was a short, broad woman with nice, ninepin calves, too wide in the hip ever to wear trousers. Mrs Doris Aucamp caught the look and was smiling at him, not taking it up but not offended – kindly amused: of course, as well as having been a jail-bird, she was also a writer. He hadn't read her; but it was a well-known name.

I'll go – it's for me.

There were times when Pattie leapt up because she had the instinct that some irreparable usurpation would take place if anyone other than herself were to open the door upon the face she expected, or respond with a voice other than hers to the summons of the telephone. A word of criticism of one of her friends roused a fierce solidarity. 'Oh Kip's not what you think at all. People get it all wrong. People just don't understand. He wouldn't trust anyone else. You have to be one of us.'

Her mother slapped down a cat who was trying to filch off a plate. 'Of course. Every set of friends has private dependencies that make it hang together. Why do I put up with Scoresby? Why does any of his pals?' The man she spoke of was a long-time friend, long-time alcoholic.

Rob was finely paring the wart on the inner side of his third finger, right hand. He looked up a moment, saw that man, who sometimes played chess with him, lying as he had once found him in a lumpy pool of pink vomit in the bathroom. He turned the blade towards his finger once more; everyone told him it was dangerous to cut warts, but he was getting rid of his by persistently slicing them away, right down to the healthy flesh, without squeamishness.

'It's not that so much. I mean, you think it's peculiar because I bring someone home and don't know his surname – even if we don't know each other personally, *we know* –'

'– But you don't really think it's a matter of age? There're people under thirty you couldn't trust as far as I could throw this greedy, shameless cat – mmh?'

'No – I'm sorry – in some ways *you* just can't –'

Her mother nodded her head as if in sympathy for some disability. 'You know what Lévi-Strauss says? Something, something ... "as man moves forward he takes with him all positions he's occupied in the past and all those he'll occupy in the future". Wait, I'll get it.' They heard her running upstairs; padding down more slowly, probably leafing through the book on the way. She stood behind her daughter, silently following the passage over the girl's shoulder. *As he moves forward within his environment, Man takes with him all the positions that he has occupied in the past, and all those that he will occupy in the future. He is everywhere at the same time, a crowd which, in the act of moving forward, yet recapitulates at every instant every step that it has ever taken in the past.*

The girl put the book down; the two of them looked into each other, but it became purely a moment of physical comprehension: Pattie saw that the skin of her mother's forehead would never have the shine of tautness again, the mother saw that little scars of adolescent turmoil had left their imperfections on the slightly sulky jaw-line that attracted men.

No – it's all right, I'll go. I'm expecting a friend.

Some of the girls feared themselves pregnant, one or two had had abortions, and there were even beginning to be a few contemporaries who got married and furnished flats. Pattie knew that if she became pregnant, her mother could deal with the situation; on the other hand, if she got married and bought furniture, well, that was all right, too.

'Isn't there anything else?'

Her mother was putting flea powder on the cats: Liz and Burton, Snorer, and the mother cat of all three, Puss. Snorer's name was really Schnorrer, dubbed for his greedy persistence at table by the Jewish professor who – the girl understood, looking back at things she hadn't known how to interpret then – had been her mother's lover for a time. Dolly, the black servant, had heard the name as Snorer; and so it had become that, just as the professor was now become a family friend, like Scoresby, only less troublesome.

'No. You meet them years later and they tell you their son is married, their daughter's engaged. All smiles, big surprise.'

'Except you. You count yourself outside.' The girl had trudged the summer through in a pair of Greek sandals whose soles had worn away completely beneath each big toe. She was examining with respect these alien, honest-workmanlike extremities of herself, thickened, ingrained with city dirt round the broken nails, assertive as the mechanic's black-ringed finger-nails that can never be scrubbed to deny their toil. After a pause: 'People say that story you wrote was about me.'

'Which story?'

'The one about the donkey.'

'It wasn't about you, it was about me.'

'But I saved up for a donkey?'

'Never. It was something I told you about myself.'

You go.

No, you.

Rob did not know that Snorer was not the cat's name any more than he knew that Julius, the professor, had not always been an old family friend. He didn't answer the phone because he was not yet interested in girls, and his boy friends used the kitchen door, coming tramping in past Dolly without knocking. Dolly's man repaired bicycles on the pavement outside the local hardware shop, and she treated the boys like the potential good customers they were, sycophantically addressing them as 'My *baasie*', 'Master' Johnny or Dick, although her employer didn't allow her to corrupt the young people of the house in this way into thinking themselves little white lordlings. '"Master" my eye! Really, Dolly! You should be putting them across your knee and warming their behinds. Nothing's ever going to change for the blacks, here, until people like you understand that nobody's born "master", never mind white kids in short pants.' But Dolly was unresponsive, for another reason. She resented having been given, with equal forthrightness, an ultimatum about closing her backyard trade in beer.

When the children of the house were small the front door had opened often upon black faces. The children had sat on the knees and laughed at the jokes of black men and women who were their mother's friends and political associates. Pattie remembered some of them quite well; where was so-and-so now, she would sometimes remark; what happened to so-and-so? But all were in exile or prison. She had, tentatively, through her own student set, a different sort of association. The political movements were dead, the university was closed to black students, but there were Africans, usually musicians, with whom was shared the free-for-all of jazz, the suspension from reality in the smoke of the weed – white hangers-on, black hangers-on, there: it depended whose world you decided it was. She even went once or twice on a jaunt to one of the black states over the border, and there met Africans who were not creatures of the night but students, like herself.

'If I fall for a black one, how would we manage?'

'You must leave the country.' Before the mother or anyone else could answer, Rob had spoken.

He put down the coloured supplement on vintage cars he was studying. His gaze was hidden under lowered lids, but his head was slightly inclined to the polarity of his mother as she sat, a cigarette comfortably between her stained first and third fingers, her square-jawed, sunburned face looking on with a turned-down neutral smile. They were waiting for her to speak, but she said nothing. At last she put out her hand and passed it again and again through the boy's hair, firmly, as the cats loved to be raked along the fur of their backs.

'There's a nice, God-fearing guardian of the white race growing up.' Andrew had dropped in to pick up his allowance; he addressed the room after his younger brother had left it.

Mrs Doris Aucamp remained serenely in her silence; as her Professor Julius had once remarked, she could turn bullets to water. She irritated her elder son by giving him the brief, head-tilted, warm glance, old childish balm for sibling fears of favoured dispensation granted the last-born.

'Sorry, no dice, my little brother doesn't think we should do it.' Pattie was amused. 'Poor kid.'

'A man once gave me up because I didn't know the boiling point of water.' But the elder son didn't accept his mother's diversion of subject; in his turn, did not appear to hear.

'Fahrenheit or centigrade?' A Peace Corps girl from Uganda, in the house for the time being, was eager to show herself to be on the family wavelength.

'Neither – I'm sure that was it. Couldn't get over it. Thought he'd found a real intellectual to appreciate him, and then discovers she doesn't even know a thing like that.'

'Black or white?' Pattie asked.

There was laughter. 'Oh he was white, very white.'

When the two of them were alone together, the daughter returned to the subject. She did not know, for sure, of anyone since Julius. 'When you were young? – The man with the boiling water?'

'Oh no, only a few years ago.'

The girl was looking for a number in the telephone directory. She covered her silence by saying kindly, politely, 'What is the boiling point of water, anyway? I've forgotten.'

'Oh I found out quickly enough. Two hundred and twelve Fahrenheit.' Mrs Doris Aucamp had the smoker's laugh that turns to coughing.

The number Pattie tried was busy. Resting on the receiver fingers wearing as many rings as a Renaissance pope, she said of her little brother, 'It's just that he wants God-to-keep-his-hand-over-us.'

'Of course.' The expression was a family one, derived from a grandmother who mistook superstition for piety.

'Poor little devil.' The girl spoke dreamily.

You go. Go on. It'll never be for me.

When their mother was out, no one – certainly not Dolly – would answer the bell for Pattie. One afternoon it was a student friend standing there; come to tell her one of their friends had been killed. He and some others had been climbing with the girl the day before on a Sunday picnic, and she had slipped and fallen before their eyes. They picked her up fifteen minutes later at the bottom of a waterfall, her neck broken.

Mrs Doris Aucamp was waylaid by Dolly as she got out of the car in the garage. She thought for a moment Dolly had been drinking again, but it was not drink that widened her nostrils with drama but the instinct of all servants to enter swiftly into those fearful emotions that they can share with employers, because there, down among death and disaster, there are no privileges or exemptions to be claimed by anyone.

'The friend with the big eyes. The one that always laugh – that Kathy. She's die. It's true.' A big shuddering sigh took the black woman by the throat.

In the doorway of the living-room the mother stood before her daughter and the young man, two faces for which there was no expression to meet the fact of death. They merely looked ashamed. There were tins of beer and cigarettes about. Their eyes were upon her, waiting.

She must have a face for this, of course.

But she stood, with the cats winding themselves about her calves. She said, 'Oh *no*?' People said that in books they had all read or films they'd seen. Then she saw the untidy hair and rosy nose of her daughter, alive, and, hand over her open mouth a moment, emotion came for what hadn't happened just as if it had: it could have been this one, mine. There was no face to meet that at the door.

The three of them sat drinking beer, breaking the awkward silences by repeating small certainties left by the girl who had died. 'She was here for supper last week. Didn't she forget a raincoat?'

'It's behind the door in my room. I noticed it this morning, it smells of her –'

'She always looked just like that when she was asleep. Honestly, it was just the same. Limp. Soft.' The young man himself looked afraid; sleeping with her, making love to her, then, he had been holding death in his arms?

He was a witty young man whose instincts were always to puncture the hot air of a distrusted solemnity. As the talk drifted away from the dead girl, tugged back to her, away again, he dashed off one of his wry mimicries of someone, and they found themselves laughing a little, slightly drunk by now, anyway. There was a closeness between them, a complicity of generations.

It had grown dark. Mrs Doris Aucamp got up to pull the curtains and wandered off upstairs by way of the kitchen, telling Dolly there would be an extra mouth at dinner. And then she met her younger son; he was repairing Dolly's radio. 'I wish my darned sister would leave my things alone. I look all over the house for my small pliers, and where are they? Lying around in the mess in her room, of course.'

'Well, don't make a fuss now. You see, darling, Kathy –'

'I heard about it.'

'It isn't the time. She's upset.'

There were shiny patches on his thin, dirty fingers where the warts had been pared away. The patches were water marked, like moire, in a design of whorls unique to him out of all the millions of human beings in the world. He was carefully, exasperatedly scraping the insulation tape from the wire. He lifted his face and the preoccupation fell away. He said, 'She wasn't crying at all. She and Davy were yapping in there, quite ordinary. And then when one of her girl friends phoned she started to make herself cry over the phone, she put it on.' His face was without malice, clear, open, waiting.

His mother said, 'I wanted to cry – for a moment.'

He asked, 'Did you believe in it?'

'What?'

He gave a little jerk to his shoulder. '*It*. I mean, you didn't see that girl lying dead.'

'Davy did.' She searched his eyes to see if the explanation was one. He said nothing.

She said, hesitantly, 'Davy says she was the same as when she was asleep. It didn't seem she was dead.'

He nodded his head: *you see* – in the manner of one who accepts that no one will have an explanation for him.

This time she did not put out her hand to touch him. She wandered back into the dark hall of the house, her bent head making a double chin; the followers of those African prophets who claimed bullets could be turned to water had, after all, fallen everywhere on battlefields, from the Cape to Madagascar.

Inkalamu's Place

Inkalamu Williamson's house is sinking and I don't suppose it will last out the next few rainy seasons. The red lilies still bloom as if there were somebody there. The house was one of the wonders of our childhood and when I went back to the territory last month for the independence celebrations I thought that on my way to the bauxite mines I'd turn off the main road to look for it. Like our farm, it was miles from anywhere when I was a child, but now it's only an hour or two away from the new capital. I was a member of a United Nations demographic commission (chosen to accompany them, I suppose, because of my old connection with the territory) and I left the big hotel in the capital after breakfast. The Peking delegation, who never spoke to any of us and never went out singly, came down with me in the lift. You could stare at them minutely, each in turn, neither they nor you were embarrassed. I walked through the cocktail terrace where the tiny flags of the nations stood on the tables from last night's reception, and drove myself out along the all-weather road where you can safely do eighty and drive straight on, no doubt, until you come out at the top of the continent – I only think of these things this way now; when I grew up here, this road didn't go anywhere else but home.

I had expected that a lot of the forest would have been cut down, but once outside the municipal boundary of the capital, it was just the same as always. There were no animals and few people. How secretly Africa is populated; when I got out of the car to drink coffee from my flask, I wanted to shout: Anybody there? The earth was neatly spaded back from the margins of the tar. I walked a few steps into the sunny forest, and my shoes exploded twigs and dry leaves like a plunderer. You must not start watching the big, egg-timer-bodied ants: whole afternoons used to go, like that.

The new tarred road cuts off some of the bends of the old one, and when I got near the river I began to think I'd overshot the turn-off to Inkalamu's place. But no. There it was, the long avenue of jacarandas plunging into the hilly valley, made unfamiliar because of a clearing beside the main road and a cottage and little store that never used to be there. A store built of concrete blocks, with iron bars on the windows, and a veranda: the kind of thing that the Africans, who used to have to do their buying from Indians and white people, are beginning to go in for in the territory, now. The big mango tree was still there – a home-made sign was nailed to it: KWACHA BEER ALL BRANDS CIGARETTES. There were hens, and someone whose bicycle seemed to have collapsed on its side in the heat. I said to him, 'Can I go up to the house?'

He came over holding his head to one shoulder, squinting against the flies.

'Is it all right?'

He shook his head.

'Does someone live in the house, the big house?'

'Is nobody.'

'I can go up and look?'

'You can go.'

Most of the gravel was gone off the drive. There was just a hump in the middle that scraped along the underside of the low American car. The jacarandas were enormous; it was not their blooming time. It was said that Inkalamu Williamson had made this mile-and-a-half-long avenue to his house after the style of the carriageway in his family estate in England; but it was more likely that, in the elevation of their social status that used to go on in people's minds when they came out to the colonies, his memory of that road to the great house was the village boy's game of imagining himself the owner as he trudged up on an errand. Inkalamu's style was that of the poor boy who has found himself the situation in which he can play at being the lordly eccentric, far from aristocrats who wouldn't so much as know he existed, and the jeers of his own kind.

I saw this now; I saw everything, now, as it had always been, and not as it had seemed to us in the time when we were children. As I came in sight of the shrubbery in front of the house, I saw that the red amaryllis, because they were indigenous anyway, continued to bloom without care or cultivation. Everything else was blurred with overgrowth. And there was the house itself; sagging under its own weight, the thatch over the dormer windows sliding towards the long grass it came from. I felt no nostalgia, only recognition.

It was a red mud house, as all our houses were then, in the early thirties, but Inkalamu had rather grandly defied the limitations of mud by building it three storeys tall, a sand-castle reproduction of a large, calendar-picture English country house, with steep thatch curving and a wide chimney at either end, and a flight of steps up to a portico. Everyone had said it would fall down on his head; it had lasted thirty years. His mango and orange trees crowded in upon it from the sides of the valley. There was the profound silence of a deserted man-made place – the silence of absence.

I tried to walk a little way into the mango grove, but year after year the crop must have been left to fall and rot, and between the rows of old trees hundreds of spindly saplings had grown up from seed, making a dark wood. I hadn't thought of going into the house, but walked round it to look for the view down the valley to the mountains that was on the other side; the rains had washed a moat at the foot of the eroded walls and I had to steady myself by holding on to the rusty elbows of plumbing that stuck out. The house was intimately close to me, like a body. The lop-sided wooden windows on the ground floor with their tin panes, the windows of the second floor with their panes of wire mesh, hung half-open like the mouths of old people asleep. I found I could not get all the way round because the bush on the valley side had grown right to the walls and instead tried to pull myself up and look inside. Both the mud and wattle gave way under my feet, the earth mixture crumbling and the supporting structure – branches of trees neither straightened nor dressed – that it had plastered, collapsing, hollowed by ants. The house had not fallen on Inkalamu and his black children (as the settlers had predicted) but I felt I might pull it down upon myself. Wasps hovered at my mouth and eyes, as if they, too, wanted to look inside: me. Inkalamu's house, that could have housed at least ten people, was not enough for them.

At the front again, I went up the steps where we used to sit scratching noughts and crosses while my father was in the house. Not that our families had been friends; only the children, which didn't count – my father and mother were white, my father a member of the Legislative Assembly, and Inkalamu's wives were native women. Sometimes my father would pay a call on Inkalamu, in the way of business (Inkalamu, as well as being a trader and hunter – the Africans had given him the name Inkalamu, 'the lion' – was a big landowner, once) but my mother never accompanied him. When my brothers and I came by ourselves, Inkalamu's children never took us to the house; it didn't seem to be *their* home in the way that our small farm-house was our home, and perhaps their father didn't know that we came occasionally, on our own, to play, any more than our mother and father knew we secretly went there. But when we were with my father – there was a special attraction about going to that house openly, with him – we were always called in, after business was concluded, by Inkalamu Williamson, their white father, with his long yellow curly hair on to his shoulders, like Jesus, and his sun-red chest and belly folded one upon the other and visible through his unbuttoned shirt. He gave us sweets while those of his own children who had slipped inside stood in the background. We did not feel awkward, eating in front of them, for they were all shades of brown and yellow-brown, quite different from Inkalamu and my father and us.

Someone had tied the two handles of the double front door with a piece of dirty rag to prevent it from swinging open, but I looped the rag off with a stick, and it was easy to push the door and go in. The place was not quite empty. A carpenter's bench with a vice stood in the hall, some shelves had been wrenched from the wall and stood on the floor, through the archway into the sitting-room I saw a chair and papers. At first I thought someone might still be living there. It was dim inside and smelled of earth, as always. But when my eyes got accustomed to the dark I saw that the parts of the vice were welded together in rust and a frayed strip was all that was left on the Rexine upholstery of the chair. Bat and mouse droppings carpeted the floor. Piles of books looked as if they had been dumped temporarily during a spring-cleaning; when I opened one the pages were webbed together by mould and the fine granules of red earth brought by the ants.

The Tale of a Tub. Mr Perrin and Mr Traill. Twenty Thousand Leagues under the Sea. Little old red Everymans mixed up with

numbers of *The Farmer's Weekly* and *Titbits*. This room with its
crooked alcoves moulded out of mud and painted pink and green,
and its pillars worm-tracked with mauve and blue by someone who
had never seen marble to suggest marble to people who did not
know what it was – it had never looked habitable. Inkalamu's roll-
top desk, stuffed like a pigeon-loft with accounts ready to take off in
any draught, used to stand on one of the uneven-boarded landings
that took up more space than the dingy coops of rooms. Here in the
sitting-room he would perform formalities like the distribution of
sweets to us children. I don't think anyone had ever actually sat
between the potted ferns and read before a real fire in that fireplace.
The whole house, inside, had been curiously uninhabitable; it looked
almost the real thing, but within it was not the Englishman's castle
but a naïve artifact, an African mud-and-wattle dream – like the VC-
10 made of mealie stalks that a small African boy was hawking
round the airport when I arrived the previous week.

A grille of light gleamed through the boards over my head. When
Inkalamu went upstairs to fetch something, his big boots would send
red sand down those spaces between the boards. He was always
dressed in character, with leather leggings, and the cloudy-faced old
watch on his huge round wrist held by a strap made of snake-skin. I
went back into the hall and had a look at the stairs. They seemed all
right, except for a few missing steps. The banisters made of the
handrails of an old tram-car were still there, and as I climbed, flakes
of the aluminium paint that had once covered them stuck to my
palms. I had forgotten how ugly the house was upstairs, but I
suppose I hadn't been up very often; it was never clear whether
Inkalamu's children actually lived in the house with him or slept
down at the kraal with their mothers. I think his favourite daughters
lived with him sometimes – anyway, they wore shoes, and used to
have ribbons for their hair, rather pretty hair, reddish-dun and curly
as bubbles; I hadn't understood when I was about six and my
brothers rolled on the floor giggling when I remarked that I wished I
had hair like the Williamson girls. But I soon grew old enough to
understand, and I used to recount the story and giggle, too.

The upstairs rooms were murmurous with wasps and the little
windows were high as those of a prison-cell. How good that it was

all being taken apart by insects, washed away by the rain, disappearing into the earth, carried away and digested, fragmented to compost. I was glad that Inkalamu's children were free of it, that none of them was left here in this house of that 'character' of the territory, the old Africa hand whose pioneering spirit had kept their mothers down in the compound and allowed the children into the house like pets. I was glad that the school where they weren't admitted when *we* were going to school was open to their children, and our settlers' club that they could never have joined was closed, and that if I met them now they would understand as I did that when I was the child who stood and ate sweets under their eyes, both they and I were what our fathers, theirs and mine, had made of us ... And here I was in Inkalamu Williamson's famous bathroom, the mark of his civilization, and the marvel of the district because those very pipes sticking out of the outside walls that I had clung to represented a feat of plumbing. The lavatory pan had been taken away but the little tank with its tail of chain was still on the wall, bearing green tears of verdigris. No one had bothered to throw his medicines away. He must have had a year or two of decline before he died, there must have been an end to the swaggering and the toughness and the hunting trips and the strength of ten men: medicines had been dispensed from afar, they bore the mouldering labels of pharmacists in towns thousands of miles away – Mr Williamson, the mixture; the pills, three times a day; when necessary; for pain. I was glad that the Williamsons were rid of their white father, and could live. Suddenly, I beat on one of the swollen windows with my fist and it flung open.

The sight there, the silence of it, smoking heat, was a hand laid to quiet me. Right up to the house the bush had come, the thorn trees furry with yellow blossom, the overlapping umbrellas of rose, plum and green *msasa*, the shouldering mahogany with castanet pods, and far up on either side, withdrawn, moon-mountainous, the granite peaks, lichen-spattered as if the roc perched there and left its droppings. The exaltation of emptiness was taken into my lungs. I opened my mouth and received it. Good God, that valley!

And yet I did not stand there long. I went down the broken stairs and out of the house, leaving the window hanging like the page of an open book, adding my destruction to all the others just as careless, that were bringing the house to the ground; more rain would come in, more swifts and bats to nest. But it is the ants who bring the grave to the house, in the end. As I pushed the swollen front doors roughly closed behind me I saw them, in their moving chain from life to death, carrying in the grains of red earth that will cover it.

They were black, with bodies the shape of egg-timers. I looked up from them, guilty at waste of time, when I felt someone watching me. In the drive there was a young man without shoes, his hands arranged as if he had an imaginary hat in them. I said good morning in the language of the country – it suddenly came to my mouth – and he asked me for work. Standing on the steps before the Williamsons' house, I laughed: 'I don't live here. It's empty.'

'I have been one years without a work,' he said mouthingly in English, perhaps as a demonstration of an additional qualification.

I said, 'I'm sorry. I live very far from here.'

'I am cooking and garden too,' he said.

Then we did not know what to say to each other. I went to the car and gave him two shillings out of my bag and he did what I hadn't seen since I was a child, and one of Inkalamu's servants used to take something from him – he went on his knees, clapped once, and made a bowl of his hands to receive the money.

I bumped and rocked down the drive from that house that I should never see again, whose instant in time was already forgotten, renamed, like the public buildings and streets of the territory – it didn't matter how they did it. I only hoped that the old man had left plenty of money for those children of his, Joyce, Bessie – what were the other ones' names? – to enjoy now that they were citizens of their mothers' country. At the junction with the main road the bicycle on its side and the man were still there, and a woman was standing on the veranda of the store with a little girl. I thought she might have something to do with the people who owned the land, now, and that I ought to make some sort of acknowledgement for having entered the property, so I greeted her through the car window, and she said, 'Was the road very bad?'

'Thank you, no. Thank you very much.'

'Usually people walks up when they come, now. I'm afraid to let them take the cars. And when it's been raining!'

She had come down to the car with the smile of someone for whom the historic ruin is simply a place to hang the washing. She was young, Portuguese, or perhaps Indian, with piled curls of dull hair and large black eyes, inflamed and watering. She wore tarnished gilt ear-rings and a peacock brooch, but her feet swished across the sand in felt slippers. The child had sore eyes, too; the flies were at her.

'Did you buy the place, then?' I said.

'It's my father's,' she said. 'He died about seven years ago.'

'Joyce,' I said. 'It's Joyce!'

She laughed like a child made to stand up in class. 'I'm Nonny, the baby. Joyce is the next one, the one before.'

Nonny. I used to push her round on my bicycle, her little legs hanging from the knee over the handlebars. I told her who I was, ready to exchange family news. But of course our families had never been friends. She had never been in our house. So I said, 'I couldn't go past without going to see if Inkalamu Williamson's house was still there.'

'Oh yes,' she said.'Quite often people comes to look at the house. But it's in a terrible mess.'

'And the others? Joyce, and Bessie, and Roger –?'

They were in this town or that; she was not even sure which, in the case of some of them.

'Well, that's good,' I said. 'It's different here now, there's so much to do, in the territory.' I told her I had been at the independence celebrations; I was conscious, with a stab of satisfaction at the past, that we could share now as we had never been able to.

'That's nice,' she said.

'– And you're still here. The only one of us still here! Is it a long time since it was lived in?' The house was present, out of sight, behind us.

'My mother and I was there till – how long now – five years ago,' – she was smiling and holding up her hand to keep the light from hurting her eyes – 'but what can a person do there, it's so far from the road. So I started this little place.' Her smile took me into the confidence of the empty road, the hot morning, the single customer with his bicycle. 'Well, I must try. What can you do?'

I asked, 'And the other farms, I remember the big tobacco farm on the other side of the river?'

'Oh that, that was gone long before he died. I don't know what happened to the farms. We found out he didn't have them any more, he must have sold them, I don't know ... or what. He left the brothers a tobacco farm – you know, the two elder brothers, not from my mother, from the second mother – but it came out the bank had it already. I don't know. My father never talk to us about these business things, you know.'

'But you've got this farm.' We were of the new generation, she and I. 'You could sell it, I'm sure. Land values are going to rise again. They're prospecting all over this area between the bauxite mines and the capital. Sell it, and – well, do – you could go where you like.'

'It's just the house. From the house to the road. Just this little bit,' she said, and laughed. 'The rest was sold before he died. It's just the house, that he left to my mother. But you got to live, I mean.'

I said warmly. 'The same with my father! Our ranch was ten thousand acres. And there was more up at Lebishe. If he'd have hung on to Lebishe alone we'd have made a fortune when the platinum deposits were found.'

But of course it was not quite the same. She said sympathetically, 'Really!' to me with my university-modulated voice. We were smiling at each other, one on either side of the window of the big American car. The child, with bows in its hair, hung on to her hand; the flies bothered its small face.

'You couldn't make some sort of hotel, I suppose.'

'It's in a mess,' she said, assuming the tone of a flighty, apologetic housewife. 'I built this little place here for us and we just left it. It's so much rubbish there still.'

'Yes, and the books. All those books. The ants are eating them.' I smiled at the little girl as people without children of their own do. Behind, there was the store, and the cottage like the backyard quarters provided for servants in white houses. 'Doesn't anyone want the books?'

'We don't know what to do with them. We just left them. Such a lot of books my father collected up.' After all, I knew her father's eccentricities.

'And the mission school at Balondi's been taken over and made into a pretty good place?' I seemed to remember that Joyce and one of the brothers had been there; probably all Inkalamu's children. It was no longer a school meant for black children, as it had been in our time. But she seemed to have only a polite general interest: 'Yes, somebody said something the other day.'

'You went to school there, didn't you, in the old days?'

She giggled at herself and moved the child's arm. 'I never been away from here.'

'Really? Never!'

'My father taught me a bit. You'll even see the schoolbooks among that lot up there. Really.'

'Well, I suppose the shop might become quite a nice thing,' I said.

She said, 'If I could get a licence for brandy, though. It's only beer, you see. If I could get a licence for brandy . . . I'm telling you, I'd get the men coming.' She giggled.

'Well, if I'm to reach the mines by three, I'd better move,' I said.

She kept smiling to please me; I began to think she didn't remember me at all; why should she, she had been no bigger than her little daughter when I used to take her on the handlebars of my bicycle. But she said, 'I'll bring my mother. She's inside.' She turned and the child turned with her and they went into the shade of the veranda and into the store. In a moment they came out with a thin black woman bent either by age or in greeting – I was not sure. She wore a head-cloth and a full long skirt of the minutely patterned blue-and-white cotton that used to be in bales on the counter of every store, in my childhood. I got out of the car and shook hands with her. She clapped and made an obeisance, never looking at me. She was very thin with a narrow breast under a shrunken yellow blouse pulled together by a flower with gaps like those of missing teeth in its coloured glass corolla. Before the three of them, I turned to the child rubbing at her eyes with hands tangled in the tendrils of her hair. 'So you've a daughter of your own now, Nonny.'

She giggled and swung her forward.

I said to the little girl, 'What's hurting you, dear? – Something wrong with her eyes?'

'Yes. It's all red and sore. Now I've got it too, but not so bad.'

'It's conjunctivitis,' I said. 'She's infected you. You must go to the doctor.'

She smiled and said, 'I don't know what it is. She had it two weeks now.'

Then we shook hands and I thought: I mustn't touch my face until I can wash them.

'You're going to Kalondwe, to the mine.' The engine was running. She stood with her arms across her breasts, the attitude of one who is left behind.

'Yes, I believe old Doctor Madley's back in the territory, he's at the WHO centre there.' Dr Madley had been the only doctor in the district when we were all children.

'Oh yes,' she said in her exaggeratedly interested, conversational manner. 'He didn't know my father was dead, you know, he came to see him!'

'I'll tell him I've seen you, then.'

'Yes, tell him.' She made the little girl's limp fat hand wave goodbye, pulling it away from her eyes – 'Naughty, naughty.' I suddenly remembered – 'What's your name now, by the way?'; the times were gone when nobody ever bothered to know the married names of women who weren't white. And I didn't want to refer to her as Inkalamu's daughter. Thank God she was free from him, and the place he and his kind had made for her. All that was dead, Inkalamu was dead.

She stood twiddling her ear-rings, bridling, smiling, her face not embarrassed but warmly bashful with open culpability, 'Oh, just Miss Williamson. Tell him Nonny.'

I turned carefully on the tar, I didn't want to leave with my dust in their faces. As I gathered speed I saw in the mirror that she still had the child by the wrist, waving its hand to me.

The Bride of Christ

Lyndall Berger, at sixteen, wrote to her parents for permission to be confirmed.

'Are you mad?' Sidney's gaze was a pair of outspread arms, stopping his wife short whichever way she might turn.

'Well, I know. But it never enters your mind that for someone – I'm not saying for *her* – it could be necessary; real, I mean. When one says "no", one must concede that. Otherwise she must put the refusal down to rationalist prejudice. You see what I mean?'

'Saved them all the abracadabra at the synagogue for this. Mumbo jumbo for abracadabra.'

It was Shirley who had agreed when the child went to boarding school that she could go to church with the other girls if she felt like it – just to see what it was all about. She bought her, at the same time, a Penguin on comparative religion; in the holidays she could read James Parkes on the origins of Judaism and Christianity, right-hand lower bookshelf near the blue lamp. Shirley did not know whether the child had ever read either; you were in the same position as you were with sex; you gave them the facts, and you left an unspoken unanswerable question. How does it feel to want to perform this strange act? How does it feel to have faith?

'It's like cutting her skirts up to her thigh. She wants to be confirmed because her friends are going to be. The answer is no.'

His wife's face winced in anticipation of the impact of this sort of dismissal. 'Of course it's no. But we must show her the respect of giving her the proper reasons. I'll talk to her when she's home next Sunday.'

Shirley had meant to take her daughter for a walk in the veld, but it wasn't necessary because Sidney and Peter, their other child, went off to play golf anyway. Shirley was not slow to take a stand on the one ground that stood firm beneath her feet. 'You've been going to church for over a year now. I suppose you haven't failed to notice that all those nicely dressed ladies and gentlemen of the congregation are white? A church isn't a cinema, you know – I say this because we get used to seeing only white people in public places like that, and it's quite understandable that one begins to take it for granted. But a church is different, you know that; the church preaches brotherhood, and there's no excuse. Except prejudice. They pray to God, and they take the body of Christ into their mouths, but they don't want to do it next to a black man. You must have thought about it often.'

'I think about it all the time,' the girl said. They were peeling mushrooms; she didn't do it well; she broke off bits of the cap along with the skin she rolled back, but her mother didn't complain.

'That's why Sidney and I don't go to synagogue or church or anything – one of the reasons. Daddy wouldn't belong to any religion wherever he lived – that you know – but perhaps I might want to if I lived anywhere else, not here. I couldn't sit with them in their churches or synagogues here.'

'I know.' Lyndall did not look up.

'I wonder how you feel about this.' No answer. Shirley felt there should be no necessity to spell it out, but to force the child to speak, she said, 'How can you want to join the establishment of the Church when there's a colour bar there?'

'Well, yes, I know –' Lyndall said.

Her mother said of the mushroom stalks, 'Just break them off; I'll use them for soup.'

They returned to the silence between them, but a promising silence, with something struggling through it.

'I think about it every time I'm in church – I'm always – but it's got nothing to do with Christ, Mummy. It's not his fault' – she paused with shame for the schoolgirl phrasing before this woman, her mother, who inevitably had the advantage of adult articulateness – 'not Christ's fault that people are hypocrites.'

'Yes, of course, that's the point I'm trying to make for you. I can understand anyone being attracted to the Christian ethic, to Christ's teaching, to the idea of following him. But why join the Church; it's done such awful things in his name.'

'That's got nothing to do with Christ.'

'You associate yourself with them! The moment you get yourself confirmed and join the Church, you belong along with it all, from

168

the Crusaders and the Spanish Inquisition to the good Christian Nazis, and the good Christians of the Dutch Reformed Church who sprinkle pious sentiments over the colour bar the way the Portuguese bishops used to baptize slaves before they were shipped from West Africa – you belong along with them just the way you do in church with the nice ladies in smart hats who wouldn't want a black child sitting beside theirs in school.'

Lyndall was afraid of her mother's talk; often the constructions she had balanced in her mind out of her own ideas fell down before her mother's talk like the houses made of sticks and jacaranda feathers that used to turn to garden rubbish beneath the foot of an unrecognizing grown-up.

She was going to be quite good-looking (Shirley thought so), but the conflict of timidity and determination gave her the heavy-jawed look of a certain old uncle, a failure in the family, whom Shirley remembered from her own childhood.

'What about Garth and Nibs.' It was a statement not a question. The couple, Anglican ex-missionaries who had both been put under ban for their activities as members of the Liberal Party, were among the Bergers' closest friends.

'Yes, Garth and Nibs, and Father Huddleston and Bishop Reeves and Crowther and a lot of other names. Of course there are Anglicans and Catholics and Methodists who don't preach brotherhood and forget it when it comes to a black face. But the fact is that they're the rarities. Odd men out. The sort of people you'll be worshipping Christ with every Sunday are the people who see no wrong in their black "brothers" having to carry a pass. The same sort of people who didn't see anything wrong in your great-grandparents having to live in a ghetto in Galicia. The same people who kept going to church in Germany on Sundays while the Jews were being shovelled into gas ovens.'

She watched her daughter's face for the expression that knew *that* was coming; couldn't be helped, it had to be dragged up, again and again and again and again and again – like Lear's 'nevers' – no matter how sick of it everyone might be.

But the child's face was naked.

'Darling' – the words found release suddenly, in helplessness – 'I really can understand how you feel. I'm not just talking; I can tell you that if I had a religion at all it could only be Christ's; I've never been able to understand why the Jews didn't accept him, it's so logical that his thinking should have been the culmination – but I know I couldn't become a Christian, couldn't . . .'

The child didn't help her.

'Because of *that*. And the other things. That go with it. It's like having one drop of coloured blood in your veins. You'd always have to admit it, I mean, wouldn't you? You'd always want to tell people first. Everything'd have to begin from there. Well, it's just the same if you're a Jew. People like us – colour and race, it doesn't mean a damn thing to me, but it can only not mean a thing if I begin from there, from having it known that I'm Jewish. I don't choose to belong with the ladies who separate the meat and the milk dishes and wear their Sunday best to synagogue, but I can't not choose the people who were barred from the universities – they were, just like the Africans, here – and killed by the Germans – you understand?' Her voice dropped from an apologetic rise; she hadn't wanted to bring that in, again. Lyndall was rubbing rolls of dirt on her sweating hands. She blinked jerkily now and then as the words pelted her. 'And you, you belong along with that too, d'you understand, you'll always belong with it. Doesn't matter if you're confirmed a hundred times over. And another thing – it's all part of the same thing, really. If you were to become a Christian, there would always be the suspicion in people's mind that you'd done it for social reasons.'

In her innocence, the child opened her lips on a gleam of tooth, and frowned, puzzled.

Shirley felt ashamed at what was at once trivial and urgently important. 'Clubs and so on. Even certain schools. They don't want to admit Jews. Oh, it's a bore to talk about it. When you think what Africans are debarred from. But at the same time – one wants *all* the pinpricks, one must show them one won't evade a single one. How can I explain – pride, it's a kind of pride. I couldn't turn my back on it.'

The child moved her head slowly and vehemently in understanding, as she used to do, near tears, when she had had a dressing-down.

'Lyndall,' her mother said, 'You'd have to be a real Christian, an every-minute-of-the-day, every-day-of-the-week Christian, before I could think of letting you be converted. You'd have to take all this on you. You'd have to know that the person kneeling beside you in church might make some remark about Jews one day, and you wouldn't be able to let it pass like a Christian; you'd have to say, I'm Jewish. I'd want you to take the kicks from both sides. It would be the only way.'

'Oh, but I will, I promise you, Mummy!' The child jumped clumsily, forgetting she was almost grown-up, forgetting her size, and gave her mother the hard kisses of childhood that landed on cheek and chin. The bowl of mushrooms turned over and spun loudly like a top coming to rest, and scrabbling for the mushrooms, looking up from under the hair that fell forward over her face, she talked: 'Father Byrd absolutely won't allow you to be confirmed until you're sure you're ready – I've had talks with him three times – he comes to the school on Thursdays – and I know I'm ready, I feel it. I promise you, Mummy.'

Shirley was left with the empty bowl; she urgently wanted to speak, to claim what had been taken out of her hands; but all she did was remove, by pressure of the pads of her fingers, the grit in the fungus dew at the bottom of the bowl.

Of course Lyndall had to be baptized, too. They hadn't realized it, or perhaps the child had wanted to break the whole business gently, one piece of preposterousness at a time. She had been named originally for that free spirit in Olive Schreiner's book, a shared feeling for which had been one of the signs that brought her parents together. Her mother attended both the baptismal and confirmation ceremonies; it was understood that Sidney, while granting his daughter her kind of freedom, would not be expected to be present. For the confirmation Lyndall had to have a sleeveless white dress with a long-sleeved bolero; all the other girls were having them made like that. 'So's you can wear the dress for parties afterwards,' she said.

'One never wears these dresses for anything afterwards,' said her mother. Eighteen years in a plastic bag, the zipper made tarnish marks on the wedding dress.

Lyndall also had to have a veil, plain muslin, held in place with bronze bobby pins.

'The bride of Christ,' said Sidney when, trying it on, she had left the room. At least he had managed not to say anything while she was there; Shirley looked up for a second, as if he had spoken to her thoughts. But he was alone in his own.

'She's not going into a nunnery,' she said.

Yet why did she feel such a cheat with him over this thing? He could have stopped the child if he'd been absolutely convinced, absolutely adamant. The heavy father. How much distaste he had – they had – for the minor tyrannies . . . It was all very well to set children free; he wouldn't compromise himself to himself by accepting that he might have to use the power of authority to keep them that way.

Lyndall was weeping when the bishop in his purple robes called her name and blessed her in the school chapel. The spasm on the rather large child's face under the ugly veil as she rose from her knees produced a nervous automatic counterspasm within her mother; the child was one of those who hadn't cried beyond the grazed-knees stage. Shirley stirred on her hard chair as if about to speak to someone, even to giggle . . . but she was alone: on the one side, somebody's grandmother with a pearl ear-ring shaking very slightly; on the other, a parent in dark grey hopsack. Afterwards there was tea and cake and an air of mild congratulation in the school hall. Meeting over a communal sugar bowl, Shirley and another woman smiled at each other in the manner of people who do not know one another's names. 'A big day in their lives, isn't it? And just as well to get it over with so they can settle down to work before the exams, I was just saying . . .' Shirley smiled and murmured the appropriate half-phrases. The white dresses swooped in and out among the mothers and fathers. Bobbing breasts and sturdy hams, or thin waists and blindly nosing little peaks just touching flat bodices – but nubile, nubile. That was Sidney's explanation for the whole thing: awakening sexuality finding an emotional outlet; they do not love Christ, they are in love with him, a symbolic male figure, and indeed, what about Father What-not with his pale, clean priest's hands, appearing every Thursday among three hundred females?

Father Byrd was gaily introducing the bishop to a parent in a blue swansdown hat. The bishop had disrobed, and now appeared in the assembly like an actor who has taken off his splendid costume and make-up. The confirmants were displaying presents that lay in cotton wool within hastily torn tissue paper; they raced about to give each other the fancy cards they had bought. Lyndall, with a deep, excited smile, found her mother. They kissed, and Lyndall clung to her. 'Bless you, darling, bless you, bless you,' Shirley said. Lyndall kept lifting her hair off her forehead with the back of a mannered hand, and was saying with pleased, embarrassed casualness, 'What chaos! Could you see us shaking? I thought I'd *never* – we could hardly get up the steps! Did you see my *veil*? Roseann's was down to her nose! What chaos! Did you see how we all bunched together? Father Byrd told us a million times . . .' Her eyes were all around the room, as if acknowledging applause. She showed her mother her cards, with the very faint suggestion of defiance; but there was no need – with heads at an angle so that both could see at the same time, they looked at the doggerel in gilt script and the tinsel-nimbused figures as if they had never wrinkled their noses in amusement at greeting-card senti-mentality. Shirley said, 'Darling, instead of giving you some little' (she was going to say 'cross or something', because every other girl seemed to have been given a gold crucifix and chain), 'some present for yourself, we're sending a donation to the African Children's Feeding Scheme in your name. Don't you think that makes sense?'

Lyndall agreed before her mother had finished speaking: 'That's a much better idea.' Her face was vivid. She had never looked quite like that before; charming, movingly charming. Must be the tears and excitement, bringing blood to the surface of the skin. An emotional surrogate, Sidney would have said, if Shirley had told him about it. But it was something she wanted to keep; and so she said nothing, telling the others at home only about the splendour of the bishop's on-stage appearance, and the way the girls who were not confirmants hung about outside the school hall, hoping for leftover sandwiches. Her son Peter grinned – he had disliked boarding school so much that they had had to take him away. Beyond this, they had had no trouble with him at all. He certainly had not been bothered by any religious phase; he was a year older than Lyndall, and as pocket and odd-job money would allow, was slowly building a boat in a friend's backyard.

When Lyndall was home for a weekend she got up while the rest of the house was still asleep on Sunday mornings and went to Communion at the church down the road. It was her own affair; no one remarked on it one way or another. Meeting her with wine on her breath and the slightly stiff face that came from the early morning air, her mother, still in a dressing-gown, sometimes made a gentle joke: 'Boozing before breakfast, what a thing,' and kissed the fresh, cool cheek. Lyndall smiled faintly and was gone upstairs to come clattering down changed into the trousers and shirt that was the usual weekend dress of the family. She ate with concentration an enormous breakfast: all the things she didn't get at school.

Before her conversion, she and Shirley had often talked about religion, but now when Shirley happened to be reading Simone Weil's letters and told Lyndall something of her life and thought, the girl had the inattentive smile, the hardly patient inclinations of the head, of someone too polite to rebuff an intrusion on privacy. Well, Shirley realized that she perhaps read too much into this; Simone Weil's thinking was hardly on the level of a girl of sixteen; Lyndall probably couldn't follow.

Or perhaps it was because Simone Weil was Jewish. If Lyndall had shown more interest, her mother certainly would have explained to her that she hadn't brought up the subject of Simone Weil because of *that*, Lyndall must believe her; but given the lack of interest, what was the point?

During the Christmas holidays Lyndall went to a lot of parties and overslept on several Sunday mornings. Sometimes she went to a service later in the day, and then usually asked Shirley to drive her to church: 'It's absolutely boiling, trekking there in this heat.' On Christmas morning she was up and off to Mass at dawn, and when she came back, the family had the usual present-giving in the dining-room, with the servants, Ezekiel and Margaret and Margaret's little daughter, Winnie, and constant interruptions as the dustmen, the milkman, and various hangers-on called at the kitchen door for their *bonsella*, their Christmas tip. The Bergers had always celebrated

Christmas, partly because they had so many friends who were not Jews who inevitably included the Bergers in their own celebrations, and partly because, as Sidney said, holidays, saints' days – whatever the occasion, it didn't matter – were necessary to break up the monotony of daily life. He pointed out, apropos Christmas, that among the dozens of Christmas cards the Bergers got, there was always one from an Indian Muslim friend. Later in the day the family were expected at a Christmas lunch and swimming party at the Trevor-Pearses'. After a glass of champagne in the sun, Shirley suddenly said to Sidney, 'I'm afraid that our daughter's the only one of the Christians here who's been to church today,' and he said, with the deadpan, young-wise face that she had always liked so much, 'What d'you expect, don't you know the Jews always overdo it?'

The Bergers thought they would go to the Kruger Park over the Easter weekend. As children grew older, there were fewer things all the members of a family could enjoy together, and this sort of little trip was a safe choice for a half-term holiday. When they told Peter, he said, 'Fine, fine,' but before Shirley could write to Lyndall, there was a letter from her saying she hoped there wasn't anything on at half-term, because she and her school friends had the whole weekend planned, with a party on the Thursday night when they came home, and a picnic on the Vaal on Easter Monday, and she must do some shopping in town on the Saturday morning. Since Lyndall was the one who was at boarding school, there was the feeling that family plans ought to be designed to fit in with her inclinations rather than anyone else's. If Lyndall wasn't keen to go away, should they stay at home, after all? 'Fine, fine,' Peter said. It didn't seem to matter to him one way or the other. And Sidney, everyone knew, privately thought April still too hot a month for the Game Reserve. 'We can go at our leisure in the August holidays,' he said, made expansive and considerate by the reprieve. 'Yes, of course, fine,' Peter said. He had told Shirley that he and his friend expected to finish the boat and get it down for a tryout in Durban during August.

A friend at school had cut Lyndall's hair, and she came out of school as conscious of this as a puppy cleverly carrying a shoe in its mouth. Her mother liked the look of her, and Sidney said 'Thank

God' in comment on the fact that she hadn't been able to see out of her eyes before. Whatever reaction there was from her brother was elicited behind closed doors, like all the other exchanges between brother and sister in the sudden and casual intimacy that seemed to grow up between them, apparently over a record that Lyndall had borrowed and brought home. They played it over and over on Thursday afternoon, shut in Lyndall's room.

Lyndall's head was done up like a parcel, with transparent sticky tape holding strands of hair in place on her forehead and cheeks; she gave her finger-nails a coating like that of a cheap pearl necklace and then took it off again. She had to be delivered to the house where the party was being held, by seven, and explained that she would be brought home by someone else; she knew how her mother and father disliked having to sit up late to come and fetch her. Her mother successfully prevented herself from saying, 'How late will it be?' – what was the use of making these ritual responses in an unacknow-ledged ceremony of initiation to adult life? Tribal Africans took the young into the bush for a few weeks, and got it all over with at once. Those free from the rites of primitive peoples repeated plaintive remarks, tags of a litany of instruction half but never quite forgotten, from one generation to the next.

Lyndall came home very late indeed, and didn't get up until eleven next morning. Her brother had long gone off to put in a full day's work on the boat. It was hot for early autumn, and the girl lay on the brown grass in her pink gingham bikini, sunbathing. Shirley came out with some mending and said to her, 'Isn't it awful, I can't do that any more. Just lie. I don't know when it went.' Whenever the telephone rang behind them in the house, Lyndall got up at once. Her laughter and bursts of intense sibilant, confidential talk now sounded, now were cut off, as Ezekiel and Margaret went about the house and opened or closed a door or window. Between calls, Lyndall returned and dropped back to the grass. Now and then she hummed an echo of last night's party; the tune disappeared into her thoughts again. Sometimes a smile, surfacing, made her open her eyes, and she would tell Shirley some incident, tearing off a fragment from the sounds, shapes, and colours that were turning in the red dark of her closed lids.

After lunch her mother asked whether she could summon the energy for a walk down to the shops – 'You'll have an early night tonight, anyway.' They tried to buy some fruit, but of course even the Portuguese greengrocers were closed on Good Friday.

As they came back into the house, Sidney said, 'Someone phoned twice. A boy with a French name, Jean-something, Frebert, Brebert?'

Lyndall opened her eyes in pantomime astonishment; last night's mascara had worked its way out as a black dot in the inner corner of one. Then a look almost of pain, a closing away of suspicion took her face. 'I don't believe it.'

'The first time, I'd just managed to get Lemmy down on the bathroom floor,' said Sidney. The dog had an infected ear and had to be captured with cunning for his twice-daily treatment. 'You won't get within a mile of him again today.'

'Jean? He's from Canada, somebody's cousin they brought along last night. Did he say he'd phone again, or what? He didn't leave a number?'

'He did not.'

She went up to her room and shut the door and played the record. But when the telephone rang she was somehow alert to it through the noisy music and was swift to answer before either Shirley or Sidney moved to put aside their books. The low, light voice she used for talking to boys did not carry the way the exaggeratedly animated one that was for girls did. But by the time Shirley had reached the end of the chapter they had heard her run upstairs.

Then she appeared in the doorway and smiled in on the pair.

'What d'you know, there's another party. This boy Jean's just asked me to go. It's in a stable, he says; everyone's going in denims.'

'Someone you met last night?'

'*Jean*. The one Daddy spoke to. You know.'

'Such gaiety,' said Sidney. 'Well, he's not one to give up easily.'

'Won't you be exhausted?'

But Shirley understood that Lyndall quite rightly wouldn't even answer that. She gave a light, patronizing laugh. 'He says he wanted to ask me last night, but he was scared.'

'Will you be going before or after dinner?' said Shirley.

'Picking me up at a quarter past seven.'

In Shirley's silences a room became like a scene enclosed in a glass paperweight, waiting for the touch that would set the snow whirling. The suburban church bells began to ring, muffled by the walls, dying away in waves, a ringing in the ears.

'I'll give you a scrambled egg.'

Lyndall came down to eat in her dressing-gown, straight out of the bath: 'I'm ready, Ma.' Sidney was still reading, his drink fizzling flat, scarcely touched, on the floor beside him. Shirley sat down at the coffee-table where Lyndall's tray was and slowly smoked, and slowly rose and went to fetch the glass she had left somewhere else. Her movements seemed reluctant. She held the glass and watched the child eat. She said, 'I notice there's been no talk of going to church today.'

Lyndall gave her a keen look across a slice of bread and butter she was just biting into.

'I woke up too late this morning.'

'I know. But there are other services. All day. It's Good Friday, the most important day in the year.'

Lyndall put the difficulty in her mother's hands as she used to give over the knotted silver chain of her locket to be disentangled by adult patience and a pin. 'I meant to go to this evening's.'

'Yes,' said Shirley, 'but you are going to a party.'

'Oh Mummy.'

'Only seven months since you got yourself confirmed, and you can go to a party on Good Friday. Just another party; like all the others you go to.'

A despairing fury sprang up so instantly in the girl that her father looked around as if a stone had hurtled into the room. 'I knew it. I knew you were thinking that! As if I don't feel terrible about it! I've felt terrible all day! You don't have to come and tell me it's Good Friday!' And tears shook in her eyes at the shame.

Peter had come in, a presence of wood-glue and sweat, not unpleasant, in the room. Under his rough eyebrows bridged by the redness of an adolescent skin irritation, he stared a moment and then seemed at once to understand everything. He sat quietly on a footstool.

'The most important day in the year for a Christian. Even the greengrocers closed, you saw –'

'I just knew you were thinking that about me, I knew it.' Lyndall's voice was stifled in tears and anger. 'And how do you think I feel when I have to go to church alone on Sunday mornings? All on my own. Nobody knows me there. And that atmosphere when I walk into the house and you're all here. How d'you think I *feel*?' She stopped to sob dramatically and yet sincerely; her mother said nothing, but her father's head inclined to one side, as one offers comfort without asking the cause of pain. 'And when you said that about the present – everyone else just got one, no fuss. Even while I was being confirmed I could feel you sitting there, and I knew what you were thinking – how d'you think it is, for me?'

'Good God,' Shirley said in the breathy voice of amazement, 'I came to the confirmation in complete sincerity. You're being unfair. Once I'd accepted that you wanted to be a real Christian, not a social one –'

'You see? You see? You're always at me –'

'At you? This is the first time the subject's ever come up.'

The girl looked at them blindly. 'I know I'm a bad Christian! I listen to them in church, and it just seems a lot of rubbish. I pray, I pray every night –' Desperation stopped her mouth.

'Lyndall, you say you want Christ, and I believe you,' said Shirley.

The girl was enraged. 'Don't say it! You don't, you don't, you never did.'

'Yet you make yourself guilty and unhappy by going out dancing on the day that Christ was crucified.'

'Oh, why can't you just leave her alone?' It was Peter, his head lifted from his arms.

His mother took the accusation like a blow in the chest.

Sidney spoke for the first time; to his son. 'What's the matter with you?'

'Just leave her alone,' Peter said. 'Making plans, asking questions. Just leave people alone, can't you?'

Sidney knew that he was not the one addressed, and so he answered. 'I don't know what you're getting hysterical about, Peter. No one's even mentioned your name.'

'Well, we talk about you plenty, behind your back, to our friends, I can tell you.' His lips pulled with a trembling, triumphant smile. The two children did not look at each other.

'Coffee or a glass of milk?' Shirley said into the silence, standing up.

Lyndall didn't answer, but said, 'Well, I'm not going. You can tell him I'm sick or dead or something. Anything. When he comes.'

'I suggest you ring up and make some excuse,' said Shirley.

The girl gestured it away; her fingers were limply twitching. 'Don't even know where to get him. He'll be on his way now. He'll think I'm mad.'

'I'll tell him. I'm going to tell him just exactly what happened,' said Peter, looking past his mother.

She went and stood in the kitchen because there was nobody there. She was listening for the voices in the living-room, and yet there was nothing she wanted to hear. Sidney found her. He had brought Lyndall's tray. 'I don't understand it,' he said. 'If the whole thing's half-forgotten already, why push her into it again? For heaven's sake, what are you, an evangelist or something? Do you have to take it on yourself to make converts? Since when the missionary spirit? For God's sake, let's leave well alone. I mean, anyone would think, listening to you in there –'

His wife stood against the dresser with her shoulders hunched, pulling the points of her collar up over her chin. He leaned behind her and tightened the dripping tap. She was quiet. He put his hand on her cheek. 'Never mind. High-handed little devils. Enough of this God-business for today.'

He went upstairs and she returned to the living-room. Lyndall was blowing her nose and pressing impatiently at the betrayal of tears that still kept coming, an overflow, to her brilliant, puffy eyes.

'You don't know how to get hold of the boy?' Shirley said.

There was a pause. 'I told you.'

'Don't you know the telephone number?'

'I'm not going to phone Clare Pirie – he's her cousin.'

'It would be so rude to let him come for you for nothing,' said Shirley. Nobody spoke. 'Lyndall, I think you'd better go.' She stopped, and then went on in a tone carefully picking a way through presumption, 'I mean, one day is like another. And these dates are arbitrary, anyway, nobody really knows when it was, for sure – the ritual observance isn't really the thing – is it? –'

'Look what I look like,' said the girl.

'Well, just go upstairs now' – the cadence was simple, sensible, comforting, like a nursery rhyme – 'and wash your face with cold water, and brush your hair, and put on a bit of make-up.'

'I suppose so. Don't feel much like dancing,' the girl added, offhand, in a low voice to her mother, and the two faces shared, for a moment, a family likeness of doubt that the boy Peter did not see.

A Meeting in Space

Every morning he was sent to the baker and the French children slid out of dark walls like the village cats and walked in his footsteps. He couldn't understand what they said to each other, but he thought he understood their laughter: he was a stranger. He looked forward to the half-fearful, disdainful feeling their presence at his back gave him, and as he left the house expected at each alley, hole and doorway the start of dread with which he would see them. They didn't follow him into the baker's shop. Perhaps the baker wouldn't have them – they looked poor, and the boy knew, from the piccanins at home, that poor kids steal. He had never been into a bakery at home in South Africa; the baker-boy, a black man who rode a tricycle with a rattling bin on the front, came through the yard holding the loaves out of the way of the barking dogs, and put two white and one brown on the kitchen-table. It was the same with fruit and vegetables; at home the old Indian, Vallabhbhai, stopped his greengrocer's lorry at the back gate, and his piccanin carried into the kitchen whatever you bought.

But here, the family said, part of the fun was doing your own shopping in the little shops that were hidden away by the switchback of narrow streets. They made him repeat over and over again the words for asking for bread, in French, but once in the baker's shop he never said them, only pointed at the loaf he wanted and held out his hand with money in it. He felt that he was someone else, a dumb man perhaps. After a few days, if he were given change he would point again, this time at a bun with a glazing of jam. He had established himself as a customer. The woman who served chattered at him, smiled with her head on one side while she picked the money out of his palm, but he gave no sign of response.

There was another child who sometimes turned up with the usual group. He would hail them loudly, from across a street, in their own language, and stalk along with them for a bit, talking away, but he looked different. The boy thought it was just because this one was richer. Although he wore the usual canvas shoes and cotton shorts, he was hung about with all sorts of equipment – a camera and two other leather cases. He began to appear in the bakery each morning. He stood right near, as if the dumb person were also invisible, and peering up experiencedly under a thick, shiny fringe of brown hair, looked along the cakes on top of the counter while apparently discussing them in a joking, familiar way with the woman. He also appeared unexpectedly in other places, without the group. Once he was leaning against the damp archway to the tunnel that smelled like a school lavatory – it was the quick way from the upper level of streets to the lower. Another time he came out of the door of the streaky-pink-painted house with the Ali Baba pots, as if he must have been watching at the window. Then he was balancing along the top of the wall that overlooked the pitch where in the afternoons the baker and other men played a bowling game with a heavy ball. Suddenly, he was outside the gate of the villa that the family were living in; he squatted on the doorstep of the house opposite, doing something to the inside of his camera. He spoke: 'You English?'

'Yes – not really – no. I mean, I speak English, but I come from South Africa.'

'Africa? You come from *Africa*? That's a heck of a way!'

'Fifteen hours or so. We came in a jet. We actually took a little longer because, you see, something went wrong with the one engine and we had to wait three hours in the middle of the night in Kano. Boy, was it hot, and there was a live camel wandering around.' The anecdote cut itself off abruptly; the family often said long-winded stories were a bore.

'I've had some pretty interesting experiences myself. My parents are travelling round the world and I'm going with them. Most of the time. I'll go back home to school for a while in the Fall. Africa. Fantastic. We may get out there sometime. D'you know anything about these darned Polaroids? It's stuck. I've got a couple of pictures of you I must show you. I take candid shots. All over the place. I've got another camera, a Minox, but I mostly use this one here because it develops the prints right in the box and you can give them to people right off. It's good for a laugh. I've got some pretty interesting pictures, too.'

'Where was I – in the street?'

'Oh I'm taking shots all the time. All over the place.'

'What's the other case?'

'Tape-recorder. I'll get you on tape, too. I tape people at Zizi's Bar and in the *Place*, they don't know I'm doing it, I've got this mi-nute little mike, you see. It's fan-tastic.'

'And what's in here?'

The aerial was pulled out like a silver wand. 'My transistor, of course, my beloved transistor. D'you know what I just heard? – "Help!" Are the Beatles popular down in Africa?'

'We saw them in London – live. My brother and sister and me. She bought the record of "Help!" but we haven't got anything to play it on, here.'

'Good God, some guys get all the breaks! You *saw* them. You notice how I've grown my hair? Say, look, I can bring down my portable player and your sister can hear her record.'

'What time can you come?'

'Any time you say. I'm easy. I've got to go for this darned French lesson now, and I *have* to be in at noon so that old Madame Blanche can give me my lunch before she quits, but I'll be around in-definitely after that.'

'Straight after lunch. About two. I'll wait for you here. Could you bring the pictures, as well – of me?'

Clive came racing through the tiny courtyard and charged the fly-screen door, letting it bang behind him. 'Hey! There's a boy who can speak English! He just talked to me! He's a real Amurr-rican – just wait till you hear him. And you should see what he's got, a Polaroid camera – he's taken some pictures of me and I didn't even know him – and he's got a tiny little tape-recorder, you can get people on it when they don't know – and the smallest transistor I've ever seen.'

His mother said, 'So you've found a pal. Thank goodness.' She was cutting up green peppers for salad, and she offered him a slice on the point of her knife, but he didn't see it.'

'He's going round the world, but he goes back to America to school sometimes.'

'Oh, where? Does he come from New York?'

'I don't know, he said something about Fall, I think that's where the school is. The Fall, he said.'

'That's not a place, silly – it's what they call autumn.'

The shower was in a kind of cupboard in the kitchen-dining room, and its sliding door was shaken in the frame, from inside. The impatient occupant got it to jerk open: she was his sister. 'You've found what?' The enormous expectancy with which she had invested this holiday, for herself, opened her shining face under its plastic mob-cap.

'We can hear the record, Jen, he's bringing his player. He's from America.'

'How old?'

'Same as me. About.'

She pulled off the cap and her straight hair fell down, covering her head to the shoulders and her face to her eyelashes. 'Fine,' she said soberly.

His father sat reading *Nice-Matin* on one of the dining-table chairs, which was dressed, like a person, in a yellow skirt and a cover that fitted over its hard back. He had – unsuccessfully – put out a friendly foot to trip up the boy as he burst in, and now felt he ought to make another gesture of interest. As if to claim that he had been listening to every word, he said, 'What's your friend's name?'

'Oh, I don't know. He's American, he's the boy with the three leather cases –'

'Yes, all right –'

'You'll see him this afternoon. He's got a Beatle cut.' This last was addressed to the young girl, who turned, half-way up the stone stairs with a train of wet footprints behind her.

But of course Jenny, who was old enough to introduce people as adults do, at once asked the American boy who he was. She got a very full reply. 'Well, I'm usually called Matt, but that's short for my second name, really – my real names are Nicholas Matthew Rootes Keller.'

'Junior?' she teased. 'The Third?'

'No, why should I be? My father's name is Donald Rootes Keller. I'm named for my grandfather on my mother's side. She has one hell of a big family. Her brothers won five decorations between them, in the war. I mean, three in the war against the Germans, and two in the Korean War. My youngest uncle, that's Rod, he's got a hole in his back – it's where the ribs were – you can put your hand in. My hand, I mean' – he made a fist with a small, thin, tanned hand – 'not an adult person's. How much more would you say my hand had t'grow, I mean – would you say half as much again, as much as that? – to be a full-size, man's hand –' He measured it against Clive's; the two ten-year-old fists matched eagerly.

'Yours and Clive's put together – one full-size, king-size, man-size paw. Clip the coupon now. Enclose only one box top or reasonable facsimile.'

But the elder brother's baiting went ignored or misunderstood by the two small boys. Clive might react with a faint grin of embarrassed pleasure and reflected glory at the reference to the magazine ad culture with which his friend was associated by his brother Mark. Matt went on talking in the innocence of one whose background is still as naturally accepted as once his mother's lap was.

He came to the villa often after that afternoon when the new Beatle record was heard for the first time on his player. The young people had nothing to do but wait while the parents slept after lunch (the *Place*, where Jenny liked to stroll, in the evenings, inviting mute glances from boys who couldn't speak her language, was dull at that time of day) and they listened to the record again and again in the courtyard summer-house that had been a pig-sty before the peasant cottage became a villa. When the record palled, Matt taped their voices – 'Say something African!' – and Mark made up a jumble of the one or two Zulu words he knew, with cheerleaders' cries, words of abuse, and phrases from familiar road signs, in Afrikaans. '*Sakabona Voetsak hambakahle hou links malingi mushle – Vrystaat!*' The brothers and sister rocked their rickety chairs back ecstatically on two legs when it was played, but Matt listened with eyes narrowed and tongue turned up to touch his teeth, like an ornithologist who is bringing back alive the song of rare birds. 'Boy, thanks. Fan-tastic. That'll go into the documentary I'm going to make. Partly with my father's movie camera, I hope, and partly with my candid stills. I'm working on the script now. It's in the family, you see.' He had already explained that his father was writing a book (several books, one about each country they visited in fact) and his mother was helping. 'They keep to a strict schedule. They start work around noon and carry on until about one a.m. That's why I've got to be out of the house very early in the morning and I'm not supposed to come back in till they wake up for lunch. And that's why I've got to keep out of the house in the afternoons, too; they got to have peace *and* quiet. For sleep *and* for work.'

Jenny said, 'Did you see his shorts – that Madras stuff you read about? The colours run when it's washed. I wish you could buy it here.'

'That's a marvellous transistor, Dad.' Mark sat with his big bare feet flat on the courtyard flagstones and his head hung back in the sun – as if he didn't live in it all the year round, at home; but this was France he basked in, not sunlight.

'W-e-ll, they spoil their children terribly. Here's a perfect example. A fifty-pound camera's a toy. What's there left for them to want when they grow up?'

Clive would have liked them to talk about Matt all the time. He said, 'They've got a Maserati at home in America, at least, they did have, they've sold it now they're going round the world.'

The mother said, 'Poor little devil, shut out in the streets with all that rubbish strung around his neck.'

'Ho, rubbish, I'm sure!' said Clive, shrugging and turning up his palms exaggeratedly. 'Of course, hundreds of dollars of equipment are worth nothing, you know, nothing at all.'

'And how much is one dollar, may I ask, mister?' Jenny had learned by heart, on the plane, the conversion tables supplied by the travel agency.

'I don't know how much it is in our money – I'm talking about America –'

'You're not to go down out of the village with him, Clive, ay, only in the village,' his father said every day.

He didn't go out of the village with the family, either. He didn't go to see the museum at Antibes or the potteries at Vallauris or even the palace, casino, and aquarium at Monte Carlo. The ancient hill village inside its walls, whose disorder of streets had been as confusing as the dates and monuments of Europe's overlaid and overlapping past, became the intimate map of their domain – his and Matt's. The alley cats shared it but the people, talking their unintelligible tongue, provided a babble beneath which, while performed openly in the streets, his activities with Matt acquired secrecy: as they went about, they were hidden even more than by the usual self-preoccupation of adults. They moved from morning till night with intense purpose; you had to be quick around corners, you mustn't be seen crossing the street, you must appear as if from nowhere among the late afternoon crowd in the *Place* and move among them quite unobtrusively. One of the things they were compelled to do was to get from the church – very old, with chicken-wire where the stained glass must have been, and a faint mosaic, like a flaking transfer – to under the school windows without attracting the attention of the children. This had to be done in the morning, when school was in session; it was just one of the stone houses, really, without playgrounds: the dragging chorus of voices coming from it reminded him of the schools for black children at home. At other times the village children tailed them, jeering and mimicking, or in obstinate silence, impossible to shake off. There were fights and soon he learned to make with his fingers effective insulting signs he didn't understand, and to shout his one word of French, their bad word – *merde*!

And Matt talked all the time. His low, confidential English lifted to the cheerful rising cadence of French as his voice bounced out to greet people and rebounded from the close walls back to the privacy of English and their head-lowered conclave again. Yet even when his voice had dropped to a whisper, his round dark eyes, slightly depressed at the outer corners by the beginning of an intelligent frown above his dainty nose, moved, parenthetically alert, over everyone within orbit. He greeted people he had never seen before just as he greeted local inhabitants. He would stop beside a couple of sightseers or a plumber lifting a manhole and converse animatedly. To his companion standing by, his French sounded much more French than when the village children spoke it. Matt shrugged his shoulders and thrust out his lower lip while he talked, and if some of the people he accosted were uncomfortable or astonished at being addressed volubly, for no particular reason, by someone they didn't know, he asked them questions (Clive could hear they were questions) in the jolly tone of voice that grown-ups use to kid children out of their shyness.

Sometimes one of the inhabitants, sitting outside his or her doorway on a hard chair, would walk inside and close the door when Matt called out conversationally. 'The people in this town are really psychotic, I can tell you,' he would say with enthusiasm, dropping back to English. 'I know them all, every one of them, and I'm not kidding.' The old women in wrinkled black stockings, long aprons and wide black hats who sat on the *Place* stringing beans for Chez Riane, the open-air restaurant, turned walnut-meat faces and hissed toothlessly like geese when Matt approached. Riane ('She topped the popularity poll in Paris, can you believe it? It was just about the time of the Flood, my father says'), a woman the size of a prize fighter who bore to the displayed posters of herself the kinship of a petrified trunk to a twig in new leaf, growled something at Matt from the corner of her vivid mouth. 'I've got some great pictures of *her*. Of course, she's a bit *passée*.'

They got chased when Matt took a picture of a man and a girl kissing down in the parking area below the château. Clive carried his box camera about with him, now, but he only took pictures of the cats. Matt promised that Clive would get a shot of the dwarf – a real man, not in a circus – who turned the spit in the restaurant that served lamb cooked the special way they did it here, but, as Matt said, Clive didn't have the temperament for a great photographer. He was embarrassed, ashamed, and frightened when the dwarf's enormous head with its Spanish dancer's sideburns reddened with a temper too big for him. But Matt had caught him on the Polaroid; they went off to sit in someone's doorway hung with strips of coloured plastic to keep out flies, and had a look. There was the dwarf's head, held up waggling on his little body like the head of a finger-puppet. 'Fan-tastic.' Matt was not boastful but professional in his satisfaction. 'I didn't have a good one of him before, just my luck, we hadn't been here a week when he went crazy and was taken off to some hospital. He's only just come back into circulation, it's a good thing you didn't miss him. You might've gone back to Africa and not seen him.'

The family, who had admired the boy's Madras shorts or his transistor radio, enjoyed the use of his elegant little record player, or welcomed a friend for Clive, began to find him too talkative, too often present, and too much on the streets. Clive was told that he *must* come along with the family on some of their outings. They drove twenty miles to eat some fish made into soup. They took up a whole afternoon looking at pictures. 'What time'll we be back?' he would rush in from the street to ask. 'I don't know – sometime in the afternoon.' 'Can't we be back by two?' 'Why on earth should we tie ourselves down to a time? We're on holiday.' He would rush back to the street to relay the unsatisfactory information.

When the family came home, the slim little figure with its trappings would be ready to wave at them from the bottom of their street. Once in the dark they made him out under the streetlight that streaked and flattened his face and that of the village half-wit and his dog; he looked up from conversation as if he had been waiting for a train that would come in on time. Another day there was a message laid out in the courtyard with matches end-to-end: WILL SEE YOU LATER MATT.

'What's the matter with those people, they don't even take the child down to the beach for a swim,' said the mother. Clive heard, but was not interested. He had never been in the pink house with the Ali Baba pots. Matt emerged like one of the cats, and he usually had money. They found a place that sold bubblegum and occasionally they had pancakes – Clive didn't know that that was what they were going to be when Matt said he was going to buy some crêpes and what kind of jam did Clive like? Matt paid; there was his documentary film, and he was also writing a book – 'There's a lot of money in kids' books actually written by a kid,' he explained to the family. It was a spy story – 'Really exotic.' He expected to do well out of it, and he might sell some of his candid shots to *Time* and *Life* as well.

But one particularly lovely morning Clive's mother said as if she couldn't prevent herself, perhaps Matt would like to come with the family to the airport? The boys could watch the jets land while the grownups had business with the reservation office. 'Order yourselves a lemonade if you want it,' said the father; he meant that he would pay when he came back. They drank a lemonade-and-ice-cream each and then Matt said he'd like a black coffee to wash it down, so they ordered two coffees, and the father was annoyed when he got the bill – coffee was nothing at home, but in France they seemed to charge you for the glass of water you got with it.

'I can drink five or six coffees a day, it doesn't bother my liver,' Matt told everyone. And in Nice, afterwards, trailing round the Place Masséna behind Jenny, who wanted to buy a polo shirt like the ones all the French girls were wearing, the boys were not even allowed to go and look at the fountain alone, in case they got lost. Matt's voice fell to a whisper in Clive's ear but Clive hardly heard and did not answer: here, Matt was just an appendage of the family, like any other little boy.

It was Saturday and when they drove home up the steep road (the half-wit and his dog sat at the newly installed traffic light and Matt, finding his voice, called out of the window a greeting in French) the village was already beginning to choke with weekend visitors. Directly lunch was down the boys raced to meet beneath the plaque that commemorated the birth in this street of Xavier Duval, Resistance fighter, killed on the 20th October, 1944. Clive was there first and, faithfully carrying out the technique and example of his friend, delightedly managed to take a candid shot of Matt before Matt realized that he was observed. It was one of the best afternoons they'd had. 'Saturdays are always good,' said Matt. 'All these psychotic people around. Just keep your eyes open, brother. I wrote Chapter Fourteen of my book at lunch. Oh, it was on a tray in my room – they were out until about four this morning and they didn't get up. It's set in this airport, you see – remember how you could just see my mouth moving and you couldn't hear a thing in the racket with that jet taking off? – well, someone gets murdered right there drinking coffee and no one hears the scream.'

They were walking through the car-park, running their hands over the nacre-sleek hoods of sports models, and half-attentive to a poodle-fight near the *petanque* pitch and a human one that seemed about to break out at the busy entrance to the men's lavatories that tunnelled under the *Place*. 'Ah, I've got enough shots of delinquents to last me,' Matt said. In accord they went on past the old girl in flowered trousers who was weeping over her unharmed, struggling poodle, and up the steps to the *place*, where most of the local inhabitants and all the visitors, whose cars jammed the park and stopped up the narrow streets, were let loose together, herded by Arab music coming from the boutique run by the French Algerians, on the château side, and the recorded voice, passionately hoarse, of Riane in her prime, from the direction of Chez Riane. The dwarf was there, talking between set teeth to a beautiful blonde American as if he were about to tear her apart with them; her friends were ready to die laughing, but looked kindly in order not to show it. The old women with their big black hats and apron-covered stomachs took up space on the benches. There were more poodles and an Italian greyhound like a piece of wire jewellery. Women who loved each other sat at the little tables outside Riane's, men who loved each other sat in identical mauve jeans and pink shirts, smoking outside Zizi's Bar. Men and women in beach clothes held hands, looking into the doorways of the little shops and bars, and pulling each other along as the dogs pulled along their owners on fancy leashes. At the Crêperie, later, Matt pointed out Clive's family, probably eating their favourite liqueur pancakes, but Clive jerked him away.

They watched *petanque* for a while; the butcher, a local champion, was playing to the gallery, all right. He was pink and wore a tourist's fish-net vest through which wisps of reddish chest-hair twined like a creeper. A man with a long black cape and a huge cat's whisker moustache caused quite a stir. 'My God, I've been trying to get him for weeks –' Matt ducked, Clive quickly following, and they zigzagged off through the *petanque* spectators. The man had somehow managed to drive a small English sports car right up on to the *Place*; it was forbidden, but although the part-time policeman who got into uniform for Saturday afternoons was shouting at him, the man couldn't be forced to take it down again because whatever gap it had found its way through was closed by a fresh influx of people. 'He's a painter,' Matt said. 'He lives above the shoemaker's, you know that little hole. He doesn't ever come out except Saturdays and Sundays. I've got to get a couple of good shots of him. He looks to me the type that gets famous. Really psychotic, eh?' The painter had with him a lovely, haughty girl dressed like Sherlock Holmes in a man's tweeds and deerstalker. 'The car must be hers,' said Matt. 'He hasn't made it, yet; but I can wait.' He used up almost a whole film: 'With a modern artist, you want a few new angles.'

Matt was particularly talkative, even going right into Zizi's Bar to say hello her husband, Emile. The family were still sitting at the Crêperie; the father signed to Clive to come over and at first he took no notice. Then he stalked up between the tables. 'Yes?'

'Don't you want some money?'

Before he could answer, Matt began jerking a thumb frantically. He ran. His father's voice barred him: 'Clive!' But Matt had come flying: 'Over there – a woman's just fainted or died or something. We got to go –'

'What *for*?' said the mother.

'God almighty,' said Jenny.

He was gone with Matt. They fought and wriggled their way into the space that had been cleared, near the steps, round a heavy woman lying on the ground. Her clothes were twisted; her mouth bubbled. People argued and darted irresistibly out of the crowd to do things to her; those who wanted to try and lift her up were pulled away by those who thought she ought to be left. Someone took off her shoes. Someone ran for water from Chez Riane but the woman couldn't drink it. One day the boys had found a workman in his blue outfit and cement-crusted boots lying snoring near the old pump outside the Bar Tabac, where the men drank. Matt got him, too; you could always use a shot like that for a dead body, if the worst came to the worst. But this was the best ever. Matt finished up what was left of the film with the painter on it and had time to put in a new one, while the woman still lay there, and behind the noise of the crowd and the music the see-saw hoot of the ambulance could be heard, coming up the road to the village walls from the port below. The ambulance couldn't get on to the *Place*, but the men in their uniforms carried a stretcher over people's heads and then lifted the woman aboard. Her face was purplish as cold hands on a winter morning and her legs stuck out. The boys were part of the entourage that followed her to the ambulance, Matt progressing with sweeping hops, on bended knee, like a Russian dancer, in order to get the supine body in focus at an upward angle.

When it was all over, they went back to the Crêperie to relate the sensational story to the family; but they had not been even interested enough to stay, and had gone home to the villa. 'It'll be really *something* for you to show them down in Africa!' said Matt. He was using his Minox that afternoon, and he promised that when the films were developed, he would have copies made for Clive. 'Darn it, we'll have to wait until my parents take the films to Nice – you can't get them developed up here. And they only go in on Wednesdays.'

'But I'll be gone by then,' said Clive suddenly.

'Gone? Back to Africa?' All the distance fell between them as they stood head-to-head jostled by the people in the village street, all the distance of the centuries when the continent was a blank outline on the maps, as well as the distance of miles. 'You mean you'll be back in *Africa*?'

Clive's box camera went into his cupboard along with the other souvenirs of Europe that seemed to have shed their evocation when they were unpacked amid the fresh, powerful familiarity of home. He boasted a little, the first day of the new term at school, about the places he had been to; but within a few weeks, when cities and palaces that he had seen for himself were spoken of in history or geography classes, he did not mention that he had visited them and, in fact, the textbook illustrations and descriptions did not seem to be those of anything he knew. One day he searched for his camera to take to a sports meeting, and found an exposed film in it. When it was developed, there were the pictures of the cats. He turned them this way up and that, to make out the thin, feral shapes on cobblestones and the disappearing blurs round the blackness of archways. There was also the picture of the American boy, Matt, a slim boy with knees made big out of focus, looking – at once suspicious and bright – from under his uncut hair.

The family crowded round to see, smiling, filled with pangs for what the holiday was and was not, while it lasted. 'The *Time-Life* man himself!' 'Poor old Matt – what was his other name?' 'You ought to send it to him,' said the mother. 'You've got the address? Aren't you going to keep in touch?'

But there was no address. The boy Matt had no street, house, house in a street, room in a house like the one they were in. 'America,' Clive said, 'he's in America.'

Otherwise Birds Fly In

Toni and Kate still saw each other regularly once or twice a year.

One would have quite expected Toni to be out of sight, by now; Kate would have accepted this as inevitable, if it had happened, and have looked up with affection at the bright passage of the little satellite among other worlds. Yet since Toni's extraordinary marriage, their alliance had survived their slummy bachelor-girlhood together, just as it had survived school. Perhaps it was because both had had no family to speak of, and had thought of themselves as independent rather than as good as orphaned. Certainly nothing else clung to either from the school in the Bernese Oberland where they had been part of an international community of five- to eighteen-year-olds displaced by war and divorce – their parents' war, and the wars between their parents. Kate was born in 1934, in Malta, where her father was an English naval officer. He was blown up in a submarine in the early forties, and her mother married an American major and went to live in St Louis; somehow Kate was ceded to Europe, got left behind at the École Internationale, and spent her holidays with her grandmother in Hertfordshire. Toni had a father somewhere – at school, when her mail arrived, she used to tear off the beautiful stamps from Brazil, for the collection of a boy she was keen on: days would go by before she would take her father's letter from the mutilated envelope. As she grew old enough to be knowing, she gathered that her English mother had gone off with someone her family loathed; though what sort of man that would be, Toni could not imagine, because her mother's family were English socialists of the most peace-proselytizing sort – indeed, this made them choose to let her grow up in an international school in a neutral country, their hostage to one world.

At the school, Toni and Kate were 'friends' in the real, giggly, perfectly exclusive, richly schoolgirl sense of the word. Kate played the flute and was top in maths. Toni was the best skier in the school and too busy keeping up with her passionate pen-friend correspondence in four languages to do much work. The things they did well and in which each was most interested, they could not do together, and yet they were a pair, meeting in a euphoric third state each alone conjured up in the other. In their last year their room was decorated with a packing-case bar with empty vermouth bottles that Toni thought looked crazily homely. *Mutti* (Frau Professor) Sperber used to come and sniff at them, just to make sure; now and then, as women, Toni and Kate were reminded of things like this, but they were not dependent upon 'amusing' memories for contact.

When Kate left school her grandmother paid for her to study music in Geneva. The two girls had always talked of Toni going off to ride about vast haciendas in Brazil, but as she grew up letters from her father came more and more irregularly – finally, one didn't know for certain whether he was still in Brazil, never mind the haciendas. She tried England for a few months; the English relatives thought she ought to take up nursing or work on a Quaker self-help project among the poor of Glasgow. She got back to Switzerland on a free air trip won by composing a jingle at a trade fair, and moved in with Kate, imitating for her the speech, mannerisms, and impossible kindness of the English relatives. In Geneva she seemed to attract offers of all kinds of jobs without much effort on her part. She met Kate several times a day to report, over coffee.

'To India? But who's this man?'

'Something to do with the UN delegation. His beard's trained up under his turban at the sides, like a creeper. He says I'd spend six months a year in Delhi and six here.'

She and Kate shared a flat in Geneva for five years; at least, Kate was there all the time, and Toni came and went. She spent three months in Warsaw typing material for a Frenchman who was bringing out a book on the Polish cinema. Another time she accompanied an old Australian lady home to Brisbane, and came back to Europe by way of Tokyo and Hong Kong, eking out funds by working as a hotel receptionist. An Italian film director noticed her at an exhibition and asked her what she did; she replied in her good Italian accent, with her pretty, capable grin, 'I live.' He and his mistress invited her to join a party of friends for a week in Corsica. Toni met people as others pick up food poisoning or fleas – although she was without money or position, soon a network of friends-of-friends was there across the world for her to balance on.

Between times, life was never dull at home in the tiny Geneva flat; Toni took a job as a local tourist guide and the two girls entertained their friends on beer and sausage, and, coming home late at night, used to wake up one another to talk about their love affairs. Kate had dragged on a long and dreary one with a middle-aged professor who taught composition and had an asthmatic wife. They discussed him for hours, arranging and rearranging the triangle of wife, asthma, and Kate. They could not find a satisfactory pattern. Although this was never formulated in so many words, they had plumbed (but perhaps it had been there always, instinctive basis of their being 'friends' against other indications of temperament) a touchstone in common: what finally mattered wasn't the graph of an event or human relationship in its *progress*, but the casual or insignificant sign or moment you secretly took away from it. So that they knew nothing would come of recomposing the triangle. Just as Kate understood when Toni said of the disastrous end of an affair in England with a bad poet – 'But there *was* that day in Suffolk, when we went to see the old church at the sea and he read out just as he ducked his head under the door, "Please close behind you otherwise birds fly in." That was his one good line.'

Kate had been the intellectual with talent and opportunity, when they left school. Yet it was Toni who moved on the fringe of the world of fashionable thinkers, painters, writers and politicians. Kate passed exams at the conservatoire, all right, but she was away down in the anonymous crowd when it came to scholarships and honours. Long after her days at the conservatoire were over she still dressed like a student, going happily about Geneva with her long, thick blonde hair parting on the shoulders of her old suede jacket. She was content to teach, and to continue experiments with electronic music with a young man she was, at last, in love with. Egon was living in the flat with her when the cable came: 'Arriving Sunday with friend. Take a deep breath.' At the time, Toni had her best job yet – away commuting between Paris and New York as something called per-sonal assistant to an elderly oil man with a collection of modern paintings. That Sunday night, she stood in the doorway, a carrier smelling of truffles balanced on her hip. Next to her, holding lilies and a bottle of Poire William, was a prematurely bald young man with a dark, withdrawn face that was instantly familiar. 'Where're your things?' Egon said, making to go downstairs for the luggage. 'We came as we were,' said Toni, dumping her burden and hugging him, laughing.

Food, drink, and flowers lay on the old ottoman. That was to be Toni's luggage, in future. The young man's face was familiar because he was Marcus Kelp, a second-generation shipping magnate badgered by picture magazine photographers not only because his yacht and houses were frequented by actresses, but also because he conceived and financed social rehabilitation and land reclamation schemes in countries where he had no 'interests'. He and Toni were blazingly in love with each other. She was proud that he was not a playboy; she would have married him if he had been one of his own deck-hands. Yet her child-like pleasure in the things she could, suddenly, do and buy and give away, was intoxicating. When first Kate and Egon were married, Toni used to telephone Geneva at odd hours from all over the world; but in time she no longer needed to find ways to demonstrate to herself that she could do whatever she wanted, she grew used to the conveniences of being a rich woman. She was drawn into the preoccupations of life on Marcus's scale; she went with him on his business about the world (they had houses and apartments everywhere) not allowing even the birth of her daughter to keep her at home. Later, of course, she was sometimes persuaded to accept some invitation that he had to forgo because of the necessity to be somewhere dull, and gradually, since her responsibilities towards her child and various households were taken care of by servants, she acquired a rich woman's life of her own. Yet once or twice a year, always, she arrived at Kate's for a night or a day or two, with Poire William and flowers. Egon was still at the institute for musical research; he and Kate had a car, a daily cleaning-woman, and one of those Swiss houses withdrawn behind green in summer, shutters in winter.

Kate had owed Toni a letter for months when she wrote, mentioning in a general round-up of personal news that she and Egon hoped to go to France in the spring. She was surprised when at once a letter came back from London saying wouldn't it be fun to meet somewhere and spend part of the holiday together?

It was years since Kate had spent any length of time with Toni. 'Toni and Marcus want to come with us!' she told Egon; they were very fond of Marcus, with his dry honesty and his rich man's conscience. But Toni drove alone up to the villa near Pont du Loup with her little daughter, Emma, standing beside her on the nanny's lap. 'Oh Marcus can't leave the Nagas,' Toni said. At once she went enthusiastically through the small rented house.

Later, in the content of lunch outdoors, Egon said, 'What was that about Nagaland? Since when?'

'You know how Marcus takes the whole world on his shoulders. He went to Pakistan in July, that's how it started. Now they're absolutely depending on him. Well, he doesn't know what he's missing' – Toni was already in her bikini, and the strong muscles of her belly, browned all winter in Barbados and Tunisia, contracted energetically as she thrust out her glass at arm's length for some more wine, and Kate and Egon laughed. Emma ran about, tripping on the uneven flagstones and landing hard on her frilly bottom – something she found very funny. She spoke French and only a few words of English, because the nanny was French. 'And what an accent!' Toni didn't bother for the woman to be out of earshot. 'It wouldn't have done at the École Internationale, I can tell you.' And she picked up the child and wouldn't let her go, so that they could hear her furious protests in provincial French as she struggled to get down.

Toni wanted to go to the beach right away, that afternoon. They drove down the steep roads of the river gorge to the sea they knew, from the house's terrace, as a misty borderland between horizon and sky. Sitting or standing on the stony beach was putting one's weight on a bag of marbles, but Toni carried Emma astride her neck into the water, and the two of them floundered and ducked and gasped with joy. 'I must teach her to swim. Perhaps I'll take her along to Yugoslavia this summer, after all.' Toni came out of the sea looking like a beautiful little blonde seal, the shiny brown flesh of her legs shuddering sturdily as she manoeuvred the stones. They were in their early thirties, she and Kate, and Toni was at the perfection of her feminine rounding-out. There was no slack, and there were no wrinkles; she had the physical assurance of a woman who has been attractive so long that she cannot imagine a change ahead. Kate's body had gone soft and would pass unnoticeably into middle age; the deep concentration of her blue eyes was already a contrast to her faded face and freckled lips.

Kate and Egon were stimulated – and touched – that first afternoon, by the fun of having Toni there, so quick to enjoyment, so full of attack, a presence like a spot-light bringing out colour and detail. It was exciting to find that this quality of hers was, if anything, stronger than ever; hectic, almost. They were slightly ashamed to discover how quiet-living they had become, and pleased to find that they could still break out of this with zest. They left the beach late, lingered at the fishing-harbour where Toni and Emma got into conversation with a fisherman and were given a newspaper full of fresh sardines, and half-way home in the dark they decided to have dinner at a restaurant they liked the look of. The food was remarkable, they drank a lot of pastis and wine, and Emma chased moths until she fell asleep in a chair. The nanny was disapproving when they got home and they all apologized rather more profusely than they would have thought necessary had they been sober.

In the days that followed they went to another beach, and another – they would never have been so energetic if it had not been for Toni. She anointed them with some marvellous unguent everyone used in Jamaica, and they turned the colour of a nicotine stain, in the sun. But after three days, when Kate and Egon were beginning to feel particularly drugged and well, Toni began to talk about places farther away, inland. There was a Polish painter living near Albi – it might be fun to look him up? Well, what about Arles then – had they ever eaten sausage or seen the lovely Roman theatre at Arles? And the Camargue? One must see the white horses there, eh? But even Arles was a long way, Egon said; one couldn't do it in a day. 'Why a day?' Toni said. 'Let's just get in the car and go.' And the baby? 'Emma and Mathilde will stay here, Mathilde will love to have the place to herself, to be in charge – you know how they are.'

They went off in the morning, in the spring sun with the hood of

Toni's car down. It had rained and the air smelled of herbs when they stopped to eat Kate's picnic lunch. They stood and looked down the valley where peasants were spraying the vines in new leaf, so thin, tender, and so brilliant a green that the sun struck through them, casting a shivering yellow light on hands and bare arms moving there. A long, chalky-mauve mountain rode the distance as a ship comes over an horizon. 'Is it Sainte-Victoire?' said Kate. If so, it didn't seem to be in quite the right place; she and Egon argued eagerly. Toni sat on a rock between the rosemary bushes with a glass of wine in one hand and a chunk of crust thick with cheese in the other, and grinned at them between large, sharp bites.

Egon was, as Toni said delightedly, 'quite corrupted' by the Jaguar and couldn't resist taking her up to ninety on the auto-route. Kate and Toni called him Toad and laughed to themselves at the solemn expression on his face as he crouched his tall body in the seat. They reached Arles in the middle of the afternoon and found a little hotel up in the old town. There was time to have a look at the theatre and the medieval cloister. In the Roman arena, as they walked past at dusk, a team of small boys was playing soccer. Toni stood watching the moon come up while Egon and Kate climbed to the stone roof of the church. Her back was quite still, jaunty, as she stood; she turned to smile, watching them come down out of the dark doorway. 'I can't explain,' Kate was saying, 'it seems to me the most satisfying old town I've ever been in. The way when you're in the theatre you can see the pimply spires of the medieval buildings . . . and that figure on top of the church, rising up over everything, peering over the Roman walls. The boys yelling down in the arena . . .' 'Kate, darling!' Toni smiled. 'Well, we'll see it all properly tomorrow,' Kate said. And over dinner, Egon was earnestly ecstatic: 'What I can't believe is the way the farm buildings have that perfect rectilinear relationship with the size and perspective of the fields – and the trees, yes. I thought that was simply van Gogh's vision that did it –?' He had driven very slowly indeed along the road beneath the plane trees that led from Aix to Arles. Late that night Kate leant on the window in her nightgown, looking out into the splotchy moon-and-dark of the little courtyard garden and could not come to bed.

But they left next morning straight after coffee, after all.

'We buy a *saucisson d'Arles* and we're on our way, eh? Don't you think so?' Toni drew deeply on her first cigarette and pulled the sympathetic, intimate face of accord over something that didn't have to be discussed.

Egon said, 'Whatever you girls want to do'; and Kate wouldn't have dreamt of getting them to hang on a second day in Arles just because she wanted another look at things they'd already seen. It wasn't all that important. They drove rather dreamily through the Camargue and didn't talk much – the watery landscape was conducive to contemplation rather than communication. A salt wind parted the pelt of grasses this way and that and the hackles of the grey waters rose to it. Egon said he could make out floating dark dots as waterfowl, but there was no sign of the white horses Toni wanted to see, except in the riding stables around Les Saintes-Maries-de-la-Mer. Toni disappeared into one of the village shops there and came out in a pair of skin-tight cowboy pants and a brilliant shirt, to make them laugh. The sun strengthened and they sat and drank wine; Kate wandered off and when she came back remarked that she had had a look at the ancient Norman church. Toni, with her legs sprawled before her in classic Western style, looked dashing by no other effort than her charming indolence. 'Should we see it, too?' Egon asked. 'Oh I don't think . . . there's nothing much,' Kate said with sudden shyness.

'It's nice, nice, nice, here,' Toni chanted to herself, turning her face up to the sun.

'I'm going to take a picture of you for Marcus,' said Kate.

'Shall we have some more wine?' Egon said to Toni.

She nodded her head vehemently, and beamed at her friends.

When the wine came and they were all three drinking, Egon said – 'Then let's spend the night. Stay here. We can look at the church. I suppose there's some sort of hotel.'

Kate broke the moment's pause. 'Oh I don't think we'd want to. I mean the church is nothing.'

They crossed the Rhône at Bac de Bacarin early in the afternoon. 'We should go back to Saintes-Maries in the autumn, there's something between a religious procession and a rodeo, then – let's do that,' said Toni; and Egon, just as if he could leave the institute whenever he felt like it and he and Kate had money to travel whenever they pleased, agreed – 'The four of us.'

'Yes, let's. Only Marcus hates Europe. We're supposed to be going to North Africa in October. Oh, we can eat in Marseilles tonight.' Toni had taken out the road map. 'Must eat a bouillabaisse in Marseilles. But we don't want to sleep there, mm?'

After she had bought them a wonderful dinner they lost their way in the dark making, as she suggested, for 'some little place' along the coast. They ended up at Bandol, in a hotel that was just taking the dust covers off in preparation for the season. Before morning, they saw nothing of the place but the glitter of black water and the nudging and nodding of masts under the window. In the room Kate and Egon slept in, last season's cockroaches ran out from under the outsize whore of a bed behind whose padded head were the cigarette butts of many occupants. Kate woke early in the musty room and got Egon up to come out and walk. The ugly glass restaurants along the sea-front were closed and the palms rustled dryly as they do when the air is cold. Fishermen had spread a huge length of net along the broad walk where, in a month's time, hundreds of tourists would crowd up and down. Without them the place was dead, as a person who has taken to drink comes to life only when he gets the stuff that has destroyed him. When they walked back through the remains of the hotel garden – it had almost all been built upon in the course of additions and alterations in various styles – Egon pointed out a plaque at the entrance. *Il est trois heures. Je viens d'achever 'Félicité' . . . Dieu sait que j'ai été heureuse en l'écrivant. – Katherine Mansfield. Jeudi 28 février 1918.* 'My God yes, of course, I'd forgotten,' Kate said. 'It was Bandol. She wrote "Bliss" here. This place.' Kate and Toni as young girls had felt the peculiar affinity that young girls feel for Katherine Mansfield – dead before they were born – with her meticulously chronicled passions, her use of pet-names, her genius and her suffering. Somewhere within this barracks of thick carpets and air-conditioned bars were buried the old rooms of the hotel in a garden, in a village, where she had lain in exile, coughing, waiting for letters from Bogey, and fiercely struggling to work. 'We must show Toni,' Egon said.

'No don't. Don't say anything.'

Egon looked at Kate. Her face was anxious, curiously ashamed as it had been the day before, in Les Saintes-Maries-de-la-Mer.

'I don't think she's enjoying . . . it all . . . everything, the way we are.'

'But you're the one who said we shouldn't stay, in the Camargue. You were the one –'

'I have the feeling it's not the same for her, Egon. She can't help it. She can go everywhere she likes whenever she likes. The South Seas or Corinthia – or Zanzibar. She could be there now. Couldn't she? Why here rather than there?' Her voice slowed to a stop.

Egon made as if to speak, and the impulse was crossed by counter impulses of objection, confusion.

'The world's beautiful,' said Kate.

'You're embarrassed to be enjoying yourself!' Egon accused.

The whole exchange was hurried, parenthetic, as they walked along the hotel corridors, and then suddenly suppressed as they reached their rooms and Toni herself appeared, banging her door behind her, calling out to them.

Kate said quickly, 'No, for *her*. I mean if she were to find out . . . about herself.'

They were back at the villa by evening, and all shared the good mood of being 'home' again. For the next few days, Kate and Egon were not inclined to leave the terrace; they read and wrote letters and went no farther than the shops in the village, while Toni drove up and down to the beaches with Emma and the nurse. But on the day before Toni was to leave, Kate went along with her to the beach. She and Toni ate lobster in a beach restaurant, very much at ease; all their lives, there would always be this level at which they were more at ease with each other than they would ever be with anyone else. The child and the nanny had something sent down to them on the beach. Mathilde had been promised that she would be taken into Nice to buy a souvenir for her sister, but Toni couldn't face the idea of the town, after lunch, and with the wheedling charm disguising command that Kate noticed she had learnt in the past few years, asked the nanny to take the bus: she would be picked up later, and could leave the child behind.

Wherever Toni went she bought a pile of magazines in several languages; the wind turned their pages, while the two women dozed and smoked. At one stage Kate realized that Toni was gone, and Emma. Being alone somehow woke her up; on her rubber mattress, she rolled on to her stomach and began to read antique and picture dealers' advertisements. Then the position in which she was lying brought on a muscular pain in the shoulder-blade that she was beginning to be plagued with, the last few years, and she got up and took a little walk towards the harbour. She was rotating the shoulder gently as the masseuse had told her and quite suddenly – it was as if she had thought of the child and she had materialized – there was Emma, lying in the water between two fishing boats. She was face-down, like a fallen doll. Kate half-stumbled, half-jumped into the oily water awash with fruit skins – she actually caught her left foot in a rope as she landed in the water, and, in panic for the child, threshed wildly to free herself. She reached the child easily and hauled her up the side of one of the boats, letting her roll over on to the deck, while she herself climbed aboard. All the things that ought to be done came back to her shaking hands. She thrust her forefinger like a hook into the little mouth and pulled the tongue forward. She snatched a bit of old awning and crammed it tight under the stomach so that the body would be at an angle to have the water expelled from the lungs. She was kneeling, shaking, working frantically among stinking gut and fins, and the water and vomit that poured from the child. She pressed her mouth to the small, slimy blue lips and tried to remember exactly, exactly, how it was done, how she had read about it, making a casual mental note, in the newspapers. She didn't scream for help; there was no time, she didn't even know if anyone passed on the quay – afterwards she knew there had been the sound of strolling footsteps, but the greatest concentration she had ever summoned in all her life had cut her off from everything and everyone: she and the child were alone between life and death. And in a little while, the child began to breathe, time came back again, the existence of other people, the possibility of help. She picked her up and carried her, a vessel full of priceless breath, out of the mess of the boat and on to the quay, and then broke into a wild run, running, running, for the beach restaurant.

And that had been all there was to it; as she kept telling Toni. In twenty-four hours Emma was falling hard on her bottom on the terrace again and laughing, but Toni had to be told about it, over and over, and to tell over and over how one moment Emma was playing with Birgit Sorenson's dachshund (Toni had just that minute run into the Sorensons, she hadn't known their yacht was in the harbour) and the next moment child and dog were gone. 'Then we saw the dóg up the quay towards the boathouse end –' and of course the child had gone the other way, and they didn't know it. Marcus was flying back from Pakistan; but what Toni could not face was Mathilde: 'She never looks at me, never, without thinking that it could not have happened with her; I see it in her face.'

They were sitting on the terrace in the evening, letting Toni talk it out. 'Then get rid of her,' said Kate.

'Yes, let her go,' Egon urged. 'It could have happened with anybody, remember that.'

Toni said to Kate in the dark, 'But it was you. *That* couldn't have been anyone else.'

This idea persisted. Toni believed that because it was her child who lay in the water, Kate had woken up and walked to the spot. No one else would have known, no one else could have given her child back to her. The idea became a question that demanded some sort of answer. She had to do something. She wanted to give Kate – a present. What else? As time went by the need became more pressing. She had to give Kate a present. But what? 'Why shouldn't I give them the little house in Spain?' As she said this to her husband Marcus, she instantly felt light and relieved.

'By all means. If you imagine that they would strike such a bargain.' He had listened to her account of that day, many times, in silence, but she did not know what he would say if she wanted to take Emma away with her anywhere, again.

She thought of a new car; Egon had so enjoyed driving the Jaguar. Yet the idea of simply arriving with the deed of a house or a new car filled her with a kind of shyness; she was afraid of a certain look passing between Kate and Egon, the look of people who know something about you that you don't know yourself. At last one day she felt impatiently determined to have done with it, to forget it once and for all, and she went once again through her jewellery, looking for a piece – something – something worthy – for Kate. She arrived unannounced in Geneva with a little suede pouch containing a narrow emerald-and-diamond collar. 'I've smuggled this bauble in, Kate, you do just as you like with it – sell it if you can't stand the sight of such things. But I thought it might look nice round your long neck.'

It lay on the table among the coffee-cups, and Kate and Egon looked at it but did not touch it. Toni thought: as if it might bite.

Kate said kindly, 'It's from Marcus's family. Toni, you must keep it.'

'Sell the damn thing!'

They laughed.

'Surely I'm entitled to give you something?'

They did not look at each other; Toni was watching them very carefully.

'Toni,' Kate said, 'you've forgotten my Poire William and the flowers.'

A Satisfactory Settlement

A sagging hulk of an American car, its bodywork like coloured tinfoil that has been screwed into a ball and smoothed out, was beached on the axle of a missing wheel in a gutter of the neighbourhood. Overnight, empty beer cartons appeared against well-oiled wooden gates; out-of-works loped the streets and held converse on corners with nannies in their pink uniforms and houseboys in aprons. In dilapidated out-buildings dating from the time when they housed horses and traps, servants kept all sorts of hangers-on. The estate agent had pointed out that it was one of the quiet old suburbs of Johannesburg where civil servants and university lecturers were the sort of neighbours one had – but of course no one said anything about the natives.

The child was allowed to ride his bicycle on the pavement and he liked to go and look at the car. He and his mother knew none of their neighbours yet, and in the street he simply thought aloud: he said to a barefoot old man in an army greatcoat, 'There's a dead rat by the tree at the corner. I found it yesterday.' And the old man clapped his hands slowly, with the gum-grin of ancients and infants: '*S'bona*, my *baasie*, may the Lord bless you, you are big man.' Under one of the silky oaks of the pavement the child said to a man who had been lying all morning in the shade with a straw hat with a Paisley band over his eyes, and a brand-new transistor radio playing beside his head, 'Did you steal it?'

The man said without moving, 'My friend, I got it in town.' The furze of beard and moustache were drawn back suddenly in a lazy yawn that closed with a snap.

'I saw a dead rat there by the corner.'

'The crock's been pushed to Tanner Road.'

'There's a native boy's got a ten transistor.'

His mother was not interested in any of this intelligence. Her face was fixed in vague politeness, she heard without listening to what was said, just as he did when she talked on the telephone: '... no question of signing *anything* whatever until provision's made . . . my dear Marguerite, I've been fooled long enough, you can put your mind at rest . . . only in the presence of the lawyers . . . the door in his face, that's . . . cut out the parties he takes to the races every Saturday, and the flush dinners, then, if he can't afford to make proper provision . . . *and*, I said, I want a special clause in the maintenance agreement . . . medical expenses *up till the age of twenty-one . . .*'

When his mother was not talking to Marguerite on the telephone it was very quiet in the new house. It was if she were still talking to Marguerite in her mind. She had taken the white bedside radio from her room in the old house – daddy's house – to a swop shop and she had brought home a grey portable typewriter. It stood on the dining-table and she slowly picked out letters with her eyes on the typing manual beside her. The tapping became his mother's voice, stopping and starting, hesitantly and dryly, out of her silence. She was going to get a job and work in an office; he was going to a new school. Later on when everything was settled, she said, he would sometimes spend a weekend with daddy. In the meantime it was the summer holidays and he could do what he liked.

He did not think about the friends he had played with in the old house. The move was only across the town, but for the boy seas and continents might have been between, and the suburb a new country from where Rolf and Sheila were a flash of sun on bicycles on a receding horizon. He could not miss them as he had done when they had been in the house next door and prevented, by some punishment or other, from coming over to play. He wandered in the street; the rat was taken away, but the old man came back again – he was packing and unpacking his paper carrier on the pavement: knotted rags, a half-loaf of brown bread, snuff, a pair of boots whose soles grinned away from the uppers, and a metal funnel. The boy suddenly wanted the funnel, and paid the old man fifteen cents for it. Then he hid it in the weeds in the garden so that his mother wouldn't ask where he'd got it.

The man with the transistor sometimes called out, 'My friend, where are you going?' 'My friend, watch out for the police!'

The boy lingered a few feet off while the man went on talking and laughing, in their own language, with the group that collected outside the house with the white Alsatian.

'Why d'you say that about the policeman?'

The man noticed him again, and laughed. 'My friend, my friend!'

Perhaps the old man had told about the funnel; a funnel like that might cost fifty cents. In a shop. The boy didn't really believe about the policeman; but when the man laughed, he felt he wanted to run away, and laugh back, at the same time. He was drawn to the house with the white Alsatian and would have liked to ride past without hands on the handlebars if only he hadn't been afraid of the Alsatian rushing out to bite the tyres. The Alsatian sat head-on-paws on the pavement among the night-watchman and his friends, but when it was alone behind the low garden wall of the house it screamed, snarled and leapt at the women who went by in slippers and cotton uniforms gaping between the buttons, yelling 'Voetsak!' and 'Suka!' at it. There were also two women who dressed as if they were white, in tight trousers, and had straightened hair and lipstick. One afternoon they had a fight, tearing at each other, sobbing, and swearing in English. The Alsatian went hysterical but the night-watchman had him by the collar.

The old car actually got going – even when the wheel was on, there was still the flat battery, and he put down his bike and helped push. He was offered a ride but stood shaking his head, his chest heaving. A young man in a spotless white golf-cap and a torn and filthy sweater wanted to buy his watch. They had been pushing side by side and they sat in the gutter, smiling like panting dogs. 'I pay you five pounds!' The slim, sticky black hand fingered his wrist, on which the big watch sat a bit off-centre.

'But where have you got five pounds?'

'How I can say I buy from you if I can't have five pounds? I will pay five pounds!'

The impossible size of the sum, quoted in old currency, as one might talk wildly of ducats or doubloons, hung in credible bluff between them. He said of his watch: 'I got it for Christmas.' But what was Christmas to the other?

'Five pounds!'

A nanny pushing a white child in a cart called out something in their language. The hand dropped the skinny wrist and a derisive tongue-click made the boy feel himself dismissed as a baby.

He did not play in the garden. His toys all had been brought along but there was no place for them yet; they stood about in his room with the furniture that had been set here or there by the movers. His mother dragged his bed under the window and asked, 'Is that where you want it?' And he had said, 'I don't know where it's supposed to be.'

The bicycle was the only thing he took out with him into the street. It was a few days before the car turned up again. Then he found it, two blocks away. This time it had two flat tyres and no one did anything about them. But a house down there was one of those with grass planted on the pavement outside and the garden-boy let him go back and forth once or twice with the petrol-motor mower. He went again next day and helped him. The garden-boy wanted to know if his father smoked and asked him to bring cigarettes. He said, 'My father's not here but when we're settled I'll ask for some for you.' He hardly ever went out now without meeting the old man somewhere; the old man seemed to expect him. He brought things out of his paper carrier and showed them to the boy, unwrapped them from rags and the advertising handouts that drift to city gutters. There was a tin finger, from a cigar, a torch without switch or glass, and a broken plastic duck: nothing like the funnel. But the old man, who had the lint of white hairs caught among the whorls on his head, spread the objects on the pavement with the confidence of giving pleasure and satisfaction. He took the boy's hand and put in it the base of some fancy box; this hand on the boy's was strong, shaky, and cold, with thick nails the colour of the tortoise's shell in the old house. The box-base had held a perfume bottle and was covered with stained satin; to the boy it was a little throne but he didn't want it, it was a girl's thing. He said with an exaggerated shrug, 'No money.' 'Yes, my *baasie*, only shilling, shilling. The Lord bless you, *Nkosana*. Only shilling.'

The old man began to wrap it all up again; the base, the duck, the torch and the tin finger. Afterwards, the boy thought that next time he might take the tin cigar finger for, say, two-and-a-half cents, or three. He'd have to buy something. As he rode back to the new house, there was the angle of a straw hat with a Paisley band in a little group chatting, accusing and laughing, and he called out, 'Hullo, my friend!'

'Yes, my friend!' the greeting came back, though the man didn't look round at him.

Then he thought he saw, without the white cap, the one who wanted to buy his watch, and with a hasty wobble of pleasurable panic he rode off fast down the hill, lifting his hands from the bars a moment in case somebody was looking, and taking a chance on the white Alsatian.

When she was not at the typewriter she was on her knees for hours at a time, sorting out boxes and suitcases of things to be got rid of. She had gone through the stuff once when she packed up and left, setting aside hers from his and being brought up short when she came upon some of the few things that seemed indisputably theirs and therefore neither to be disposed of nor rightfully claimed by either. Now she went through all that was hers, and this time, on a different principle of selection, set aside what was useful, relevant and necessary from what was not. All the old nest-papers went into the dustbin: letters, magazines, membership cards, even photographs. Her knees hurt when she rose but she sometimes went on again after she and the child had eaten dinner, and he was in bed.

During the day she did not go out except for consultations with the lawyers and if Marguerite phoned at night to hear the latest, she sat down at the telephone with a gin and bitter lemon – the first opportunity she'd had to think about herself, even long enough to pour a drink. She had spoken to no one round about and awareness of her surroundings was limited to annoyance latent in the repetition of one worn, close-harmony record, mutedly blaring again and again from nearby – a gramophone in some native's *khaya*. But she was too busy getting straight to take much notice of anything; the boy was getting a bit too much freedom – still, he couldn't come to any harm, she supposed he wouldn't go far away, while out of the way. She hadn't seen any of the good friends, since she'd left, and that was fine. There'd been altogether too much talk and everyone ready to tell *her* what she ought to do, one day, and then running off to discuss the 'other side of the story' the next – naturally, it all got back to her.

Marguerite was quite right. She was simply going ahead to provide a reasonable, decent life for herself and her child. She had no vision of this life beyond the statement itself, constantly in her mind like a line of doggerel, and proclaimed aloud in the telephone conversations with Marguerite, but she was seized by the preoccupations of sorting out and throwing away, as if someone had said: dig here.

She walked round the house at night before she went to bed, and checked windows and doors. Of course, she was used to that; but when, as had so often happened, she was left alone in the other house, there were familiar servants who could be trusted. There was no one to depend on here; she had taken the first girl who came to the back door with a reference. It was December and the nights were beautiful, beautiful: she would notice, suddenly, while pulling in a window. Out there in the colour of moonstone nothing moved but the vibration of cicadas and the lights in the valley. Both seemed to make shimmering swells through the warm and palpable radiance. Out there, you would feel it on bare arms while you danced or talked, you could lie on your back on hard terrace stone and feel the strange vertigo of facing the stars.

It was like a postcard of somewhere she had been, and had no power over her in the present. She went to bed and fell asleep at once as if in a night's lodging come upon in the dark.

But after the first few days something began to happen in the middle of the night. It happened every night, or almost every night (she was not sure; sometimes she might have dreamt it, or run, in the morning, the experience of two nights into one). Anyway, it happened often enough to make a pattern of the nights and establish, through unease, a sense of place that did not exist in the light of day.

It was natives, of course; simply one of the nuisances of this quiet neighbourhood. A woman came home in the early hours of the morning from some shebeen. Or she had no home and was wandering the streets. First she was on the edge of a dream, among those jumbled cries and voices where the lines of conscious and subconscious cross. Then she drew closer and clearer as she approached the street, the house, the bed – to which the woman lying there was herself returning, from sleep to wakefulness. There was the point at which the woman in the bed knew herself to be there, lying awake with her body a statue still in the attitude of sleep, and the shadowy room standing back all round her. She lay and listened to the shouts, singing, laughter and sudden cries. It was a monologue; there was no answer, no response. No one joined in the singing and the yells died away in the empty streets. It was impossible not to listen because, apart from the singing, the monologue was in English – always when natives were drunk or abusive they seemed to turn to English or Afrikaans; if it had been in their language she could have shut it out with a pillow over her ears, like the noise of cats. The voice lurched and rambled. Just when it seemed to be retreating, fading round a corner or down the hill, there would be a short, fearful, questioning scream, followed by a waiting silence: then there it was, coming back, very near now, so near that slithering footsteps and the loose slap of heels could be heard between the rise and fall of accusations, protests, and wheedling obscenities. '. . . telling LIARS. I . . . you . . . don't say me I'm cunt . . . and telling liars . . . L-I-A-RS . . . you know? you know? . . . I'm love for that . . . LIARS . . . the man he want fuck . . . LI-A-A-RS . . . my darling I'm love . . . AHH hahahahha-hahoooooee . . . YOU RUBBISH! YOU HEAR! YOU RUBBISH . . .'

And then slowly it was all gathered together again, it staggered away, the whole muddled, drunken burden of it, dragged off some-where, nowhere, anywhere it could not be heard any more. She lay awake until the streets had stifled and hidden it, and then she slept.

Until the next night.

The summons was out of the dark as if the voice came out of her own sleep like those words spoken aloud with which one wakes oneself with a start. YOU RUBBISH . . . don't say me . . . he want . . . L-I-A-R-S . . . don't say me.

Or the horrible jabber when a tape recorder is run backwards. Is that my voice? Shrill, ugly; merely back-to-front? L-I-A-R-S. The voice that had slipped the hold of control, good sense, self-respect, proper provision, the future to think of. My darling I'm love for that. Ahhhhhhhahahhaoooooeee. Laughing and snivelling; no answer: nobody there. No one. In the middle of the night, night after night, she forgot it was a native, a drunken black prostitute, one of those creatures with purple lips and a great backside in trousers who hung about after the men. She lay so that both ears were free to listen and she did not open her eyes on the outer dark.

Then one night the voice was right under her window. The dog next door was giving deep regular barks of the kind that a dog gives at a safe distance from uncertain prey, and between bouts of fisting on some shaky wooden door the voice was so near that she could hear breath drawn for each fresh assault. 'YOU HEAR? I tell you I'm come find . . . YOU HEAR-R-R . . . I'm come give you nice fuck . . . YOU-OOO HE-ARR?' The banging must be on the door of the servant's room of the next-door house; the dividing wall between the two properties was not more than twenty feet from her bedroom. No one opened the door and the voice grovelled and yelled and obscenely cajoled.

This time she got up and switched on the light and put on her dressing-gown, as one does when there is a situation to be dealt with. She went to the window and leant out; half the sky was ribbed with cloud, like a beach in the moonlight, and the garden trees were thickly black – she could not see properly into the neighbour's over the creeper-covered wall, but she held her arms across her body and called ringingly, 'Stop that! D'you hear? Stop it at once!'

There was a moment's silence and then it all began again, the dog punctuating the racket in a deep, shocked bay. Now lights went on in the neighbour's house and there was the rattle of the kitchen door being unbolted. A man in pyjamas was in her line of vision for a moment as he stood on the back steps. 'Anything wrong?' The chivalrous, reassuring tone between equals of different sex.

'In your yard,' she called back. 'Some drunken woman's come in from the street.'

'Oh my God. Her again.'

He must have been barefoot. She did not hear anyone cross the yard but suddenly his voice bellowed, 'Go on, get out, get going . . . I don't care what you've come for, just get on your feet and *hamba* out of my yard, go on, quickly, OUT!' 'No, master, that boy he –' 'Get up!' 'Don't swear me –' There was a confusion of the two voices with his quick, hoarse, sober one prevailing, and then a grunt with a sharp gasp, as if someone had been kicked. She could see the curve of the drive through the spaced shapes of shrubs and she saw a native woman go down it, not one of the ladies in trousers but an ordinary servant, fat and middle aged and drunk, in some garment still recognizably a uniform. 'All right over there?' the man called.

'Thanks. Perhaps one can get some sleep now.'

'You didn't send for the police?'

'No, no, I hadn't done that.'

All was quiet. She heard him lock his door. The dog gave a single bark now and again, like a sob. She got into the cool bed and slept.

The child never woke during the night unless he was ill but he was always up long before any adult in the mornings. That morning he remembered immediately that he had left his bicycle out all night and went at once into the garden to fetch it. It was gone. He stared at the sodden long grass and looked wildly round from one spot to another. His mother had warned him not to leave anything outside because the fence at the lower end of the garden, giving on a lane, was broken in many places. He looked in the shed although he knew he had not put the bicycle there. His pyjamas were wet to the knees from the grass. He stuffed them into the laundry basket in the bathroom and put on a shirt and trousers. He went twice to the lavatory, waiting for her to get up. But she was later than usual that morning, and he was able to go into the kitchen and ask the girl for his breakfast and eat it alone. He did not go out; quietly, in his room, he began to unpack and set up the track for his electric racing cars. He put together a balsawood glider that somehow had never been assembled, and slipped off to throw it about, with a natural air, down the end of the garden where the bicycle had disappeared. From there he was surprised to hear his mother's voice, not on the telephone but mingled with other voices in the light, high way of grown-up people exchanging greetings. He was attracted to the driveway; drawn to the figures of his mother, and a man and woman dressed for town, pausing and talking, his mother politely making a show of leading them to the house without actually inviting them in. 'No, well, I was saying to Ronald, it's all right if one's an old inhabitant, you know –' the woman began, with a laugh, several times without being allowed to finish. '– a bit funny, my asking that about the police, but really, I can assure you –' 'Oh no, I appreciated –' '– assure you they're as much use as –' 'It *was*, five or six years ago, but it's simply become a hang-out –' 'And the women! Those creatures in Allenby Road! I was saying, one feels quite ashamed –' 'Well I don't think I've had an unbroken night's sleep since I moved in. That woman yelling down the street at two in the morning.' 'I make a point of it – don't hang about my property, I tell them. They're watching for you to go out at night, that's the thing.' 'Every single morning I pick up beer cartons *inside* our wall, mind you –'

His mother had acknowledged the boy's presence, to the others, by cupping her hand lightly round the back of his head. 'And my bicycle's been stolen,' he said, up into their talk and their faces.

'Darling – where?' His mother looked from him to the neighbours, presenting the sensation of a fresh piece of evidence. 'You see?' said the man. 'There you are!'

'Here, in the garden,' he said.

'There you are. Your own garden.'

'*That* you must report,' said the woman.

'Oh really – on top of everything else. Do I have to go myself, or could I phone, d'you think?'

'We'll be going past the police station on the hill, on our way to town. Ronald could just stop a minute,' the woman said.

'You give me the particulars and I'll do it for you.' He was a man with thick-soled, cherry-dark shoes, soaring long legs, an air-force moustache and a funny little tooth that pressed on his lip when he smiled.

'What was the make, again – d'you remember?' his mother asked him. And to the neighbours, 'But please come inside –. Won't you have some coffee, quickly? I was just going to make myself – oh, it was a Raleigh, wasn't it? Or was that your old little one?' They went into the house, his mother explaining that she wasn't settled yet.

He told them the make, serial number, colour, and identifying dents of his bicycle. It was the first time he and his mother had had visitors in this house and there was quite a flurry to find the yellow coffee-cups and something better than a plastic spoon. He ran in and out helping, and taking part in the grown-up conversation. Since they had only just got to know him and his mother, these people did not interrupt him all the time, as the friends who came to the other house always had. 'And I bet I know who took it, too,' he said. 'There's an old native boy who just talks to anybody in the street. He's often seen me riding my bike down by the house where the white dog is.'

Why Haven't You Written?

His problem was hardening metal; finding a way to make it bore, grind, stutter through auriferous and other mineral-bearing rock without itself being blunted. The first time he spoke to the Professor's wife, sitting on his left, she said how impossible that sounded, like seeking perpetual motion or eternal life – nothing could bear down against resistance without being worn away in the process? He had smiled and they had agreed with dinner-table good humour that she was translating into abstract terms what was simply a matter for metallurgy.

They did not speak now. He did not see her face. All the way to the airport it was pressed against his coat-muffled arm and he could look down only on the nest of hair that was the top of her head. He asked the taxi driver to close the window because a finger of cold air was lifting those short, overlaid crescents of light hair. At the airport he stood by while she queued to weigh-in and present her ticket. He had the usual impulse to buy, find something for her at the last minute, and as usual there was nothing she wanted that he could give her. The first call came and they sat on with his arm round her. She dared not open her mouth; misery stopped her throat like vomit: he knew. At the second call, they rose. He embraced her clumsily in his coat, they said the usual reassurances to each other, she passed through the barrier and then came back in a crazy zigzag like a mouse threatened by a broom, to clutch his hand another time. Ashamed, half-dropping her things, she always did that, an unconscious effort to make no contact definitively the last.

And that was that. She was gone. It was as it always was; the joking, swaggering joy of arrival carried with it this reverse side; in their opposition and inevitability they were identical. He was used to it, he should be used to it, he should be used to never getting used to it because it happened again and again. The mining group in London for whom he was consultant tungsten carbide metallurgist sent him to Australia, Peru, and – again and again – the United States. In seven or eight visits he had been in New York for only two days and spent a weekend, once, in Chicago, but he was familiar with the middle-sized, Middle West, middle-everything towns (as he described them at home to friends in London) like the one he was left alone in now, where he lived in local motels and did his work among mining men and accepted the standard hospitality of good business relations. He was on first-name terms with his mining colleagues and their wives in these places and at Christmas would receive cards addressed to his wife and him as Willa and Duggie, although, of course, the Middle Westerners had never met her. Even if his wife could have left the children and the Group had been prepared to pay her fare, there wasn't much to be seen in the sort of places in America his work took him to.

In them, it was rare to meet anyone outside the mining community. The Professor's wife on his left at dinner that night was there because she was somebody's sister-in-law. Next day, when he recognized her standing beside him at the counter of a drug-store she explained that she was on a visit to do some research in the local university library for her husband, Professor Malcolm, of the Department of Political Science in the university of another Middle Western town not far away. And it was this small service she was able to carry out for the Professor that had made everything possible. Without it, perhaps the meetings at dinner and in the drug-store would have been the only times, the beginning and the end: the end before the beginning. As it was, again and again the Professor's wife met the English metallurgist in towns of Middle Western America, he come all the way from London to harden metal, she come not so far from home to search libraries for material for her husband's thesis.

It was snowing while a taxi took him back along the road from the airport to the town. It seemed to be snowing up from the ground, flinging softly at the windscreen, rather than falling. To have gone on driving into the snow that didn't reach him but blocked out the sight of all that was around him – but there was a dinner, there was a report he ought to write before the dinner. He actually ground his teeth like a bad-tempered child – always these faces to smile at, these reports to sit over, these letters to write. Even when she was with him, he had to leave her in the room while he went to friendly golf games and jolly dinners with engineers who knew how much *they* missed a bit of home life when they had to be away from the wife and youngsters. Even when there were no dinner parties he had to write reports late at night in the room where she lay in bed and fell asleep, waiting for him. And always the proprietorial, affectionately reproachful letters from home: ... *nothing from you ... For goodness' sake, a line to your mother ... It would cheer up poor little mumpy Ann no end if she got a postcard ... nothing for ten days, now, darling, can't help getting worried when you don't ...*

Gone: and no time, no peace to prepare for what was waiting to be realized in that motel room. He could not go back to that room right away. Drive on with the huge silent handfuls of snow coming at him, and the windscreen wipers running a screeching finger-nail to and fro over glass: he gave the driver an address far out of the way, then when they had almost reached it said he had changed his mind and (to hell with the report) went straight to the dinner although it was much too early, 'For heaven's sakes! Of *course* not. Fix yourself a drink, Duggie, you know where it all is by now ...' The hostess was busy in the kitchen, a fat beautiful little girl in leotards and dancing pumps came no farther than the doorway and watched him, finger up her nose.

They always drank a lot in these oil-fired igloos, down in the den where the bar was, with its collection of European souvenirs or home-painted Mexican mural, up in the sitting-room round the colour TV after dinner, exchanging professional jokes and anecdotes. They found Duggie in great form: that dry English sense of humour. At midnight he was dropped between the hedges of dirty ice shovelled on either side of the motel entrance. He stood outside the particular door, he fitted the key and the door swung open on an absolute assurance – the dark, centrally heated smell of Kim Malcolm and Crispin Douglas together, his desert boots, her hair lacquer, zest of orange peel, cigarette smoke in cloth, medicated nasal spray, salami, newspapers. For a moment he didn't turn on the light. Then it sprang from under his finger and stripped the room: gone, empty, ransacked. He sat down in his coat. What had he done the last time? People went out and got drunk or took a pill and believed in the healing sanity of morning. He had drunk enough and he never took pills. Last time he had left when she did, been in some other place when she was in some other place.

She had put the cover on the typewriter and there was a dustless square where the file with material for Professor Malcolm's thesis used to be. He took his notes for his report out of the briefcase and rolled a sheet of paper into the typewriter. Then he sat there a long time, hands on the machine, hearing his own breathing whistling slightly through his blocked left nostril. His heart was driven hard by the final hospitable brandy. He began to type in his usual heavy and jerky way, all power in two forefingers.

In the morning – in the morning nothing could efface the hopeless ugliness of that town. They laughed at it and made jokes about the glorious places he took her to. She had said, if we could stay with each other for good, but only on condition that we lived in this town? She had made up the scene: a winter day five years later, with each insisting it was the other's turn to go out in the freezing slush to buy drink and each hurling at the other the reproach – it's because of *you* I got myself stuck here. She was the one who pulled the curtain aside on those streets of shabby snow every morning, on the vacant lots with their clapboard screens, on the grey office blocks with lights going on through the damp-laden smog as people began the day's work, and it was she who insisted – be fair – that there was a quarter-of-an-hour or so, about five in the evening, when the place had its moment; a sort of Arctic spectrum, the fire off a diamond, was reflected from the sunset on the polluted frozen river, upon the glass faces of office blocks, and the evening star was caught hazily in the industrial pall.

In the morning frozen snot hung from the roofs of wooden houses. A company car drove him to his first appointment. Figures in the street with arms like teddy bears, the elbow joints stiffened by layers of clothing. A dog burning a patch of urine through the snow. In the cafeteria at lunch (it was agreed that it was crazy, from the point of view of everyone's waistline, to lay on an executive lunch for him every day) he walked past Lily cups of tuna fish salad and bowls of Jell-O, discussing percussive rock drilling and the heat treatment of steel. Some drills were behaving in an inexplicable manner and he was driven out to the mine to see for himself. A graveyard all the way, tombstones of houses and barns under snow. Sheeted trees. White mounds and ridges whose purpose could only be identified through excavation, like those archaeological mounds, rubbish heaps of a vanished culture silted over by successive ones. He did not know why the tungsten carbide-tipped drills were not fulfilling their promised performance; he would have to work on it. He lied to one generous colleague that he had been invited to dinner with another and he walked about the iron-hard streets of the downtown area (the freeze had crusted the slush, the crust was being tamped down by the pressure of feet) with his scarf over his mouth, and at last ended up at the steak house where they used to go. Because he was alone the two waitresses talked to each other near him as if he were not there. Each table had a small glass box which was a selector for the juke-box; one night she had insisted that they ought to hear a record that had been the subject of controversy in the newspapers because it was supposed to include, along with the music, the non-verbal cries associated with love-making, and they had laughed so much at the groans and sighs that the bloody slabs of meat on the wooden boards got cold before they ate them. Although he thought it senseless to fill himself up with drink he did finish the whole bottle of wine they used to manage between them. And every night, making the excuse that he wanted to 'work on' the problem of the drill, pleading tiredness, lying about an invitation he didn't have, he went from brutal cold into fusty heat and out to brutal cold again, sitting in bars and going to the steak house or the Chinese restaurant and then back to bars again, until the final confrontation with cold was only half-felt on his stiff hot face and he trudged back along planes of freezing wind to the motel room or sat behind a silent taxi driver, sour to have to be out on such nights, as he had sat coming home alone from the airport with the snow flinging itself short of his face.

The freeze continued. The TV weatherman gabbling cheerily before his map showed the sweep of great snowstorms over whole arcs of this enormous country. On the airport she had left from, planes were grounded for days. The few trains there were, ran late. In addition, there was a postal strike and no letters; nothing from England, but also nothing from her, and no hope of a phone call, either, because she had flown straight to join the Professor at his mother's home in Florida and she could neither telephone from the house nor hope to get out to do so from elsewhere at night, when he was in the motel room; they dared not risk a call to the Company during the day. He moved between the room – whose silence, broken only by Walter Cronkite and the weatherman, filled with his own thoughts as if it were some monstrous projection, a cartoon balloon, issuing from his mind – he moved between that room and the Japanese-architect-designed headquarters of the Company, which existed beneath blizzard and postal strike as an extraordinary bunker with contemplative indoor pools, raked-stone covered courtyards, cheerful rows of Jell-O and tuna fish salad. He woke in the dark mornings to hear the snow plough grinding along the streets. Men struck with picks into the rock of ice that covered the sidewalks a foot solid. The paper said all post offices were deep in drifts of accumulated mail, and sealed the mouths of all mail boxes. England did not exist and Florida – was there really anyone in Florida? It was a place where, the weatherman said, the temperature was in the high seventies, and humid. She had forgotten a sheet of notes that must have come loose from the file, and the big yellow fake sponge (it was what she had been buying when they found themselves together in the drug-store of that other Middle Western town) that she now always brought along. She would be missing the sponge, in Florida, but there was no way to get it to her. He kept the sponge and the sheet of paper on the empty dressing-table. Overnight, every night, more snow fell. Like a nail he was driven deeper and deeper into isolation.

He came from dinner with the Chief Mining Engineer and his party at the country club (the Chief Mining Engineer always took his wife out to eat on Saturday nights) and was possessed by such a dread of the room that he told the taxi driver to take him to the big chain hotel, that had seventeen floors and a bar on top. It was full of parties like the one he had just left; he was the only solitary. Others did not look outside, but fiddling with a plastic cocktail stirrer in the shape of a tiny sword he saw through the walls of glass against which the blue-dark pressed that they were surrounded by steppes of desolation out there beyond the feebly lit limits of the town. Wolves might survive where effluvia from paper mills had made fish swell up and float, and birds choked on their crops filled with pesticide-tainted seeds. He carried the howl somewhere inside him. It was as close as that slight whistling from the blocked sinus in his left nostril. When the bar shut he went down with those chattering others in an elevator that cast them all back into the street.

The smell in the motel room had not changed through his being alone there. He felt so awake, so ready to tackle something, some work or difficulty, that he took another drink, a big swallow of neat whisky, and that night wrote a letter to Willa. I'm not coming back, he said. I have gone so far away that it would be stupid to waste it – I mean the stage I've reached. Of course I am sorry that you have been such a good wife, that you will always be such a good wife and nothing can change you. Because so long as I accept that you are a good wife, how can I find the guts to do it? I can go on being the same thing – your opposite number, the good husband, hoping for a better position and more money for us all, coming on these bloody dreary trips every winter (why don't they ever send me in good weather). But it's through subjecting myself to all this, putting up with what we think of as these partings for the sake of my work, that I have come to understand that they are not partings at all. They are nothing like partings. Do you understand?

It went on for two more pages. When he had finished he put it in an airmail envelope, stamped it, went out again – he had not taken off his coat or scarf – and walked through the ringing of his own footsteps in the terrible cold to where he remembered there was a mail box. Like all the others, the mouth was sealed over by some kind of gummed tape, very strong stuff reinforced by a linen backing. He slit it with a piece of broken bottle he found in the gutter, and pushed the letter in. When he got back to the room he still had the bit of glass in his hand. He fell asleep in his coat but must have woken later and undressed because in the morning he found himself in bed and in pyjamas.

He did not know how drunk he had been that night when he did it. Not so drunk that he was not well aware of the chaos of the postal strike; everyone had been agreeing at the country club that most of the mail piled up at the GPO could never be expected to reach its destination. Not so drunk that he had not counted on the fact that the letter would never get to England. – Why, he had broken into the mail box, and the boxes were not being cleared. – Just drunk enough to take what seemed to him the thousand-to-one chance the letter might get there. Suppose the army were to be called in to break the strike, as they had been in New York? Yet, for several days, it did not seem to him that *that* letter would ever be dispatched and delivered – that sort of final solution just didn't come off.

Then the joke went round the Company headquarters that mail was moving again: the Company had received, duly delivered, one envelope – a handbill announcing a sale (already over) at a local department store. Some wit from the administration department put it up in the cafeteria. He suddenly saw the letter, a single piece of mail, arriving at the house in London. He thought of writing – no, sending a cable – now that communications were open again, instructing that the letter was to be destroyed unopened.

She would never open a letter if asked not to, of course. She would put it on the bedside-table at his side of the bed and wait for a private night-time explanation, out of the hearing of the children. But suppose the letter had been lost, buried under the drifts of thousands, mis-sorted, mis-dispatched – what would be made of a mystifying cable about a letter that had never come? The snow was melting, the streets glistened, and his clothes were marked with the spray of dirty water thrown up by passing cars. He had impulses – sober ones – to write and tell the Professor's wife, but when she unexpectedly did manage to telephone, the relief of pleasure at her voice back in the room so wrung him that he said nothing, and decided to say nothing in letters to her either; why disturb and upset her in this particularly disturbing and upsetting way.

He received a letter from London a fortnight old. There must have been later ones that hadn't turned up. He began to reason that if the letter did arrive in London, he might just manage to get there before it. And then? It was unlikely that he would be able to intercept it. But he actually began to hint to the colleagues at the Company that he would like to leave by the end of the week, be home in England for the weekend, after all, after six weeks' absence. The problem of the drill's optimum performance couldn't be solved in a day, anyway; he would have to go into the whole business back at the research laboratory in London. The Chief Mining Engineer said what a darned shame he had to leave now, before the greens were dry enough for the first eighteen holes of the year.

He forced himself not to think about the letter or at least to think about it as little as possible for the remaining days. Sometimes the idea of it came to him as a wild hope, like the sound of her voice suddenly in the room, from Florida. Sometimes it was a dry anxiety: what a childish, idiotic thing to have done, how insane to risk throwing everything away when, as the Professor's wife often said, nobody was being hurt: Professor Malcolm, the children, Willa – none of them. Resentment flowed into him like unreasonable strength – *I am being hurt!* Not so drunk, after all, not so drunk. Yet, of course, he was afraid of Willa, ranged there with two pretty children and a third with glasses blacked out over one eye to cure a squint. What could you do with that unreasonable life-saving strength? – Against that little family group? And, back again to the thought of the Professor's wife, his being afraid disgusted him. He spoke to her once more before he left, and said, Why do we have to come last? Why do we count least? She accepted such remarks as part of the ragged mental state of parting, not as significant of any particular development. He put the phone down on her voice for the last time for this time.

He took the plane from Chicago late on Friday afternoon and by midnight was in early-morning London. No school on Saturdays and Willa was there with the children at Heathrow. Airports, airports. In some times and places, for some men, it was the battlefield or the bullring, the courtroom or the church; for him it was airports. In that architectural mode of cheap glamour suited only to bathos his strongest experiences came; despair could not be distinguished from indigestion induced by time-change, dread produced the same drawn face as muscle cramp, private joy exhibited euphoria that looked no different from that induced by individual bottles of Moët et Chandon. These were the only places where he ever wanted to weep, and no places could have been more ridiculous for this to happen to him.

Willa had a new haircut and the children were overcome with

embarrassment by the eternal ten yards he had to walk towards them, and then flung themselves excitedly at him. Willa hugged his arm and pressed her cheek against that coat-sleeve a moment; her mouth tasted of the toothpaste that they always used at home. The last phone call – only nine hours ago, that's all it was – receded into a depth, a distance, a silence as impossible to reach down through as the drifts of snow and piled-up letters . . . No letter, of course; he saw that at once. His wife cooked a special lunch and in the afternoon, when the children had gone off to the cinema with friends, he did what he must, he went to bed with her.

They talked a lot about the postal strike and how awful it had been. Nothing for days, more than two weeks! His mother had been maddening, telephoning every day, as if the whole thing were a conspiracy of the wife to keep the mother out of touch with her son. Crazy! And her letters – had he really got only one? She must have written at least four times; knowing that letters might not arrive only made one want to write more, wasn't it perverse? Why hadn't he phoned? – Not that she really wanted him to, it was so expensive . . . by the way, it turned out that the youngest child had knock knees, he would have to have remedial treatment. – Well, that was what he had thought – such an extravagance, and he couldn't believe, every day, that a letter might not come. She said, once: It must have been quite a nice feeling, sometimes, free of everything and everyone for a change – peaceful without us eh? And he pulled down his mouth and said, Some freedom, snowed under in a motel in that God-forsaken town. But the mining Group was so pleased with his work that he was given a bonus, and that pleased her, that made her feel it was worth it, worth even the time he had had to himself.

He watched for the postman; sometimes woke up at night in a state of alarm. He even arranged, that first week, to work at home until about midday – getting his reports into shape. But there was nothing. For the second week, when he was keeping normal office hours, he read her face every evening when he came home; again, nothing. Heaven knows how she interpreted the way he looked at her: he would catch her full in the eyes, by mistake, now and then, and she would have a special slow smile, colouring up to her scrubbed little ear-lobes, the sort of smile you get from a girl who catches you looking at her across a bar. He was so appalled by that smile that he came home with a bunch of flowers. She embraced him and stood there holding the flowers behind his waist rocking gently back and forth with him as they had done years ago. He thought – wildly again – how she was still pretty, quite young, no reason why she shouldn't marry again.

His anxiety for the letter slowly began to be replaced by confidence: it would not come. It was hopeless – safe – that letter would never come. Perhaps he had been very drunk after all; perhaps the mail box was a permanently disused one, or the letter hadn't really gone through the slot but fallen into the snow, the words melting and wavering while the ink ran with the thaw and the thin sheets of paper turned to pulp. He was safe. It was a good thing he had never told the Professor's wife. He took the children to the Motor Show, he got good seats for Willa, his mother and himself for the new *Troilus and Cressida* production at the Aldwych, and he wrote a long letter to Professor Malcolm's wife telling her about the performance and how much he would have loved to see it with her. Then he felt terribly depressed, as he often did lately now that he had stopped worrying about the letter and should have been feeling better, and there was nowhere to go for privacy, in depression, except the lavatory, where Willa provided the colour supplements of the Sunday papers for reading matter.

One morning just over a month after her husband had returned from the Middle West, Willa picked up the post from the floor as she brought the youngest home from school and saw a letter in her husband's handwriting. It had been date-stamped and re-date-stamped and was apparently about six weeks old. There is always something a bit flat about opening a letter from someone who has in the meantime long arrived and filled in, with anecdote and his presence, the time of absence when it was written. She vaguely saw herself producing it that evening as a kind of addendum to their forgotten emotions about the strike; by such small shared diversions did they keep their marriage close. But after she had given the little one his lunch she found a patch of sun for herself and opened the letter after all. In that chilly spring air, unaccustomed warmth seemed suddenly to become aural, sang in her ears at the pitch of cicadas, and she stopped reading. She looked out into the small garden amazedly, accusingly, as if to challenge a hoax. But there was no one to answer for it. She read the letter through. And again. She kept on reading it and it produced almost a sexual excitement in her, as a frank and erotic love letter might. She could have been looking through a keyhole at him lying on another woman. She took it to some other part of the garden, as the cat often carried the bloody and mangled mess of its prey from place to place, and read it again. It was a perfectly calm and reasonable and factual letter saying that he would not return, but she saw that it was indeed a love letter, a love letter about someone else, a love letter such as he had never written to her. She put it back in the creased and stained envelope and tore it up, and then she went out the gate and wandered down to the bus stop, where there was a lamp-post bin, and dropped the bits of paper into its square mouth among the used tickets.

FOR THE BEST IN PAPERBACKS, LOOK FOR THE

In every corner of the world, on every subject under the sun, Penguin represents quality and variety—the very best in publishing today.

For complete information about books available from Penguin—including Pelicans, Puffins, Peregrines, and Penguin Classics—and how to order them, write to us at the appropriate address below. Please note that for copyright reasons the selection of books varies from country to country.

In the United Kingdom: For a complete list of books available from Penguin in the U.K., please write to *Dept E.P., Penguin Books Ltd, Harmondsworth, Middlesex, UB7 0DA.*

In the United States: For a complete list of books available from Penguin in the U.S., please write to *Dept BA, Penguin*, Box 120, Bergenfield, New Jersey 07621-0120.

In Canada: For a complete list of books available from Penguin in Canada, please write to *Penguin Books Canada Ltd, 10 Alcorn Avenue, Suite 300, Toronto, Ontario, Canada M4V 3B2.*

In Australia: For a complete list of books available from Penguin in Australia, please write to the *Marketing Department, Penguin Books Ltd, P.O. Box 257, Ringwood, Victoria 3134.*

In New Zealand: For a complete list of books available from Penguin in New Zealand, please write to the *Marketing Department, Penguin Books (NZ) Ltd, Private Bag, Takapuna, Auckland 9.*

In India: For a complete list of books available from Penguin, please write to *Penguin Overseas Ltd, 706 Eros Apartments, 56 Nehru Place, New Delhi, 110019.*

In Holland: For a complete list of books available from Penguin in Holland, please write to *Penguin Books Nederland B.V., Postbus 195, NL-1380AD Weesp, Netherlands.*

In Germany: For a complete list of books available from Penguin, please write to *Penguin Books Ltd, Friedrichstrasse 10-12, D-6000 Frankfurt Main I, Federal Republic of Germany.*

In Spain: For a complete list of books available from Penguin in Spain, please write to *Longman, Penguin España, Calle San Nicolas 15, E-28013 Madrid, Spain.*

In Japan: For a complete list of books available from Penguin in Japan, please write to *Longman Penguin Japan Co Ltd, Yamaguchi Building, 2-12-9 Kanda Jimbocho, Chiyoda-Ku, Tokyo 101, Japan.*

FOR THE BEST IN PAPERBACKS, LOOK FOR THE

"Nadine Gordimer writes more knowingly about South Africa than anyone else." —Anatole Broyard, The New York Times

☐ **MY SON'S STORY**

Told through the eyes of a young boy, this is the story of what he knows and what he imagines of political and erotic liberation, of the contention between family life and political action, of sexual jealously between father and adolescent son, and of the power of apartheid in South Africa today. Wrenching and passionate, this tale reveals Gordimer's keen insight into human nature. *288 pages ISBN: 0-14-015975-4*

☐ **JUMP AND OTHER STORIES**

In sixteen new stories ranging from the dynamics of family life to the worldwide confusion of human values, Nadine Gordimer gives us access to many lives in places as far apart as suburban London, exotic Mozambique, a mythical island, and turbulent South Africa. Moving, incisive, and with strong moral resonance, Gordimer's stories offer a portrait of life as it is lived now, at the end of our century. *272 pages ISBN: 0-14-016534-7*

☐ **JULY'S PEOPLE**

As South Africa turns into a raging battleground between blacks and whites, the liberal white Smales family members are led to refuge by their servant, July. What happens to them — the shifts in character and relationships — provides an unforgettable look into the terrifying tacit understandings and misunderstandings between blacks and whites. *176 pages ISBN: 0-14-006140-1*

☐ **SELECTED STORIES**

Nadine Gordimer herself has selected these stories, in which she brings to life unforgettable characters from every corner of society. From the Zaire River to black Johannesburg to the hushed gardens of the white suburbs, she brilliantly depicts the African landscape they inhabit. The momentous implications of these superbly constructed tales are universal. *448 pages ISBN: 0-14-006737-X*

☐ **BURGER'S DAUGHTER**

Rosa Burger is left alone after her father's death in prison — alone to find her own identity in the turbulent political environment of South Africa and to explore the intricacies of what it actually means to be Burger's daughter. Moving through an overwhelming flood of sensuously described memories that will not release her, she arrives at last at a fresh understanding of her life. *368 pages ISBN: 0-14-005593-2*

FOR THE BEST IN PAPERBACKS, LOOK FOR THE

□ SOMETHING OUT THERE

This powerful collection of short stories and a novella reflects Nadine Gordimer's extraordinary ability to illuminate the connection between the personal and the political in the divided society of South Africa. With compassion and scrupulous honesty, Gordimer penetrates to the core of the human heart, revealing the subtlest feelings of her characters — black and white, revolutionaries and racists, adulterers, spinsters, and lovers.

208 pages   ISBN: 0-14-007711-1

□ A SPORT OF NATURE

Hillela is Nadine Gordimer's "sport of nature": a spontaneous mutation, a new type of untainted person, seductive and intuitively gifted for life. *A Sport of Nature* is the bold, sweeping story of her rise from obscurity to an unpredictable kind of political power. *368 pages   ISBN: 0-14-008470-3*